THE SENTHIEN

BOOK ONE OF THE
DESCENDANTS OF EARTH

BY TARA JADE BROWN

BROWN DOVE
PUBLISHING

ISBN: 978-3-9524946-0-8

Editor: Sarah Kolb-Williams
Book cover design: Deranged Doctor Design
Print formatting: Streetlight Graphics

BROWN DOVE
PUBLISHING

www.browndovepublishing.com

To my Mom and Dad

CHAPTER 1

My feet are bare.

I'm standing on a hard, dark surface. Soft orange light casts shadows on rough black walls around me.

And he is here, standing in front of me.

Again.

His body is close to mine.

Too close.

No two individuals in Uni would break the interpersonal space like this.

Yet he does.

And I want it.

I keep looking at him.

Dark hair. Dark eyes. Bronze-colored skin.

I gaze at his lips, feeling the strange need to come even closer, to break the interpersonal space even more.

My heartbeat picks up.

I'm confused.

And then, he does the same thing he always does before I snap out of my Vision. He comes closer and places his warm palm on my cheek.

He slowly bends his face toward mine and kisses me.

A strong electric sensation pulses through my body, snapping me out of my Vision and jolting me back into wakefulness.

I opened my eyes to the complete darkness surrounding me. I might as well have kept them closed; it wouldn't have made any difference. My heart still pounded—an aftereffect of my recurring dream. I placed my palm on my chest, feeling the drumming beneath my rib cage. I swallowed, trying to keep my fast breathing inaudible, hoping it wouldn't be detected by the AI sensors. I put my arms next to my body, closed my eyes, and with deliberate intent and flawlessly trained willpower, I relaxed all of my muscles, gradually bringing my heartbeat back to normal.

Behind my eyelids, I still saw him. None of my dreams had ever affected my body in the way this one did. And I didn't understand any of it.

It couldn't possibly have been the future that I was seeing. He was a Human. And my Descendant ranking gave me no common ground with them.

I will never meet a Human.

I will never meet him.

I sighed silently just as the lights turned on. I pressed my eyelids together, covering them with the heels of my palms. It gave me a moment to get used to the sudden brightness, the unnatural end of dark, the abrupt start of another day.

"It is 81-03.7405. Good morning, Dana. I hope you have

had a productive dream. Would you like me to prepare a report recording?" the pleasant female voice of the apartment AI asked.

"No!" I quickly moved my arms and opened my eyes—and then realized that I'd been a little too quick to answer. "Thank you, but... no," I said in a calmer voice. "I did not have any productive dreams last night."

There was a small break, and then the AI said, "A report of *No Visions* will be submitted. Thank you."

I knew it was a computer, but I couldn't help but think I heard a hint of disappointment in her voice. I decided not to dwell on it.

I got up swiftly and walked to the E-bathroom, not turning back to the sounds of the bed being folded under the floor behind me. The bathroom door slid to the side as the lights inside turned on at the same time. I waited for a fraction of a second and then stepped into the E-shower.

Thousands of tiny electric shocks pinched spots all over my body, stimulating the muscles underneath. My eyes were closed and my lips pressed tightly together as I waited for the mandatory morning session to finish. Not for the first time, I wished I lived on a planet with stronger gravity.

After seven passes, electric stings were replaced by soft water drops.

I sighed in relief.

The water-shower.

I loved it.

I let the stream of water fall on my cheeks, sliding down my neck, continuing the journey over my body. The water-shower stopped automatically after five passes. I opened my eyes, trying not to be disappointed.

The semitransparent wall in front of me slid open and I

walked into a small cabin, each corner one IP distance from the center. The doors behind me closed and warm air started blowing from tiny holes out of four white corner pillars. I closed my eyes as the water drops disappeared from my skin and my heavy hair dried.

I thought of my dream again.

I had seen him so many times I knew all the details of his face by heart. And then, I thought about the kiss. I touched my lips with the tips of my fingers, trying to bring back the feelings. It was amazing—such a simple touch bringing more sensations than anything else I had ever felt.

Who was he?

Does he exist, or is he only a product of my imagination?

The air stopped blowing just as the last drop dried and the opaque glass door on the other side opened. I sighed, then walked into my brightly lit living quarters.

"Clothes," I ordered to the apartment's AI, and a cupboard containing several different skinsuits opened from the wall. I chose the whitest skinsuit I could find, although I knew it would still be dark compared to Boolean clothing. I dressed quickly.

My skinsuit was simple, with no additional attachments, pockets, or straps. For a short port trip, I wouldn't need any.

"E-band."

A small flat drawer next to the wardrobe extended outward. On its surface were seven nicely aligned arm computers standing in their chargers. I picked up the white one, secured it on my left forearm, and swiped the screen to bring it out of standby.

I glanced at the food processor but decided against eating. I strapped up my boots and left the apartment.

CHAPTER 2

"Dora Dana Dasnan. We acknowledge your presence on our premises. The distinguished head of our institute will join you in the library," said the tall, thin, white-faced woman, welcoming me as I exited the porting chamber. Her slick black hair was wrapped at the back of her neck. Like all Booleans, she had no eyebrows, and her eyes were completely black, with no white inside. This made it very difficult to tell where she was looking.

As always, it made me feel uncomfortable.

My face, however, stayed calm. Relaxing my facial muscles, I responded in a well-trained monotonous tone, "I acknowledge your hospitality."

"Please, follow me," she said and moved her arm toward the hallway door.

I made a step forward, careful not to break the IP distance.

"We strongly recommend that our visitors always stay with accompanying personnel and never walk through any of our premises unattended."

I stopped in front of the doors and looked at her. Checking the plate name on her white skinsuit, I said, "TA-645, I have been on your premises before. I am aware of your regulations."

Her black eyes stared at me for a few moments.

It seems that responding to an assertive remark wasn't integrated into her genotype.

"We enforce this on every visit," she said. "The communication of the regulation is obligatory."

I took a breath to answer but then stopped, turning toward the door. *Careful, Dora…*

"Of course, TA-645. Please, lead me to the library."

TA-645 turned toward the door too and pressed her palm on the small scanning plate next to it. The door slid open and we stepped into a bright white hallway. It was high, with sufficient width to take a group of six people without compromising their IP space.

We passed many doors, all of them tightly sealed. Each was scan-protected, and they all looked alike, with no indication of a name or a room number.

And just like every time before, the corridors were empty.

Although I was used to that, it made me feel uneasy, as if the genetically grown technical assistant and I were the only ones in this institute. TA-645 did not talk, but from the corner of my eye I could see her head was strangely twisted in my direction rather than facing the path.

I tried to ignore her.

The whiteness of the hallways was disturbing. It made me lose all sense of what was closer and what was farther away. I closed my eyes to refocus and then opened them again.

After a few turns, we stopped next to a door, and TA-645 pressed her finger on a small panel and left it there for a moment. After a faint clicking sound, her identity was confirmed, and the doors slid open.

The room we entered was a library. White walls, white chairs, white desks, each with an empty holographic screen. Three walls were completely covered in rows of tightly packed chips stored in their slots. It vaguely reminded me of the old libraries I'd seen in the history recap classes, though these images were a lot more colorful than this one here. I was sure all the information on the chips was accessible through the main computer, but the library, it seemed, had to look presentable.

"Dana, please have a seat. Dr. Zamnan Second will be with you shortly. Should you be interested in light informational material, some articles are highlighted in green." She tapped a finger on an empty white screen next to the door and several chips on the wall to my right lit up green.

"I wish you a productive conversation during your stay at the Boolean Institute," she said and stepped toward the door. She placed her palm on the scanning screen and the doors slid open.

In that moment, I saw a group of six women passing the corridor. The first one was clearly Boolean, but the rest had beige-colored suits and much darker skin than any of the Descendant races.

Humans?

Their heads were hanging low, as if they couldn't lift them up. And then, in one short moment, one of them looked sideways and saw me. Her eyes were wide open, her neck and jaw muscles tight. Having had only rare opportunities to observe Human facial expressions, I wasn't sure what it meant, but my gut feeling told me that she was scared. Very scared.

TA-645 looked back at me with her wide black eyes and then stepped out without saying a word. The door closed, and there was a perfect silence. I exhaled loudly. I needed some kind of a sound to distract me.

I looked around the white room, then sat at the first holo screen. Rather than scrolling through some "light informational material" as TA-645 recommended, I decided to go over the Vision I recently had—the Vision I wanted to share with Dr. Zamnan Second.

> Dr. Zamnan stares at the holo screen data in front of him. He turns to TA-002 and says, "This will make our production unyielding. Do we have any reserves?"
>
> "No, distinguished Dr. Zamnan. We already used them."
>
> "We need to notify the High Priest. The seeding needs to be increased dramatically if we are to obtain the same level of production. Place all our remaining yield into the Mind."

This Vision was puzzling. I understood that the High Zlathar Priest should know about current genetic experiments, particularly if one of those projects had presented the Booleans with problems or challenges. *But what does the Mind have to do with all of this?*

The Mind belonged to the Loreans. They engineered it, they maintained it, they improved it, and all of this information was strictly confidential. They had the absolute intellectual property, even over the Zlathars.

So what experiments are the Booleans doing that has to do with the Mind?

The sliding door silently opened and a tall, thin man with long dark hair strapped at the back of his neck walked in. He smiled in the typical Boolean way, his lips spreading only sideways instead of up. I never thought this expression looked happy—or comfortable, for that matter. I stood up to greet him.

"Dora Dana Dasnan. I acknowledge your presence," he said, his black eyes on me as he walked toward me. He stopped outside the standard IP distance, but for some reason, I felt uncomfortable.

"Dr. Zamnan Second, it is an honor to be at your institute, as always."

"What can we help you with, Dana?"

"There is a Vision I thought you should be aware of," I said flatly.

His calm, unemotional face grew even calmer as he relaxed all his facial muscles.

"I am ready to hear your recent Vision."

I lifted my left forearm and swiped the E-band screen, sending the holo report to the first table screen on the right. The holo projection of my torso appeared above the table, bringing some color to the white surroundings.

Pale oval face, high cheekbones, and long, dark gray hair.

Like all other Senthiens, my eyes were bright green with the whites lightly green as well. The only unusual things about my face were my lips. Senthiens normally had dark, almost purplish, thin lips. But mine were soft, red, and full.

I glanced at Dr. Zamnan from the corner of my eyes and automatically pressed my lips together to make them look thinner.

The monotonous voice of my report recording echoed slightly in the library room until it was finished, and the projection disappeared.

Dr. Zamnan Second still looked at the empty white holo screen.

I kept watching him, but he didn't move. I realized there was something else that made Booleans so unusual: they never blink. I felt a slight shiver rising up my back, but my face remained calm.

Dr. Zamnan Second slowly turned his head toward me but didn't say anything.

"Is this information helpful?" I asked.

"At the moment, I do not have the knowledge to confirm your Vision. Our institute is free of any problematic issues."

"Are there any experiments currently being conducted that relate to the Mind?"

"The Mind is the property of Loreans. It holds no interest for us. Did all your Visions come to be?"

I remembered the Vision I had this morning—the dream—and after a slight delay, I said, "All the reported Visions have come to pass. But I have not reported a large number of Visions as of yet. I am still developing my skills."

"Yes. Understandable. You are still young," he said. "Did you communicate this to anyone in the Zlathar Council?"

"The Zlathar Council received this report, as they normally do, but I have not received any query from them for a holo communication."

"Of course," he said, but his face tightened. "There is no reason to."

He stepped toward the exit, indicating that I should follow him. My visit here, I realized, was coming to an end. As the door slid open, I asked, "Is there a specific reason you have Humans on your premises?"

He looked at me suddenly. "Humans?"

"I saw a group of Humans passing in the corridor while awaiting your arrival."

"You are mistaken. We do not have Humans anywhere in our institute. These premises are clear of all impurity. You did not see Humans."

"It was then certainly a mistake," I said, my voice as flat as

I could make it. I stepped in front of him into the corridor and Dr. Zamnan joined me. He turned toward me and spread his lips wide into a typical Boolean smile.

"Thank you for sharing your Vision with us. I regret that this had to be the first inaccurate one. I am confident that you will have many more true future Visions."

As a new TA approached, he said, "TA-3279 will accompany you to our porting chamber."

"Thank you for receiving me today. It was a pleasure to communicate with you."

He bowed slightly in response, and I bowed back. Then he turned around and walked in the opposite direction. Soon all I could see, looking back at him wearing all white, was a black head with a long, thin braid floating through the white hallway.

"Visionaire Dasnan?"

I turned toward the TA, who looked exactly like the woman who had fetched me from the porting chamber.

"Please, follow me," she said and started walking back to the chamber.

I walked next to her, ignoring her strange sideways glare and making sure my face remained calm.

My head was full of questions. Zamnan wasn't telling the truth. None of the Descendants had such pigmentation in their skin as the women I had seen. And those were not Descendants. They had to be Zema4 inhabitants.

We arrived at the chamber, and TA-3279 opened the door for me.

"Thank you for visiting our institute. Please, come back again."

"Thank you for your hospitality. May Torquemada Joseph Nadraque watch over you," I said in the traditional way, then walked into the small chamber and turned around to face the doors.

The Boolean smiled a thin, flat smile, and the doors closed.

I stretched my shoulders from their stiff position and looked around. This chamber was wide enough to allow for the teleportation of five individuals with their needed IP space. Although it seemed spacious to port only one person, this chamber was the smallest in its dimensions. Portation chambers came in sizes of such magnitude that they could hold an entire battle cruiser with its accompanying fleet.

The walls and ceiling, as well as the floor of the chamber, were all covered in semitransparent rosenquartz tiles, each with an intricate pattern of APC chips intertwined in their structure.

"The port number 445-76-498-02 to porting gate 164'55'16 will begin in three passes," the female voice of the computer announced.

I folded my arms on my chest, preparing myself for the process. It was not as unpleasant as an E-shower, although it did something far more radical. The feeling resembled the return of blood flow to an arm that had fallen asleep in an awkward position, but this experience wasn't limited to just an arm; it affected the whole body.

The pleasant rose lighting of the chamber dimmed to give way to the dark purple hue of the transfer itself as the complex energy field coordination and power cycles of the porting process began.

CHAPTER 3

"Welcome back to Senthia, Dora Dana Dasnan," the female AI voice of the porting chamber announced. "It is sixteen hours and twenty-three passes."

I shivered once, shaking off the aftermath of the port. The chamber took on a soft rose hue once more, and the doors slid open. I walked into a large tubelike corridor, brightly lit by rows of ceiling lights, busy with people.

I stopped, thinking of what to do next. Then I turned right and with firm steps walked to the Data Center Hall, passing the open entrances to Nature Hall, E-Fitness Hall, and Interactive Coupling Hall.

The DC Hall was large, three stories of galleries with transparent walls overlooking a central reception area.

I walked to the counter, and the woman lifted her gaze to me.

"Good day at Senthia. How can we help you?"

Part of her job description was to smile, and it never faltered. Her eyes were gray, her hair short and platinum blonde, and although she was sitting, her face was only a head lower than mine. Typical Jacobson traits.

"I need access to a DC room."

"What is the purpose of your visit?"

"Further Vision development. Broad search criteria."

"Of course." She looked at the holo screen in front of her, which was black from my side. She tapped a few buttons, then swiped through several holo pages before she reached down to her drawer.

She handed me an E-hook. "Floor three, right, DC room three fourteen. Please return the interface on your way out. Enjoy your stay."

I picked up the E-hook and thanked her, then walked around the counter to enter one of the four transparent elevator tubes. The door closed, the tube pushing me upward while I glanced at the people on the ground floor, entering and leaving the DC Hall.

Searching for my room, I could see the people inside other DC rooms since the walls were transparent, however their holo screens were dark when viewed from the hallway. Once I found mine, I placed my palm on the scanning panel, and entered, the door closing behind me. It was a small, with a diameter of only one IP. It was meant to be occupied by only one person in a standing position.

I put the E-hook to my left ear and the object attached itself to my head, allowing me to move freely without it falling off. A tone signaled that the connection to my nanoprobes was established.

I thought about my search criteria for a moment. Without making it too obvious, I needed to find articles about current experiments that were somehow related to the Mind and had run into problems.

"Search: Booleans. Current experiments."

Several pages with different titles piled up on the desk screen.

I swiped the screen upward to bring them in front of me on the holo screen wall.

"Advancements in Rejuvenation Procedures."

I tapped on the title, and the first page of information sheet appeared. I glanced through it.

"Thirty years regular cycle... scientist at the Boolean Institute used a novel sequence... new virus extends the rejuvenation cycle up to fifty years..."

Clear.

I tapped on "virus" to check if it had anything to do with Humans. Several new pages appeared, but none of them mentioned the Human species. I swiped all of the pages on my screen and pushed them down, minimizing them at the bottom right corner.

I looked back on the piles of information sheets that referred to the experiments.

"3-D Algae Lakes."

I looked into the file.

On most of the Uni worlds, oxygen is made by fusion plants and GMO forests in the Nature Halls. However, the amounts produced that way are not sufficient for the whole planet's population, so Booleans devised a system of algae lakes, which produce the majority of oxygen. Recently, they seemed to have developed a novel structure where algae grow on several levels, therefore producing more oxygen than a 2-D surface previously had.

It didn't seem like there were any yield issues here.

I clicked on "algae."

"Skin products... raw food material..."

I read through.

Clear.

Humans were not good test subjects either, because their metabolism is too different from ours. In addition, Booleans have been using in vitro cell-culture preps using Descendant cells for centuries. They wouldn't need Humans for that.

I swiped the screens down, and all the pages disappeared in front of me.

"What else? What about Zamnan Second?" I mused and swiped up some more pages from the search pile I had on the desk.

"Dr. Zamnan Second wins the Uni Award for Novel Research in epigenetics and mutagenesis."

Yes. Yet again.

Both Zamnan First and Zamnan Second received multiple awards from Zlathars for the development of the Descendant species. All the species in Uni were once Humans. With the targeted mutagenesis during the voyage of the Seedships, led by Dr. Zamnan First, most of the Descendant species were already being developed, though the current range of species took another thousand years to reach their final stage. The large population of original Humans rebelled against Descendants, but they were defeated by Zlathar forces and placed on the concentration planet Zema4, where they are still kept under surveillance.

I looked back at the holo screen.

This was not the information I was looking for. I touched a pile of information sheets on the desk and made a fist to mimic crumpling paper. All the sheets of the previous search disappeared.

"In the Vision, Zamnan Second showed apprehension regarding the Mind. I need to view Loreans," I said out loud, and typed: *Loreans. Mind. Yield.*

Several pages piled up in front of me.

"The high-security Mind central station is being transported to a new location."

I shook my head slightly and read the line again.

Unclear.

This information did not make sense.

The location of the Mind was a tightly kept secret; only high-ranking Loreans and Zlathars knew about it. If it was a secret, then why write about a change of location in the first place?

Unless…

Unless this was to dissuade anyone else who would want to search for it.

I closed my eyes, letting my nanoprobes recalculate the possibilities. Then I nodded and opened my eyes.

Yes, possible… but then, who? And why?

I looked back to the article and read through the rest. As expected, it was short and didn't give away any useful information. The Mind was too valuable to make something of such importance public knowledge. The only issue was that it hindered the creation of my future Visions. If I did not receive correct data, I could not recalculate possible future options.

I shook my head and raised my hand to the screen, but just before I swiped it away, a line at the end of the article caught my attention:

"…with the smooth new transition. Moreover, there was no delay in chip delivery. The replacements continue on schedule."

Replacements? Of APC chips?

Definitely unclear!

I did not know that APC chips had to be replaced. There should be no need to do so. Most of the synthetic materials produced at Uni last for several millennia. *Why, then, would they need to replace them?*

I looked back at the board and typed "APC chips" to access more information. All of a sudden, there was a faint buzzing sound, and all my screens went black. I looked up, confused.

Then I tapped on the holo wall.

Nothing.

I tapped on the table desk.

Still nothing.

I pressed the E-hook on my left ear and said out loud, "The DC room is dysfunctional. I need assistance."

There was a short break, and then the voice of the woman at the reception replied, "Yes, I see it on the screen. It seems there's a power outage in your DC room."

"Could I change to a different room?"

"We are closing in a few passes. But I can book one DC room for you tomorrow, if there is a need for it."

I took a moment before responding. "Yes, please, book the DC room for me at zero-eight-hundred."

"One room is booked. Thank you for your time, and we apologize for the inconvenience."

"I thank you." I clicked off the E-hook and walked out, joining a group of Senthiens leaving the DC Hall.

I entered my apartment and the lights automatically switched on, then walked into my living room, unzipped my boots, and stripped off my clothes. As I bent down to collect them, I stopped, frowning.

Power outage?

I had never experienced a problem with the power. Anywhere.

I stepped toward the wall. "Recycle bin."

A section of the wall opened outward, and I dropped my clothes in the bin. The wall closed.

The power failed just when I wanted to look further into APC chips. Should I not have access to this information?

I uploaded all the information on APC chips that was available on my nanoprobes.

They were designed and synthetically manufactured by Loreans, and were ingrained into rosenquartz tiles, which were the building blocks of portation chambers. But I had no information what the APC chips actually were. I never thought it was of any importance. Until now.

I closed my eyes and let my nanoprobes recalculate.

The APC chips…

The delivery…

The replacements…

The APC chips…

The yield…

The yield?

I opened my eyes. Zamnan was worried about the yield. *What kind of yield?*

I had no way of knowing. Booleans work with a variety of living materials for their research. Any one of them could have been the problem. But whatever it was, it seemed very important. *Place all our remaining yield into the Mind,* he'd said. And whatever they were missing, it was linked to the Mind. Then I thought of another sentence in the article: "…*there was no delay in APC chip delivery. The replacements continue on schedule.*" But what if that wasn't true? What if the APC chip replacements were actually *not* on schedule?

Was Zamnan talking about a yield of APC chips?

No, this can't be. Yield implies growth—growth of something living, not something that has been synthetically manufactured.

I shook my head and exhaled loudly.

This seemed too large a concept to process in a conscious state. I hoped that all the newly acquired data provided enough information for a revealing Vision.

I sat on the soft bench opposite the large beige wall.

"Wall: Senthia moons," I said, and the wall dissolved into the night sky with two bright white globes, one of them smaller than the other, a slight purple haze in its white coloring.

I slowly relaxed looking at the image on the screen.

This was probably my favorite image in the library of the Descendant worlds. But the images I would never be able to see, although they were the ones I would love to see the most, were the images of Old Earth. The only ones I had ever seen were in my history recap classes more than three hundred years ago, but there had only been a few, and they were unavailable in the image library.

This wasn't surprising. The dead Earth was an all but forgotten memory of the embarrassing beginning of the Descendants' history, and anything connecting Descendants to that past was scarce.

I looked at the top right of the image to check the time. It was past nineteen hundred, the scheduled time to take an evening meal. I didn't feel hungry at all, but I was well aware that too many missed meals would be noted.

No need to cause an alarm.

I brought the food processor out of standby. It was one of the older types, but I had insisted it shouldn't be replaced by a newer version. This one produced food that still had some taste.

Although the meals it made looked like they consisted of

different foods, it was all still done out of the same basic paste, with a little bit of taste difference based on the specific nutrient content. The density of the food was also different, which kept the digestion system, gums, and teeth functional, but in the end, it all tasted similar.

I scanned through the list of meals and decided on the VEV-3, a low-carb, high-protein meal. I tapped the production button and sat on the bench opposite the image wall again, waiting for the synthesis to finish, while looking at the moons, my gaze unfocused.

There were too many open questions. Humans at the Boolean Institute; the problem with the yield, which was somehow connected to the Mind; the APC chip delivery and replacements; the power problem in the DC room…

I closed my eyes for a moment, my frown deepening. Then a moment later, I opened them.

My father!

I need to contact my father. He will advise me.

I got up, voice-opened the clothes wardrobe, and took a sleeveless evening skinsuit. Then I walked to the holo station next to my sleeping area and dialed my father.

In half a pass, the image appeared, and I heard his voice. "Dora."

"Father."

He looked the same as the last time I'd seen him: short dark gray hair, piercing green eyes, thin lips, and even younger skin than before.

"How are you, my child?"

"I am… fine."

His head tilted just slightly. "Did you have any productive Visions?"

"No. Not recently."

"I see."

"And how are you?" I asked.

"My rejuvenation cycle has finished recently."

"Do you still reject Interactive Coupling?"

"Yes, as always."

"It must be difficult."

"It is. For the body. But my mind is free."

"It's been almost four hundred years, Dad."

"Four hundred years is just a fraction of time, but an eternity without your mother."

There was a moment of silence between us.

"Dora, it was a privilege, you know this. But it was also a burden. You know this as well."

"I understand, Father."

"Why did you call?"

"A power outage."

"Yes?" His eyes narrowed.

"How often does it happen?"

"Where?"

"In a DC room. It happened while I was researching APC chips."

He inhaled sharply and stayed silent for a few moments.

"Dora, I usually take the VRA-08 meal," he said in a calm voice.

I opened my eyes wider. My heart started to race. Then I deliberately relaxed my face and regained a neutral expression.

"Yes," I said.

"The search is not important. I would recommend rejuvenation instead."

I swallowed, then said, "Thank you, Father. Will you port? Shall we see each other?"

"I still take the same meal, Dora. Remember that. It's important."

I nodded.

"Perhaps a good idea for you," he said, "would be to take a sabbatical, just like I did three hundred and ninety-three years ago." He lowered his head slightly, still looking at me, making sure I understood what he meant.

I nodded again. "Yes, Father, this might be a good age to take one."

He looked at me for a long time, his lips barely moving to the words he dare not say.

"Goodbye, my child. As your mother would say."

I pressed my lips together and closed my eyes for a moment, then said, "Goodbye, Father. Until a new holo communication."

His image disappeared, and I remained seated.

VRA-08 was a code.

It meant that we shouldn't talk about this subject anymore, because it was dangerous. And recommending rejuvenation actually meant that he was scared for my life. That, should I continue my investigation, I might not live to have my next rejuvenation cycle at all.

I closed my eyes again, thinking of his last words.

I knew what he wanted to say then, and I knew he couldn't. It was something my mother would say when I was small. She'd whisper it in my ear: *I love you.*

I stayed seated for another fifteen passes, trying to pull myself together. Finally, I got up and walked to the food processor. The food was synthesized, and the processor had kept it warm. I sat down on the bench opposite the two Senthien moons and took a bite.

In the middle of my supper, the apartment AI announced,

"It is twenty-hundred. The apartment is locked for your safety. Good night and productive dreams."

With my mouth still full of food, I looked up to the ceiling, following the direction of its voice.

My own safety?

I never really understood who would want to intrude into my living quarters when all the other Senthia inhabitants were locked into their own rooms as well.

I glanced at the time again. In fifteen passes, the lights would automatically switch off. I needed to hurry with my dinner.

I finished most of my food, placed the remains in the recycle bin, and went to the wardrobe to put away my clothes, then walked to the bedroom while sipping the teeth cleaning liquid on the way.

Within two passes, the lights turned off.

I was lying in the dark with my eyes wide open, my brain buzzing with thoughts.

Before I was born, my father had asked for permission to take a sabbatical. His request had been granted, and we spent six years on the desert world of Fraya Spark, completely secluded from Uni.

Recuperation sabbaticals are not unusual for Senthiens. It's the only time when they are free of Visions, because they are not exposed to constant new information flow that normally triggers predictive Visions. But my father had a very different reason to ask for a sabbatical. And he is still alive because no one discovered what that reason really was.

I understood why he wanted me to get away. And I hoped that I still could.

CHAPTER 4

He is a step ahead, and I am following. We are finding our way through a meshwork of the most amazing plants I have ever seen in my life. I look down at my hand and realize he's holding it. His hand is warm and his palm rough. He turns around, smiles broadly, and squeezes my hand.

The soft pressure gives me a feeling of safety, and I keep following.

"We are almost there," he says and turns around.

I am without words. I keep looking at his arm pulling me to follow him. My heartbeat is loud inside my ears, and my lips are dry. I don't understand, but I am excited.

"Now, close your eyes. I will guide you," he says, his teeth pearling on his sunbathed face.

I do what he says.

I opened my eyes to the pitch black of my apartment.
Him again.
What did that mean?
I needed a revealing Vision to tell me about APC chips, about the yield, about things I wasn't supposed to know. I needed an answer.

Instead, I had a wonderful dream of the person I would never meet.

I exhaled. The lights turned on, and I closed my eyes briefly. Then, instead of the usual question, my AI said, "Dora Dana Dasnan, please report to Senior Senthien Visionaire Councilor Ra Jodar Sennan, at the Nature Hall number zero-zero-six-three, in sixty passes."

My heart skipped a beat.

My usual meeting with Jodar was scheduled in a few days. Why now? And why was there no request for a Vision report?

A thread of anxiety wrapped around my heart, crawling under my carefully established demeanor, but this feeling wasn't new. I've been dealing with this since I was six.

I inhaled, keeping the air in my lungs for a few moments, and then breathed out, relaxing my shoulders at the same time. Once my features were completely calm, I got up and walked to my living area.

"Clothes," I commanded to the AI.

A dozen different skinsuits in the wardrobe cupboard rolled out in front of me. I put my hand on the traditional red skinsuit I was obliged to wear when meeting a Senior Senthien.

Then I looked to the right to the last skinsuit hanging at the very end and pulled it out. It was dark gray with atmospheric moisture repellant, five small pockets on the upper left thigh for food tube bars, and spider-net resistance meshwork for physical impact protection.

I paused for a moment.

Why would I choose that?

I decided to follow my instinct.

The wardrobe cupboard slid back into the wall. I put on the

skinsuit, took the matching E-band from the charging drawer, and put on my boots.

I stepped over to the food processor, slid my fingers over the glass command board, and pushed the Process button to begin the food bar synthesis. Once completed, I took five of them out and inserted them into my skinsuit pockets. Then I plaited my hair into a thick braid and headed for the exit.

I contemplated using a few passes for another search in the DC Hall, but it was still closed this early in a day. And if my father was right, perhaps it was better not to search any further. I entered the Nature Hall and then stopped, looking up.

The sky was pale blue seen through the transparent dome shield, and the grass short and faded green. Still, I could sense a higher level of oxygen in here. I took a deep breath and stepped away from the gate, following the path of neatly aligned hexagonal stones, paving a dense network of walkways around the hall.

On the left side was a small forest and on the right was a large flat plain, intertwined with pathways.

I headed left, looking at the forest: low, thin trees with smooth gray bark and geometrical pale green foliage. I walked to the edge of the forest and stopped, looking at the rows of trees.

Then I moved two steps back.

From this angle, all the trees were in one line, one row. I could only see the first one, and all the others lined up behind it. I moved forward a few steps and stopped again. A new column of trees.

Geometrical. Symmetrical. Patterned.

Every tree was surrounded by pavement from all sides, so that no visitor had to step on grass to come close to a tree.

I walked along the paths, trying to stay oblivious to where I was going, but a beeping sound from my E-band alerted me to my imminent meeting with Jodar. I turned around and walked back to the entrance of the Nature Hall.

Councilor Ra Jodar Sennan walked slowly toward me, his heavy dark red coat rustling with every step. More than one thousand years behind him, and Jodar looked younger than my father. He must have chosen a younger age when he started his first rejuvenation.

He stopped one and a half IPs away.

"You know already?" Jodar said, looking at my skinsuit.

"Councilor Jodar," I said, my tone calm and bland.

"The High Zlathar Priest, Monsignor Torquemada Joseph Nadraque, asked for your presence."

"He wishes for a holo communication?"

"No. He wishes for a personal meeting," he said and started walking.

My stomach clenched, my legs frozen to the ground. I had never met a Zlathar before. My main interaction was always through a holo communication, and even though I talked to them, I never knew what they looked like: their faces were always hidden under hooded cloaks.

Will this be the first time I'll see them for real?

I was still glued to the ground for a moment or two. Then I took a silent breath and hurried to join Jodar.

"Direct contact with Zlathars is a privilege to have," he continued. "Although perhaps initially uncomfortable."

Uncomfortable was an understatement. For the first time in my life, I was in real danger.

I tried to remain calm, not revealing any of my thoughts to Jodar. He could never find out just how uncomfortable Zlathars made me feel. Such a strong emotion was not the Senthien way.

"An initial sense of discontent does not present a challenge for me," I said in the same monotonous voice.

"So what does present a challenge, Dana?" He stopped to look at me.

"Through their *connection*, they would be aware of all my thoughts."

"Is there something to hide?" He arched his eyebrows.

"Of course not, Jodar."

"It is clear that for us"—he made a motion with his hands to encompass both of us—"privacy is completely unnecessary. This is why the Zlathars requested a personal meeting with you, Dana. With your level of Visionaire talent, you will be of great help to them."

"I am positive that I will be of service to them."

As we continued walking, I moved my gaze from Jodar's green eyes to the path in front of us. It needlessly curved back and forth across the boring plain in a regular wavy line.

After a few passes, Jodar stopped and turned halfway toward me. I faced him, leaving two IPs between us.

"There have been incidents of… port failures in the past few months," he said.

Port failures? "Does this mean the ports did not happen?"

"No. The ports happened, but the destination is unknown."

I quickly glanced at him, for a moment unable to hide my surprise, but then I moved my gaze backward to the path ahead, feigning indifference.

We continued walking.

For several passes, we remained quiet, then Jodar continued,

"The Zlathar Council is worried. The Mind has never made a port mistake before. The series of recent port failures are clearly not mistakes. They suspect sabotage."

"By who?" I said, my tone flat.

"This is currently unknown. They want to find out if it was done by Humans."

I stopped to look at him. "Humans are kept under high surveillance on Zema4. They cannot access any of the Uni computer systems."

"I realize it is highly unlikely," he said, nodding, then continued walking. "Their low intelligence and the primitive level of their social constellation makes it almost impossible for them to do so… but, Dana, do not forget that they are kept at Zema4 for a reason. Their species was and remains cruel and vicious."

"Of course, Jodar. The video of the Humans' cruelty was repeatedly shown to us during the seven years of history recap classes. I remember it clearly."

"Humans unfortunately did not reach the level of enlightenment we have," he said and continued his slow walk along the path. "We are all fortunate that Zlathars recorded the terrible deeds Humans committed to Descendants. Only our enlightened nature prevents us from exterminating them for good."

"Yes, Jodar, I do not forget."

After a few moments, he continued, "Because the Humans' wish to hurt Descendants has not faltered, the Zlathars need to interrogate you, Dana, to see if the Mind errors are linked to Humans in any way."

"I did not have any indicative Visions. I think this was clear from my reports."

"This is clearly understood from the reports you sent to the Zlathar Council. We might not recognize any indications, Dana, but Senthiens do not have such ability. Zlathars, however, are much more proficient in these areas, and with an overview of all your conscious levels when they… connect… to you… they might see something that gives them a clue. It is our duty to help them find the perpetrator causing this malfunction."

Jodar's slow steps kept moving the rough fabric of his coat around his feet, making a hard swishing sound that was slightly uncomfortable to my ears. "The port will be ready in thirty passes," he said.

My heart was drumming in my ears, but my face remained calm and aloof.

"You will be accompanied by one more person," he continued.

I nodded. "Thank you, Jodar. I will report to you upon my return."

"I thank you, Dana. May Torquemada Joseph Nadraque watch over you."

He gave a slight bow, and I returned the gesture.

He turned away and continued his walk on the wavy path farther into the center of the Nature Hall.

I watched him leave, then turned the opposite way, and for a moment or two, I wondered if it would be inappropriate to ignore the useless stone tiled path and walk a straight line to the entrance of the Hall.

I decided against it. It gave me more time to think.

The Zlathars' request had to be linked to my last reported Vision. Would they be able to see more than what I saw in my Vision when they connect? I cringed at the thought of their connection to me, feeling an uncomfortable tingling sensation at the back of my neck.

They would have access to my thoughts, my wishes, my wants and needs, to all my Visions… and my dreams.

And they would see a Human man in my mind as well. They would see me coming into contact with the only enemy Zlathars have, and as such, I would become an enemy too.

They would not realize that it was only a dream. To Zlathars, Visions and dreams look exactly the same. They could not tell the difference. And neither could I.

Was it a dream?

Or was it the future?

But even if it was the Vision, it didn't mean anything. My father taught me never to blindly trust the Visions. They are merely the most probable course of events based on the current course of events. A Vision is only one possible projection, he said.

I walked out of the Nature Hall gate and turned left in the direction of the porting chamber.

Two things were conflicting. First, I was never wrong with any of my Visions. Each and every one had come to be. But second, nothing in the current course of events indicated that I would ever meet a Human. And yet he kept coming back to me, in the early morning hours from the Visionaire depths of my mind.

I closed my eyes and shook my head to chase that thought away.

Right now, I had more pressing problems. When they connect, Zlathars will see the past as well.

They will find out everything. And I can never let that happen.

My life, and my father's life, was in grave danger.

And I desperately needed a way to hide that part of my mind from them—or avoid the port completely.

I reached the porting chamber gate and stopped.

My heart was racing. I had to exert all my willpower just to keep still.

The breeze coming from the ventilation shaft right above me cooled the beads of sweat appearing on my forehead. I wanted to turn around. I wanted to run away. I wanted to hide. Inside, I was on the edge of fleeing. But on the outside, my demeanor remained calm. I watched the closed door of the chamber gate, waiting for my porting companion to arrive.

"Dora Dana Dasnan." The flat male voice startled me and I turned to look.

"Barka Stevanion Narth," I said.

"I will be pleased to accompany you to Zlatharing."

"I acknowledge your presence and I thank you," I answered in the same monotonous tone.

He turned to the chamber gate, lifted his palm, and pressed it to the screen board.

I didn't move.

He turned his head toward me. "Dana?"

I exhaled silently and slowly lifted my hand to the screen board, but stopped before I touched it.

I can say I forgot an additional E-band battery at my premises and I need to pick it up.

I can say I accidently took the wrong skinsuit and I need to change into a new one.

I can just leave.

But—

I pressed my palm on the cold glass screen board and the gate opened.

I can't.

Escaping from the Zlathars is impossible.

We entered the porting chamber, turned toward the entrance and the gate closed.

"Dana, my rejuvenation period is approaching," Stevanion said, looking at the gate. "I would like to make a request for Interactive Coupling with you."

What?

I turned my head toward him.

He kept looking at the gate. His pose was aloof, his head just slightly turned backward, his thin nose pointing at the gate.

It took me a moment or two to gather my thoughts.

Stevanion's proposal wasn't unusual at all—I'd heard, initiated, and complied with a number of them during my cycles—but right now I had far more pressing thoughts on my mind than indulging my next post-rejuvenation hormonal craving.

"If there would be an additional wish on your side," he continued, still looking at the gate, "I would also be honored to make a contribution to the Senthien population with you at the Office of Progeny at another convenient point in time."

I moved my gaze back to the gate as well.

"I appreciate your offer, Stevanion, but my rejuvenation period has recently passed."

"The port number 409-82-833-01 to porting gate 53'0'11' will begin in three passes," the AI female voice announced.

"Perhaps the next time, then," he said.

I kept my gaze impassive. *Perhaps not.*

The chamber dimmed to dark purple.

I took a deep breath. *Here it goes.*

I clenched my fists and held my breath.

The port lasted no more then a few seconds.

The air suddenly changed, the temperature dropped, and the purple hue of the chamber disappeared. Steady, cool airflow startled both of us as we looked at each other in alarm.

The humid and low-oxygen air of the dark halls of the Zlathar world was nothing I wanted to experience, but the lack of all of the sensations I'd expected triggered an immediate alert.

We were not on the Zlathar planet!

CHAPTER 5

It took me a few moments to adjust to the dark. The surrounding was thick with vegetation of the most amazing shapes and sizes, nothing at all comparable to anything I had ever seen on any of the Descendant planets. I lifted my head to look at the ceiling.

There was none. Above me was simply the universe, a dark blue canvas with an uncountable number of stars.

Seeing the universe like this, with no shield, no screen or protection grid in between, was breathtaking.

"We are not on the Zlathar planet," Stevanion said, stating the obvious.

I looked down again. "No, we are not." My eyes scanned the surroundings, but I didn't move.

"We are not in a porting chamber, either," he continued. "It is highly improbable that any porting can come to pass in this place."

"Improbable, but evidently possible."

"How can this be?" He turned to me. "Did you have a Vision of this?"

"No, I did not. The Mind's porting errors were the reason I was requested to personally report to the Zlathar High Council. We have just experienced such an error."

"This environment does not correspond to any of my saved data. Do you have this information available?"

I didn't even try to load anything from the nanoprobes. If any images of this kind were downloaded on my knowledge base, I would have known about it. This was something I simply wouldn't have forgotten.

"No, Stevanion, I do not have any corresponding information available."

"We need to port back. We need to find a porting chamber."

I lifted my forearm to look at my E-band screen.

"We have no access to a computer frame. And my battery is almost out." I lowered my hand and looked around again.

Stevanion looked at his E-band too. "My E-band has a similar level of power. It is not usual for a battery to lose so much power during one porting procedure. Do you understand why this happened?"

"No, Stevanion, I do not."

"If inward portation is possible on this specific location, I can assume that the outward portation is possible too, wouldn't you agree?"

"I would argue the same, but neither of our E-bands have enough power to generate a hyperspace resonance field and connect to the porting channels."

"This is correct. We need to find a porting chamber," Stevanion said with finality.

"Or a strong enough source of power to load our E-bands. In both cases, we need to change our location."

"Dana, I am in agreement with you."

I lifted my head and looked up at the trees. The wind above moved the leaves in different directions and more of the night sky became visible. The next moment, a small black shadow soundlessly flew high above me. Then another one as well. My heartbeat picked up.

Should I be scared?

Are we in a dangerous place?

I lowered my head and exhaled. *We will soon find out.*

"I would recommend waiting for the daylight, Dana. The light will improve our search."

"Yes," I said and sat on the ground, looking into the sky again. Stevanion remained standing.

I didn't know where we were, and I knew this might well be a dangerous place, but somewhere deep inside me was a thrill, a hidden joy, almost an ecstasy.

I had escaped!

I didn't know how long it would last, but right now I was happy to be anywhere other than facing the High Zlathar Priest.

My eyes were still plastered across the sky. I'd been mapping the view, comparing it to all my saved maps. *Nothing.*

"Dana, what are you looking at?"

"The sky."

He looked up. "Why?"

"The stars, Stevanion. I never saw these constellations before."

Then he looked at me. "Dana, do you have maps saved on your nanoprobes? I do not port with high frequency and had no need for such an information file. Do you know where we are?"

"I have the maps, Stevanion, but these stars tell me nothing."

"This is an impossibility. All the star maps of Uni worlds are recorded."

"Perhaps we are not in Uni anymore."

"This is another impossibility, Dana. This world needs to be in Uni. Otherwise no porting would be possible."

"Stevanion, I understand your rational analysis, and I would argue the same, but the maps I have don't correspond to the image projected onto my optic nerve cam. There are no overlapping star patterns on any of the files."

A rustling sound close behind made me turn around, but it was so dark I couldn't see anything, despite enhancing my ONCs.

"It is vital that we find out where we are," Stevanion said in a lower tone, still looking at the dark shadows of the forest.

"I am in agreement. A change of location might give us more information about this world."

I pulled my knees up to my body and hugged them with both arms.

In the dark, my sight was limited, so all my other senses stretched out, feeling the new world around me. I heard a hooting sound on my left. I turned but I couldn't spot anything. After a few passes, I heard the same sound high above me on my right. I automatically turned in that direction, although I knew I wouldn't be able to see it.

I transferred the audio data for analysis and the nanoprobes came back immediately. There was not an exact overlap, but the information given was that the sound belonged to the organism called a bird. An image of the exemplar organism was projected to my ONC.

We didn't have anything like that on Senthia, but some Descendant worlds did have a large population of this type of flying organism.

My neck started to hurt from looking up, but I wanted to see them for real. After a few passes, I bowed my head, stretching my neck muscles.

That's okay. I will see them, sooner or later...

It was less than two hundred passes before the daylight started breaking behind us, revealing colors and outlining contrasts to the darkness of the night. The few sounds I heard during the night paled in comparison to the orchestra I heard now. The life in the trees was enveloped in beautiful sounds, echoing from one tree to another.

"Stevanion, I think we should start walking."

He looked down at me. "Yes. I believe we should look for higher ground. We might have a better vantage point from which to spot habitation domes."

I got up.

"I am in agreement, Stevanion," I said and started walking.

"There is a very high probability that a habitation area has at least two porting chambers," Stevanion said.

I didn't respond to him this time. I knew that all of the Uni habitats had porting chambers—but what I didn't know was if we were in fact still in Uni. And if we were outside of it, we might not find any habitats at all.

I activated the local coordinates on my nanoprobes and set up a local track path, to make sure we didn't walk in circles.

We walked not saying a word. I looked at the ground, my feet shifting dried leaves on dark brown soil, making soft rustling sounds.

I lifted my gaze to look at the forest. The trees on this planet were so much larger and more diverse than any of the trees I had seen in Descendant worlds. Tall; wide; thin; thick; smooth bark; rough bark; branches starting from the bottom of the soil; branches starting from the top of the tree; bright green; dark green; large leaves; small leaves; flat leaves striped into many green comb-like spikes.

The trees.

They were enchanting.

Who would have thought it possible? Why didn't I see this before? Where is this place?

I looked up. The sky was a beautiful deep blue. The bright star rose behind us, warming the air and the rich greenery we walked through. It was getting lighter with every pass, and slowly our shadows disappeared below our feet.

Every now and then, I closed my eyes for a moment and focused on the sounds.

It is beautiful.

I gave a silent command to my nanoprobes for audio recording. The songs were now committed to my knowledge base memory, and I could bring them back whenever I wanted.

I smiled again, just slightly.

The scents of this forest dazzled me as well. The air was full, rich, and intoxicating, almost to the level of making me nauseous.

It must be the trees.

I inhaled deeply, letting all the scents leave their traces as they passed through my nose, throat, and lungs. Keeping my eyes closed for a moment, I focused on the smells. They were truly magnificent.

"Dana, are you in good state? Your breathing has changed," Stevanion said with a typical neutral Senthien voice.

I breathed out. "I am in good state, Stevanion. Thank you for your concern," I said in the same detached tone.

We continued walking in silence.

Once again, I was distracted by the flora of this place. Everything was so green: a place where you didn't need to close your eyes and they could still rest. Almost every tree had a soft green layer covering one side of the engraved bark, and I noticed it was always facing the same direction.

I stopped for a moment and followed the green carpet with my eyes to the top of one tree and back. Stevanion passed me by. I looked at the tree, then Stevanion, and then at the tree again.

And then—I touched it. It gave way softly beneath my palm. And it felt *wonderful*.

Stevanion turned around, and I quickly removed my hand from the tree.

"Is there a particular reason you were in contact with this vegetative form?"

For a moment I was startled by his question, though it was the most logical one a fellow Senthien could ask.

"I… " I looked back at the tree again. *I wanted to know how it feels. Only… I couldn't tell him that.* "I was analyzing if the vegetation is similar to anything in the saved catalog of Uni vegetation," I said firmly as I approached him.

"That is peculiar, Dana. The analysis I do works mainly though visual comparison. Tactile sensitivity in the layers of my skin is virtually nonexistent," he said, looking down at his open palms.

I know…

I took a quick breath and continued, "The visual comparison did not give me any data. I tried to get another information point. It failed." I passed him and continued walking.

We had been walking for a while and I was getting tired. I could tell by the sliding of Stevanion's feet that he was too. For an instant, there was a slight feeling of panic arising in my mind.

How far do we need to go? Where do we need to go?

I had no answers to these questions, and no Vision to help me.

"Stevanion, we have not digested anything in the last several hundred passes." I stopped and pulled a food bar from my thigh pocket. "I suggest the intake of energy," I said, holding out one bar for him.

"Thank you, Dana. I had not thought to bring any food with me to the port. It must be your frequent porting experience that makes you prepared for different locations," he said, opening the foil.

I looked at him for a moment without responding. I had chosen this specific skinsuit and packed it with food bars, with no idea why I would need it at all. It was a gut feeling. And it was impossible for me to explain it to Stevanion.

"We have food to digest for another one and a half days." I turned away from him, looking at the wild vegetation. "But then we need to find more bars. Or a porting chamber," I said and bit into the white chewy paste.

Just as I finished the bar and folded the empty foil to put back into my pocket, a single water drop fell on the top of my head, right in the middle where my hair divided. Another drop slid from the left side of my forehead to my eyebrow, and another on the top of my nose.

I looked up. Dark gray clouds with intricate whitish patterns had closed in on the bright blue sky and sunshine to give way to a… a water-shower!

This was the only way I could describe it.

On contact, each drop was a bit cold, but then it took on the warmth of my body and spread delicately on the skin, merging with the other drops falling from the gray-patterned sky. I closed my eyes, lifted my face to the sky, and savored the feeling.

"Is this toxic for us, Dana?" Stevanion's flat tone interrupted my thoughts.

I sighed inwardly. I did not respond right away. I wanted to take a moment more to enjoy this unique experience.

Then I turned to him and said in a bland voice, "I do not believe so, Stevanion. There is no reason for this particular concern. However, with this amount of water-shower, our clothes may get wet. We should find shelter."

We continued walking for a while longer, unable to find proper cover. All the trees were marvelous, but none of them seemed to provide enough shelter. It was getting darker, too. Night was falling. I wondered how long the days lasted here. I was disoriented, not only in space, but in time as well.

The water drops were falling hard now, but my skinsuit protected me; every drop just slid off, finding its way to the ground. Stevanion, however, wasn't wearing the same suit as me, and his wet clothes started giving him chills. He was shaking.

Before nightfall, we finally found a tree with large hanging teardrop-shaped leaves, giving enough covered space for both of us, although it didn't leave much room for IP. Neither of us mentioned it, though, and we both crumpled up with our backs to the corrugated tree trunk, its large leaves protecting us completely from the rain.

We didn't talk.

I leaned on the bark and slowly drifted into sleep.

I woke up at the first light of morning. There were no clouds above, only deep, clear blue morning sky with a hint of bright light coming from this planet's star.

My suit was completely dry, but I was still very cold. This, however, had not woken me up during the night. I must have been really tired.

I lifted myself to a seated position and stretched my arms. Then I turned to the still-sleeping Stevanion. He was on his back, arms holding himself in a hug to keep warm, head tilted backward a bit with his mouth slightly open.

In more than 386 years, I had never woken up so close to anyone, so I stood up and moved away from him. Fallen leaves shuffled softly under my feet.

"Barka Stevanion Narth," I said in a neutral voice.

Stevanion didn't stir.

"Stevanion." My voice was louder.

He then moved, cleared his throat, and sat up.

"Stevanion, I believe we should continue," I said.

He looked at me and said in a flat tone, "My body temperature is not convenient."

I looked at his still-wet skinsuit.

"We should walk. The muscle contractions will induce the same effect as an E-shower and you will get warmer."

"I am in agreement with you." He stood up awkwardly, not wanting to press his hands on the soil to push himself up, and joined me.

By midday, the star was high above us and the air was warm. My pace was slow, and I was tired. I touched my lips. They felt rough and dry.

I silently communicated the symptoms to my knowledge base. The answer came back quickly: it corresponded to thirst and dehydration.

It was such a natural, basic need, yet I had never felt it like this before. It was a new and novel experience. It wasn't my nanoprobes giving me this information. It was my body advising me that the current situation was not acceptable.

How amazing is that?

This wasn't something I could record in any way, so I tried hard to memorize the feel of it.

I then turned to Stevanion. "We need to find water."

He blinked few times, trying to clear his eyes. "I do not think this place has any HO engines… "

"You would not need hydro–oxy combustion here. This planet has natural water. The water-shower from yesterday must have gone somewhere."

He nodded, then stopped walking. "My body needs a rest." He sat down on his knees, his gaze empty on the ground.

I looked ahead. "I will try to find some water and come back." I noted the coordinates of Stevanion's location on my nanoprobes and continued walking.

After only a few passes, an unusual plant caught my attention. It was only a little bit taller than the top of my head, and cup-shaped leaves were hanging down low from the green succulent trunk. They held water from last night's shower.

"Ah, the Moons of Senthia!" I whispered and walked to the plant. I held a cupped leaf in my hand, lowered it to touch my lips, and tilted it sideways so the water could flow freely into my mouth. I closed my eyes and enjoyed a thrilling sensation of the cold liquid rolling down my tongue. I drank for what seemed to be a long time. Once satisfied, I let go of the leaf and it sprang up high in the air, empty of its water weight.

I took one leaf still full of water and peeled the stem off the trunk.

The nanoprobe map led me directly back to Stevanion.

"Stevanion, I found water."

He was sitting next to a tree.

"Stevanion, I found water," I said again.

He turned toward me, looking at the leaf and then at me. "Dana, do we have any confirmation that this water is good for intake?"

His voice sounded rough, and his lips were dry and rough like mine.

"I do not have any confirmation, but we are both dehydrated. It is necessary for our bodily functions that we drink."

"Thank you, Dana, but I am unwilling to take the risk if there is no proper safety confirmation."

I lowered my hands and looked down at the leaf cup.

"If there are no health consequences to my body by tomorrow, would you then consider it nontoxic?"

"Yes."

"In this case, you would drink the water. Am I correct?"

"Yes."

"Good. Then we have agreed. Tomorrow, you will drink the water."

I looked at my straps and attachments, wondering if I could keep the water somewhere on my skinsuit, but there was nothing appropriate, so I brought the leaf to my mouth and took several deep gulps. The rest I poured on the ground.

"Let us press on. We only have two food bars left. They will last until tomorrow morning."

Stevanion got up and said, "What is your plan of movement, Dana?"

"We need to find a location where our surroundings are easily observable. We have been unable to find higher ground from which we can do this. My plan now is to walk to the end of the forest."

"Do you think this is achievable?"

I turned to him. "I do not have this information. Our best option is to try. We do not have much choice in the matter."

"I am in agreement with you," he said and turned forward to continue.

Magnificent and breathtaking as this flora was, I found it hard to keep my pace. I kept stepping over lifted roots and fallen trees, brushing past branches and leaves, pushing through the undergrowth. As the day was coming to an end, I was happy for a night's rest.

"Do you think we will have another shower above us?" I heard Stevanion ask behind me.

I looked up. Clear blue sky with no clouds in sight. The slowly folding navy blue blanket promised a clear but cold night.

"I do not think so, but it might start while we are asleep," I said. "Let us find a protected position before we rest."

Not long after, we found a tree similar to the tree that protected us the night before, only this one was somewhat different. Instead of a wooden trunk, its large leaves started at the ground and reached a few feet over our heads. The stem was dark green and hard, with overlapping scales covering the height from the ground to its leaves.

I sat close to the base. Stevanion sat as close to me as the IP distance allowed, so he could still have leaves protecting him from the possible shower.

We didn't talk.

The night fell, covering us in complete darkness. With no visible moon on this planet, stars were the only light, decorating the black vacuum like sprinkled diamond dust. I had seen stars many times before, but somehow now, from here, they looked miraculous.

From the corner of my eye, I noticed movement and looked back at Stevanion. He was shaking in his sleep. This didn't surprise me. His skinsuit had been wet throughout the previous night and most of the morning.

I looked around at the neighboring trees.

Barely visible in the night was a short but wide beige tree that I remembered from before. The bark was quite different from other trees I had seen here, and it peeled off in thin layers.

I rose, walked to the tree, and peeled off several of the large sheets. They were warm and soft to the touch. I brought them back to Stevanion, and without saying anything, I layered them on top of his body as fast as I could without them falling off and without me touching him.

I moved away quickly.

I didn't know what else to do.

I sat down leaning on the succulent green trunk, warm under my protective skinsuit, and fell asleep.

CHAPTER 6

I woke up late the next morning. The sun was already high in the bright sky and the air pleasantly warm. High in the trees, a softly humming breeze mingled with the birds' songs, and looking at it, I couldn't help but smile. I stood up and stretched, feeling my muscles aching, then looked at Stevanion. He was still asleep; soft tree sheets were spread around him on the ground and he wasn't shaking anymore. This made me feel much calmer.

After only a few moments, I heard Stevanion waking up, and as I turned to look at him, seeing his pale and tired features, I had my first Vision in the awake state.

My eyes were open, but I barely registered Stevanion's puzzled look. The sounds around me were now dimmed and replaced by tones a lot clearer and crisper than reality. A white veil from both sides of my field of vision closed off the view of my surrounding completely and displayed—the Vision. And I watched all of this through a nauseating combination of fear and curiosity.

> A man is lying still on an erected wooden bed. He is pale, his eyes closed, and I can feel the recognition rising at the back of my mind. I don't want to let it surface. I focus on the figure lying there that hardly resembles my current companion.
>
> At that moment, he coughs a heavy, throaty cough,

his face a grimace of pain. Someone else is there, too. I see the back of a woman, wearing a light brown dress. She comes to him, supports his shoulders until his coughing frenzy stops, and then helps him lie gently back on the bed. He resumes his corpselike posture, not moving, barely breathing.

"What is wrong with him?" the woman next to him asks and as she turns, I realize that it is me.

Another woman comes into my Vision scene. She has long dark hair and is also wearing loose beige clothes.

"I'm sorry, Dora," she says. "I don't know. It seems he has a flu. Just a regular flu. It normally lasts for a few days only, but it's as if his body doesn't have the means to fight it."

I look back at him.

Stevanion is dying.

Dying from a viral disease that Descendant immune systems never learned to fight.

The Vision disappeared at that moment, and I was looking right into Stevanion's wide eyes.

"You had a Vision. You can *see* while awake!" he said.

"Stevanion, we are not alone. There are people living here. And we need to find them, fast." I stood up and started walking, continuing in the same direction. Stevanion followed, trying to keep up.

"This is truly significant." He was breathing fast and talking at the same time. "This occasion is unique. This is something the High Council needs to know right away. What did you see? Which Descendants?" He caught up and looked at me.

I stopped and turned to him.

"I do not know. I can not say," I said, breaking our locked gaze. "I have never seen them before."

"But… you have been to so many Uni planets, Dana."

"They seemed… well, different."

Stevanion moved backward just a little bit with a slight sense of fear in his eyes.

"Could it be that we are in the Human settlement? Somewhere on Zema4?"

He might actually be right.

"I cannot tell. I do not know," I said out loud.

"Were the people in your Vision… amicable?"

"Yes," I said without hesitation. "And we need to find them soon. Or they us."

"Why? What is the urgency?"

I looked at him, not sure if I should tell him the truth.

"There is something else I saw."

He waited patiently and calmly, in true Senthien manner.

"Stevanion, in my Vision, you are sick. And it is caused by something on this planet. And we need to find people, soon, because they might be able to help you."

"And you are sure they will want to help us?" he asked, as if he wasn't concerned about the information about his health he just received.

"I am sure their intentions are to help us, yes."

"All right. Let us continue," he said in a flat voice as he took a step forward.

I sighed silently and continued walking. I understood him perfectly. Any Senthien would act exactly the same way, taking the Vision on an as-is basis and acting in the best possible way to enable the best possible outcome.

I took the rest of the food bars from my pocket and offered one to Stevanion. He accepted one with a bow of acknowledgment.

I hoped we would find people fast, because without food, we would not be able to last much longer.

We had been walking at a good pace for the first sixty passes, but with the lack of food and water, we got tired quickly and kept tripping over branches and holding onto trees and lianas as we passed. I was in the front, keeping leaves and bushes out of our way, when all of a sudden, I stopped in my tracks.

I was not standing on densely covered undergrowth anymore. I was standing on a beaten path.

My mind was racing.

This path has been used.

By somebody. Recently.

I quickly looked to the right and then to the left. On both sides, the forest made a green tunnel above the trail, the top of it still slightly opened to the rays of this planet's star. My heart was pounding, and I could hardly control my breathing to keep from giving away my excitement.

"We are standing on a path, Stevanion. Someone made this path."

Stevanion didn't respond.

I turned to look at him.

His eyes were closed, as if the brightness around him was blinding, and his body posture showed exhaustion.

"We will find them, Stevanion," I said with obvious emotion in my voice, my usual neutral tone gone.

He then opened his eyes and looked at me. I expected him to say something, but he didn't. There was no strength in him anymore. Then he closed his eyes again, swayed a little bit, and fell on his knees. Just before he hit the ground, I jumped toward him and caught him under his arms.

His body was pressed to mine and his head slumped over my shoulder. I closed my eyes tightly. I had to exert all my willpower to endure this lack of IP and not let him go. I sat on my knees and leaned Stevanion's head on my lap. Then I lifted my head and looked both ways on the path, wondering what to do.

At that moment, an image came to my mind, as clear as a recent memory.

A Vision. In an awake state. Again.

I closed my eyes. Keeping them open felt pointless. I dived into the subconscious display behind my eyelids I could not escape from. After a short moment, the Vision was gone.

I blinked a few times. I did not understand this at all. I never heard of anyone having Visions in an awake state—and now I'd had two of them.

Why?

Why now?

Why here?

I looked around at the green surrounding me, satiating my craving for pure nature.

It's this place.

It must be.

I took a deep breath. In some illogical way, I felt the musical harmony of the birds above binding me to this place.

Stevanion coughed and I looked down at him. He looked at me, his eyes thin slits under the bright light. I expected him to move away at this unusual proximity, or at least to comment on it, but he did neither. He closed his eyes again, tried to swallow; failing, he coughed again.

I looked at the path.

"A group of people," I said to Stevanion without looking at him. "Two… no, three, coming from… " I turned my head to the other direction. "That way. They will help us."

Then I looked down at him. "They will help you."

But he was too weak to answer. His eyes half closed, he was at the edge of consciousness. I looked up to the path again. And waited.

After less than ten passes, I heard the rough sounds of heavy feet on the trodden soil.

"Stevanion, can you stand?"

Stevanion opened his eyes and nodded. I helped him up and stood next to him, holding his arm for support. I looked back down the path. My heart was racing.

Then—they came into sight.

They were three.

And I had seen them before.

CHAPTER 7

"Hello!"

I heard the strong voice of the large man leading the group while he was still more than twenty IPs away. The group continued walking, despite my lack of response. They came to a halt at an uncomfortably close distance.

"I am Peter Wallace. This is Simon," he said, moving his hand to his right, "and Patrick." He motioned to his left.

He had a dark brown beard, which covered half of his face, and all I could clearly see were his pleasant honey-brown eyes.

"We've been looking for you for two days," he said with a smile. "Most Jumpers stay where they land, and it's easy to find them, but you… " He smiled again and shook his head. "We thought we wouldn't find you anymore."

"Until we came across your tracks on our way back," said the man who Peterwallace had introduced as Patrick.

"Fortunately, you chose the right direction. You could have gone the other way, deep into the jungle. We'd never have found you there," said Peterwallace.

Although I had seen them, and I had expected them, I was still so taken aback that I could not respond.

Peterwallace's features took on a worried expression. "Do you understand me?"

"Yes, Peterwallace. I understand you." My voice was firmer than I thought I could muster. "My name is Dora Dana Dasnan. My companion needs assistance."

Peterwallace came even closer and looked at Stevanion. He was conscious but so exhausted that he could not lift his head. The man detached a leather bottle-shaped container from his belt and opened the top. Slowly opening Stevanion's mouth with his hand, he poured in a bit of water. Stevanion swallowed two sips and then coughed.

"He's dehydrated," Peterwallace said, giving me the water bottle, and with one smooth motion he scooped Stevanion up in his arms.

"Take a sip—you need it, too!"

The idea of putting the bottleneck to my lips just after it had touched someone else's slightly revolted me.

"No, thank you, Peterwallace. I am not thirsty."

He gave me a side look but didn't comment.

"Let's go back to the village!" he said to Simon and Patrick. Then he turned to me and said, "And Dora, it's just Peter."

At first, we all walked in silence, our feet crunching the soil underneath our feet. Peter kept watching me intently, and I tried to keep my eyes on the path.

"You told me," I said after a while, still not looking at him, "that other Jumpers stay where they were ported. Which other Jumpers?"

"I thought you might be interested in that. You all are!" His smile was broad, as if revealing a best-kept secret. "You will hear more from Old Mike once we're back in the village, but in short, in the last couple of months, we've had a number of people being teleported here. Like I said, most of them are so shocked they just stay where they were dropped, and it's easy to find them. But you…" He looked at me speculatively over Stevanion's head that was drooping on his shoulder. "You didn't."

We continued for some moments in silence. He kept looking at me as we walked, and finally I said, "Why are you looking at me?"

"Oh, I'm sorry, but you… you don't look very Human. I mean, you do, sort of… but your eyes—they are *so* green. They don't look—Human. I don't mean that in a negative way," he quickly continued. "It's just… you look—alien."

"I am not an alien. I am a Senthien, a race of the Descendants." I turned my gaze back in the direction we were walking. "I guess you must have seen many Descendant porters in the last few months."

"No," he said, looking back at me. "No, all of the Jumpers were Humans."

Humans?

I stared back.

Does this mean that every mistake the Mind made was with a Human?

"I… do not understand," I said.

"Aye, me neither." He laughed. "But one thing is for sure: If you're not Human, then you and your partner here are the very first Descendants to have been ported to Earth."

I stopped in my tracks.

Earth!

The word pierced my mind, and I let out an audible gasp, my eyes wide open.

"Earth?" I whispered.

Peter stopped and looked back at me. Behind his beard, I could recognize a smile.

"Hmm—you didn't know, did ya? I guess not being a Human,

you couldn'a… well, Dora, welcome to Earth!" He continued walking to catch up with the others.

I was frozen for a moment, my gaze empty on the ground. Then, realizing I was falling behind, I pressed on.

We walked for more than two hundred passes. I was getting tired, but I didn't want to ask for a break. Peter was still carrying Stevanion, who was either unconscious or so exhausted he couldn't find the strength to protest.

The vegetation had changed as well. The trees here were very high—twenty, perhaps thirty IPs—and their trunks were thick and brown, wrinkled as the rough, dark soil we were walking on. Their bright green leafy crowns spread high up on top, completely shadowing the ground.

And then, I started recognizing a new sound, first faint and then louder and louder.

Voices.

Human voices.

I searched the surrounding area, expecting to see houses or domes or some kind of living quarters arranged on the ground, but there were none. And although the voices became so clear I could almost recognize the words, I did not see anything. All around me were high trees and fern bushes.

Peter turned toward me with a grin on his face and lifted his index finger in front of his chest. For a few moments nothing happened, and I just kept looking at him and waiting with polite patience. Realizing that I didn't understand his gesture, he said, "Look up."

Understanding now what the gesture meant, I followed the direction his finger was pointing.

I gasped.

The trees were connected with a dense net of hanging wooden bridges. The larger trees harbored broad platforms, and some of the smaller ones had tiny wooden bases that connected two bridges together.

Peter stopped next to one tree that had regularly interspaced protruding sticks, starting from the bottom of the tree and spiraling all the way to the top. They were made out of wood but were definitely not the natural part of the trunk.

"Come, Dora. Let me show you our village," he said and motioned me to follow him to the tree. He started climbing, setting his feet on the wooden protrusions, carrying Stevanion as if he was no burden at all. Simon and Patrick didn't follow, obviously waiting for me to go first.

I swallowed heavily, but my face stayed calm, my distress hidden beneath a well-trained mask.

I placed my foot on the first protrusion and carefully put my weight on it. Logic dictated that if the protrusions could hold Peter's weight together with Stevanion's, they could certainly hold the weight of someone who, coming from a lower G-field planet, was a lot lighter than any of the inhabitants of this Old Earth. Still, I needed several steps to gain confidence in these stairs that led up the tree.

When I reached the small wooden base, I was gasping for air. My muscles hurt and my windpipes burned with the fast airflow I was now forcing into my lungs.

So much for the E-showers...

They were made to strengthen muscles for routine movement on other Descendant worlds. They were not, apparently, made for climbing.

"Are you all right?" Peter asked. He made a motion as if he

was about to touch my shoulder, but thinking better of it, he let his hand drop down again.

"Yes, Peter. I. Appreciate. Your. Concern," I said, one breath between each spoken word.

"All right," he said, not looking very convinced.

After a few moments, I looked around. The large platforms I saw from below were not merely platforms. They each supported a wooden cottage. Through the windows, I could see orange-gold flickering light.

Patrick now came to our platform. With four people on this small space, I started feeling uncomfortable. We were well within one IP from one another.

"Dora, could you come with me, please?" Peter said, still holding Stevanion, and motioned with his head to follow him over the wooden bridge. I stepped onto it and felt the swaying movement that Peter made with his walking. It made me feel nauseous.

"You can hold onto the rails," said Patrick behind me.

I swallowed and grabbed the rope rails on both sides.

"Perhaps you should wait a few seconds until Peter gets across. Then it won't sway so much," he added.

I nodded and waited.

Once Peter stepped onto the cottage platform, I stepped forward.

Having the ground move below my feet was something I had never experienced before. It was thrilling and scary, but with every step I took, the more comfortable I felt. Once I reached the other platform, I heard Peter talking to someone else.

"… should definitely go to the infirmary. He needs medical care."

Stevanion was now conscious but clearly scared to protest

the body-to-body contact with Peter. The person Peter was talking to was a woman. She turned around and came closer to me, thankfully stopping one IP away. Her skin was suntanned bronze, and she had dark eyes and a strong build. Her thick dark hair was tied at the back of her neck, and she wore a loose beige dress with straps, her arms free of fabric.

"I'll come back in a moment," Peter said and turned to walk over another bridge. The woman didn't turn to Peter but kept looking at me, her eyes filled with curiosity and interest.

"Hi, Dora. I am Tania," the woman said, her voice strangely familiar, as she put her hand out toward me.

I looked at her hand, then at her.

"Where is he taking Stevanion?" I asked.

Tania pulled her hand back. "He needs to go to the infirmary. The hospital house. He seems to be dehydrated, and he will need a day or two to recover. You teleported two days ago, isn't that right?"

"That is correct."

"Hmm," said Tania, lowering her gaze. "He seems surprisingly weak after only two days without water. Did you drink anything, Dora?"

"Yes. I drank the water from the water-shower above us, which collected in the leaf of a tree. Stevanion refused."

Tania raised her eyebrows. "The water-shower? Ah, you mean the rain. Okay. Well, how about I show you to your cottage, and then you can have something to eat and drink?"

"My cottage?" I was confused. *Why would I want a cottage, and why would they have one for me at all?*

"Well, we have a few more cottages that just became available. People getting together, moving in and stuff, you know."

My gaze was as blank as my thoughts. I did not understand any of what she was saying.

"Never mind. There is a cottage that is free for you, and you are welcome to live there."

"Live? Here?" I was dumbstruck. Then I took a deep breath to center myself. Even if I wanted to stay here, hiding from the Zlathars, Stevanion didn't need to. He needed to go back to Senthia. "Stevanion… we need access to your computers. I am fairly confident that I can correct the mistake in the port," I said, keeping my tone flat and matter-of-fact.

She turned around to look at me.

"I would *love* to give you access to a computer. In fact, I would love to have access to a computer myself. But Dora, there are no working computers here. We are back in the Middle Ages."

"I do not understand. The Earth had computers before the Evacuation. Where are they now?"

"Well, the computers are still here, sort of, it's just that we can't use them. They don't work. After the Evacuation, something happened that destroyed all the electronic devices on Earth."

I took a moment to connect to my nanoprobes, searching for information about the escape from Old Earth.

"EMP."

"Pardon me?"

"Electromagnetic pulse. I do not have the full information, unfortunately, because the data on Old Earth is very scarce, but the computers are not working because of the EMP."

Tania wrinkled her nose. "Let's talk about it later. I'm sure lots of others would like to hear what you have to say. Until then," she said, "shall I show you where you can sleep?"

I nodded. "Yes, Tania, please take me to my sleeping quarters."

"Sleeping quarters," Tania repeated and smiled. "It's really quite small, you know." She started walking around her cottage to the other bridge, her feet tapping on the wooden platform. On the other side, the platform connected to the neighboring platform with another hanging bridge, only this one was made out of a row of thick wooden branches held together by a rope. On both sides of it, a mesh net of dark green vines made an elastic but resistant fence.

Tania was already on the other side. She turned around.

"It's safe, don't worry."

I stepped on the bridge and immediately felt a lot less comfortable than on the previous one I had to cross. Through the gaps beneath my feet, I could see the ground below. I grabbed the fence tighter.

Tania looked down to the ground and then back at me.

"It's about ten meters high," Tania said, realizing the thoughts that occupied me.

I didn't know what size a meter was, but ten of them looked very high.

"Look at me, it's easier."

I moved my gaze to her.

She was right. It was easier like that.

I moved on and reached the next platform.

I followed her across several bridges, when we finally stopped next to what was apparently my cottage. Tania walked to the other side and stopped next to an opening with a thick hanging curtain made of leaves. She walked in and held the curtain with her hand to let me through.

The room was a lot darker than outside. The two narrow windows did not allow much of the fading afternoon light into the cottage. Tania walked to the small wooden table next to one of the windows, then picked something up and made a short scratching sound in her hand. A flickering light appeared in front of her.

I came closer and peeked around her to see what was making the light.

In front of her on the table was a small white tube, and on the top of it was a beautiful yellow-orange light.

"A candle," Tania said, noticing my enchanted gaze. "You've never seen fire?"

I shook my head. I could not find my voice to answer her.

Tania smiled. "It's nice to see it's making such an impression on you. Uni Humans still use it on Zema4. They're not half as thrilled about it as you are."

"I have heard of it. I even downloaded some pictures of fire, but…"

"But what?"

"But I just didn't realize it moves!"

Tania laughed. "Oh, just wait until you see what Earth has in store for you!"

"In store?" I was puzzled.

"Never mind, it's an old term. Why don't you get comfortable? I'll bring you some clothes so you can change. And otherwise…" Tania looked around the room. "Just make yourself at home, okay? I'll be right back." She nodded and left.

I turned to look around the small room. Although night was falling, the candle lit the room well enough for me to take it all in. Everything around me was made out of wood: a narrow table, two chairs, a bed, and a wardrobe.

Wooden floors. Wooden walls. Wooden ceiling.

It felt warm.

It felt cozy.

And it was beautiful.

I walked over to the bed and bent down to see what its top was made of. It had two thin layers of textile on top, and below was a dense meshwork of very thin brown threads, making the surface soft but resilient.

Tania came back then. She placed a small bag and a leather bottle on the table.

"I also brought some food and water for you. You probably don't feel hungry right now, but as you relax a little bit more, you'll realize that you're starving," she said and smiled.

"And here are some clothes. I'll put them on your bed. Tomorrow morning, I'll take you to a lake pool. You can have a bath there. It's very pleasant this time of the year."

I stayed silent.

What is a pool? And what is a bath?

I quickly checked my nanoprobes. I received the images instantly, but I did not understand them. It resembled nothing I have heard or done in my life. However, I didn't let that show on my face.

Senthiens always understand.

Senthiens always know.

"Is that okay with you? Are you all right being here by yourself?" Tania said warily, as if doubting that any of what she said had reached my processing centers.

"Of course, Tania, I thank you." My voice was calm, steady and confident. "I will see you tomorrow, and we can go to a lake pool."

Tania waited for another moment and then smiled slightly, obviously not understanding what was happening behind my confident façade, but realizing that she wouldn't manage to find out much more tonight.

"Good night, Dora. Get a good rest."

"Good night."

"And Dora, before you go to bed, put the candle out."

I turned to the candle, then back to her. I did not understand what she meant.

She smiled broadly. "Blow on it to turn the fire out. All right?"

"Yes, I understand."

As she left, I felt tiny pricks of panic crawling up my throat. I did not understand several things she had talked about.

Pool? Bath? New clothes? And why can't I wear my skinsuit?

I picked up the soft, beige-colored clothes she left on the bed. I wasn't even sure how I should put them on. They were too large and would leave too much space around my body.

Did Tania want me to dress this way for sleeping?

I let them fall back onto the bed.

Sleep times at Senthia were spent with no clothes on at all, but as I thought of taking off my skinsuit, I realized that the temperatures were not tightly regulated as they were in my world. So I decided to keep the skinsuit on.

I walked over to the table to blow on the candle. My breath made the fire move even more, and the orange flickering light made beautiful shapes dance on the walls and ceiling. When the fire finally died, the room got dark, and it almost reminded me of the complete darkness of the sleeping time in my apartment. I walked over to the bed and lay down on top of the double sheets with my boots still on as well.

It took me a long time to fall asleep. My mind was full of jumbled thoughts. None of them made any sense anymore.

What was I doing here?

Why did the Mind start making mistakes?

Who were these people?

Where did they come from?

And how, for the Moons of Senthia, does Earth still exist?

Earth was dead.

It died a long time ago. What was once a vibrant green planet became a dead, dry place with no oxygen and all the oceans scorched. I remember seeing the images of Earth that were taken by the satellites, the last transmission before the Descendants left the Solar System. I remember seeing them.

So how is this possible?

My troubled thoughts wore me down until they were lost somewhere, falling away in the dark as I finally fell asleep.

CHAPTER 8

I opened my eyes to the waking traces of the dawn. I gazed idly around for a moment and then closed my eyes again, seeing behind my eyelids the residual image of the wooden ceiling above. Sunshine rays made a random pattern on the wooden cottage wall, leaving an artistic design of soft yellow-white shimmering images.

I took a deep breath.

Air.

No!

Oxygen.

It was downright intoxicating. It was rich and powerful and natural, bringing with it the fresh green smell of this planet's flora.

It was early morning. I hadn't had a Vision. The night had released me to a deep, dreamless sleep, allowing for a complete and thorough rest I hadn't felt since childhood.

I opened my eyes again, slowly, deliberately, and enjoyed the soft rise of the morning light, the natural start of the day. The Earth's day.

Earth.

Earth.

I'm on Earth.

I smiled at the thought.

I was walking on a ghost planet. A natural, green ghost planet. And no one in Uni knew about it.

If they did, would they want to come back?

Somewhere behind this cottage, I heard voices: men's voices, women's voices, and other tiny voices that might have been female but were somehow different. They were all muffled, and I assumed it was because people were still in their cottages.

A moment later, I heard soft footsteps crossing the wooden bridge and stepping onto my platform.

There was a knock on the wooden wall, just on the side of the leaf curtain. I remained silent, waiting. I didn't know what I should do, although I felt this situation needed some response.

There was another knock.

I thought about it again and decided that knocking on the wood of the bed frame might be the best reaction.

There was a soft laugh outside, and I heard Tania's voice. "May I come in?"

"Yes, Tania, please, do come in," I said and stood up.

She moved the heavy leaves and stepped forward.

"Don't worry about it. I know it's confusing for you," Tania said with an empathetic expression as she came in. "Even more so for you than for other Jumpers, I imagine. Many of the others do have some recognition of the old customs and ways. Before entering a cottage, one knocks to say, 'I am here! Can I come in?' And then the person inside comes to the door and lets them in, or gives them permission to come in. Just so you know for the future." She smiled. "How do you feel today? Did you sleep well?"

"I slept well. I appreciate your concern."

Tania looked at me, and again her face gave me the impression that I had said something unusual. I decided to ignore it. I knew it was bound to happen.

"Good, I'm glad. I see you didn't feel comfortable taking off your suit," she said, looking at my dark gray skinsuit. "It's quite understandable."

She walked to the bedside and folded over her arms the beige robes she'd left for me the night before. "I know those special suits can handle being submerged, but you should really take it off when you take a bath. It is so much better. Trust me, you will enjoy it."

She smiled and motioned for me to follow her.

I was not at all certain that I would take off my suit when we came to whatever a pool was to do whatever a bath was, but I followed her all the same.

We had to walk through the tree village and over several platforms and wooden bridges to reach one of the trees with a way down to the ground.

"Shall I go first?" Tania asked, arching her eyebrows.

"Yes, please do."

Tania started climbing down, skillfully placing her feet on the protruding wooden rods placed in the tree trunk as stairs.

"Tania, do you have information on Stevanion's health state?" I asked as I followed her.

"I went to see him just before I came to you. He's feeling better, but I think he should stay in the hospital cottage for another day or two," she said as she climbed down. When she reached the ground she looked up, waiting for me to descend, and then started walking again.

"I guess you have many questions," she said, turning her head toward me.

"Yes, Tania. I do. Have you been living here for the past five thousand years?"

"For heaven's sake, no, not at all! We were cryo-preserved. Frozen. We woke up only nine years ago."

"Was this the plan, to wake up at this specific time?"

"Oh, no! We were supposed to wake up one hundred years after the start of the cryo. But the de-freezing schedule was overridden. As far as we can tell, we weren't supposed to wake up at all."

"When was the cryo-preservation performed?"

"That was 2231. We were supposed to de-freeze in 2331."

"And the News came in 2232," I said. I didn't need to access nanoprobes for that. It was a famous year; everyone knew about it. It was the year when scientists determined that Earth had an expiry date. "By the time you were supposed to de-freeze," I said, "the Earth would have been dead, nothing but rock and sand."

She nodded. "We only found out about the News and the Evacuation when our first Jumpers came. We had no idea what had happened when we woke up."

"This means that whoever overrode the hundred-year wake-up plan did not want you to wake up on a dead planet," I said.

"Not only that. I think the idea was to save us from the solar blasts, too."

"What do you mean?"

"Well, our cryo-crèches were located in the CPC, the Cryo Preservation Center. And that was in the city... well, on the outskirts of the city, but still, the city."

I looked at her for a moment, then said, "I assume this is not where you de-froze, then."

Tania shook her head. "No. New place altogether."

She moved aside a long branch that blocked her way and held

it for me as I passed, then continued. "We were about four walking days' distance from the city, and… we were underground."

I looked at her. "Underground? That saved you from the solar storms and the EMP. That is how your cryo-crèches were still working."

Tania nodded. "We were transferred to… some kind of industrial underground installation. Well, some of us were transferred, anyway…"

"I do not understand."

"I'm not really sure myself. It was maybe fifteen to twenty meters underground, and the immediate surroundings and the staircase up to the surface all looked… industrial, or military even, I don't know."

"No, I meant: why did you say 'some of us' were transferred?"

"Ah," she said and lowered her head. "There were a lot of people who went under cryo, several hundred, I'm sure. But when we woke up, we were only two hundred."

"What happened to the rest of them?"

"I don't know. I guess the same thing that happened to the rest of the world who didn't evacuate."

I looked at her. "Did… did Jumpers tell you about Evacuation? About the *selection*?" My last words were spoken in a barely audible voice.

"Yes."

I nodded, but Tania didn't look at me.

What could I say to a person who'd been left behind? Left behind to die, like billions of other people who were not deemed valuable enough or rich enough to save—while I was the descendant of those who were?

I closed my eyes for a moment, trying to chase away this thought.

"Why did you then de-freeze—wake up—nine years ago?" I said, trying to change the subject.

She shook her head and pressed her lips together in negation. "I don't know. Perhaps it was an accident, a mistake?" She looked at me and shrugged her shoulders. "Well, whatever it was, we survived. And I am grateful for it."

Then she looked forward and continued walking.

We passed through a stretch of forest that didn't have many trees but was covered in ferns. I slid my hand over the plants, touching the soft leaves, which bent under my palm and sprang back as I released them. My mind was still overwhelmed by the stunningly diverse vegetation of this place.

"This is all new to you, isn't it?" Tania asked through a smile.

I nodded. "It is wonderful. I have never seen anything like this."

"Come. I'm sure you will find the bath wonderful as well."

After only a few more passes, we reached a small water surface, not more than four by four IPs. The water was clear and fairly shallow, with large dark stones forming clear patterns at the bottom.

"Is this a pool?" I asked.

"Well, not really," Tania said, a grin on her face. "It's more like a bathtub."

When she didn't receive any response from me, she continued. "You're used to showers, aren't you?"

"Yes. That is correct."

"And you've never had a bath?"

"No."

"Well, this is like a shower in that it's meant to make you clean, but it's much more enjoyable."

Much more enjoyable. I repeated the words in my mind,

wondering how there could be anything more enjoyable than the most pleasurable and intense tactile sensation I had experienced in Uni.

"You'll need to take off your suit."

I didn't move.

"I will not look as you take it off, I promise. But I will have to watch you while you're in the pool. It does get a bit deeper a few stones into the pool. And"—she glanced sideways at me—"I assume you don't know how to swim."

"You are right," I said in a typical calm Senthien way. "I do not know this word."

Tania seemed a bit surprised with my answer.

"Hmm, well, swimming is… I guess movements you do in water to keep yourself at the surface, with your head out of the water."

"Out of the water? What happens if you do not do these swimming movements?"

"In most cases, you drown."

"Drown," I said flatly.

"Your head goes under the water, you inhale water into your lungs, and you die because of lack of air."

"Oh," I said with a little bit less Senthien authority than I'd planned. "I guess I never really thought about dying."

"It's because you're young. Young people never think of dying. Unless something happens to make them think of death."

She lowered her gaze for a moment and her facial features changed in a way I could not decipher. Then she lifted her head and said a bit louder than before, "You seem the age of my oldest daughter. How old are you?"

"I am three hundred ninety-two standard years old."

"*What?*" Tania gasped, her eyes wide with bewilderment.

"You look extremely surprised."

"I *am* extremely surprised! You look, I don't know, like you're twenty-three or twenty-four. Not more than twenty-five!"

"That is because of rejuvenation."

"Rejuvenation?"

"Didn't Jumpers tell you about rejuvenation?"

Tania shook her head.

"Rejuvenation is a cellular healing process. It regenerates your body, taking off several dozen years of age every time it is done."

"Wow, I could use some of that." She smiled. "How does it work?"

"I do not know all the details. It is not really my expertise. It was developed by Booleans—another Descendant species—and it uses a virus carrier that accesses and infects every cell in the body, triggering major cell division over the next several days. In this process, one daughter cell takes the majority of the excess metabolites and dies, leaving the body with only new cells and virtually no waste or harmful products. The dead cells are removed by macrophages and discarded. But the details of the process are known only to the Booleans."

"That's… impressive. And how long do Descendants live?"

"A thousand, two thousand years, maybe more. The technology has improved dramatically in the last one and a half thousand years, so most individuals that came after these improvements are still alive."

"Don't you get bored with living so long?"

"No," I answered surprised by her question. "Everyone lives like that."

"Yes, I guess it's normal for you. I don't know what I would do if I was granted another hundred years of life. But then again, if you know you're going to live that long, you arrange your life accordingly."

Tania placed the beige clothes on a dark stone just outside the water.

"I guess your population must be growing really fast, with children being born and people living so long…"

"Well, the birth rate is controlled by the Office of Progeny. They keep the number of new individuals slightly above the switch-off rate."

"New individuals? You mean children?"

"Yes, children."

"Interesting. So you guys have some kind of inbuilt contraceptive system?"

"Contraceptive?"

"So you don't get babies when you have sex?"

I blinked at her. I didn't understand anything she said.

"When you have intercourse?" she explained further.

"Are you referring to Interpersonal Coupling?"

She paused for a moment and then shrugged her shoulders. "I guess that's the same thing."

"Well, this process is done every fifty or sixty years, just after rejuvenation, and every person has…"

Tania looked at me and then burst into laughter.

After a few moments of staring, I said, "I do not understand your reaction."

"I'm sorry, I just don't see how people can refrain from having sex! Every fifty years? Seriously? Isn't the orgasm one of the strongest drivers of evolution? Ensuring the survival of the species and all?"

I stayed silent, watching her. There were too many new concepts and terms for me to process in one sentence.

"Okay, let's get you out of this suit and into the water. I feel this needs several hours of explanation, and if we do that, you'll never get a bath."

She turned her back toward me and said, "Tell me once you're in the water."

I tilted my head slightly and didn't move, looking at Tania's back.

"I do not understand," I said.

"What don't you understand?" She turned her head slightly so I could hear her but she kept her back toward me.

"Why do you not want to look at me if this might cause the event of my lungs being filled with water without the ability to breathe?"

She then turned fully toward me, and after a short pause she said, "I thought you wouldn't want me to look at you while you're getting undressed."

"Why?"

"I thought you might be shy."

"I do not understand."

"Well, people are often shy about taking their clothes off in front of people they are not intimate with."

"Intimate?"

"When people feel very comfortable with each other, when all the borders are down."

"Like an IP border?"

"Yes, like for example an IP border." She looked at me intently and continued, "Are all Descendants like you?"

I nodded and unzipped my skinsuit. Tania lowered her gaze.

"The other Jumpers," I said as I took off my clothes, "the Zema4 Humans—are they like you, or like Descendants?"

"They are like us in the sense that they are shy to get undressed in public."

"Hmm." I thought about it for a moment, remembering images of my early life. "Yes," I said more to myself and then walked to the edge of the pool.

"The temperature is very comfortable," Tania said, following me to the edge, "but there are some springs on the sides of the pool that are quite hot and can burn your skin if you stay there, so be careful not to get too close to those."

I turned around to look at her, nodded, and then stepped in with one foot.

Then I stopped. The feeling was like nothing I had ever experienced. It was like getting into very warm, dense air that pushed me from all sides the same way. Every so often small bubbles of air drifted upwards, following the contours of my leg. And it tickled.

I looked at Tania and smiled.

"You like it?" she said and smiled back.

I nodded, then looked back down, seeing the unclear image of my foot under the water. I stepped in with the other foot and stayed like that for several moments. It was such an immense feeling, I was sorry I couldn't record it to my nanoprobes. I recorded the pool image, though, and then walked further into the pool, stepping down two more stones.

"You can now sit on the stone behind you. Your shoulders will still be out of the water. If you go deeper, you'd need to be able to swim," she said.

I cautiously sat down, enjoying the unexpected sensation as the water enclosed me in its pressure from my thighs to my shoulders. It was a very close and comfortable warm touch, and it was all over my body. Everything was defying the IP distance, but it was so good, I had no choice but to enjoy all the sensations I felt against my skin.

"Here," Tania said, kneeling next to me and handing me a green bar. "It's soap. Handmade. Totally organic." She winked at me.

I kept looking at her, not understanding.

"Take it," she said and shook the bar in her hand.

I took it, but it slipped from my hand and fell under the water to the stone floor next to my feet.

I bent down to fetch it, tilting my head up so I could still breathe. But my lower back moved into the stream of a hot spring and I yelped, moving my body away. My feet slipped from the stones below and the next moment, my head went under the water.

The sounds immediately changed. The clear and crisp resonance of the air turned into a muffled cadence of thousands of little green bubbles slowly floating upward. Above my head, I saw my long hair bending and twisting to a slow-moving tune. I tilted my head sideways, my hair following the motion, as I watched this fascinating performance.

The next moment, Tania grabbed me under my arms and pulled me out.

I sat back on the stones and blinked a few times to clear my eyes.

Tania's breathing was heavy. "Are you okay?"

I turned to look at her. "Yes. Of course."

"It's good that you stopped breathing!" she said. "It's a very… instinctive response. For Humans."

I looked at her, searching for deeper meaning behind her eyes, but I didn't see any.

"Thank you. For lifting my head out of the water."

Tania smiled broadly and shook her head. "You're welcome, Dora. Any time."

She then stood up and opened up a towel.

"Maybe that was enough excitement for one morning. Let's get you dry. And it's time for a fashion change, too."

I stood up, frowning at the words I didn't understand.

"Earth clothes. They are much more comfortable than a skinsuit. Trust me."

I doubted it, but decided to comply nevertheless.

CHAPTER 9

I walked very slowly, scanning and measuring every step before I placed my foot on the ground. I looked at my pale feet and my light green toenails as I pressed gently down on the dry brown soil laced with grass and fallen leaves. It didn't hurt, but it was such a strong tactile experience that I could hardly focus on anything else.

I exhaled and then bent down to put on the soft leathery shoes I was carrying in my hand. I stretched my toes inside and lifted my head, letting in the surrounding sounds: the murmur of people talking, children yelling and laughing, an amazing instrumental concerto of numerous species of birds coming from way up in the trees, the buzz of small insects.

I looked up. Two birds, one following the other, flew from one high branch to another, hiding again among the lush green of this ancient forest—untouched, uncoded, and real.

I stopped next to a group of people, women and men with suntanned skin and gray-grizzled hair. I assumed this meant they were older, but with none of these physical markers visible in any of the Descendants, there was no way for me to tell their age.

They were all sitting in a circle. Each of them was bent over a bowl, holding a large smooth rock with both hands, which they used to scrape the bottom of the bowl. I stepped closer, interested in what they were doing.

"Would you like to try?" one of the men asked, a friendly smile behind the gray beard.

"Thank you, but I can observe the process from here as well." My voice was even.

"I know you can see it. But sooner or later, you'll need to do it yourself. Everyone gets a turn." And all of them laughed.

"What are you performing?" I asked.

A woman turned toward me but continued her work. "We're making flour. This one is from maize. We'll use the flour to make bread."

I leaned in closer. The bowls weren't empty. At the bottom of each was a mixture of yellow grains and powder.

"Yes, I tried your bread yesterday evening. It was very good. Very dense."

They all laughed again. I looked around the group, not understanding the laughter, and took a small step back. Then one man lifted up his hands up in front of him, his palms white with powder.

"Hey, it's not my fault! It wouldn't rise. What could I do about it?"

"Put in some yeast, perhaps?" said a woman sitting opposite him.

"I did!" The man shook his head and said in a lower tone, "As if that's the first time I ever made bread."

"Rafael, we're joking," said a woman. "I know it sometimes doesn't work. And anyway, it was very good, perhaps even because it was so dense." Then she turned to me and asked, "You liked it, didn't you?"

"Yes."

"There you go," she said, looking at Rafael. He nodded and smiled.

The man who spoke to me first turned to Rafael and said, "There's always some joy in making fun of a famous chef. You know that, don't you?"

Rafael shook his head but was laughing now.

"You know, Tony, if I ever get to open another restaurant, you'll need to pay double for the meals!"

Tony laughed. "That's fine, buddy. It'll still be worth it!"

Then they all laughed again.

I was lost. All of this was spoken in a friendly, bantering manner, but I couldn't follow half of it, let alone understand the jokes they shared.

An alien.

After thousands of years of targeted genetic manipulation, remarkable technological achievements, and dominion over two hundred terraformed worlds, I am finally back on Earth, the original cradle of life and I'm—an alien.

Again.

I turned away from the group and continued on my way, making even larger loops around other groups I met. None of them talked to me, but almost all of them looked at me, apparently fascinated by my piercing green eyes. After a while, I stopped looking back at them, feeling self-conscious and alone.

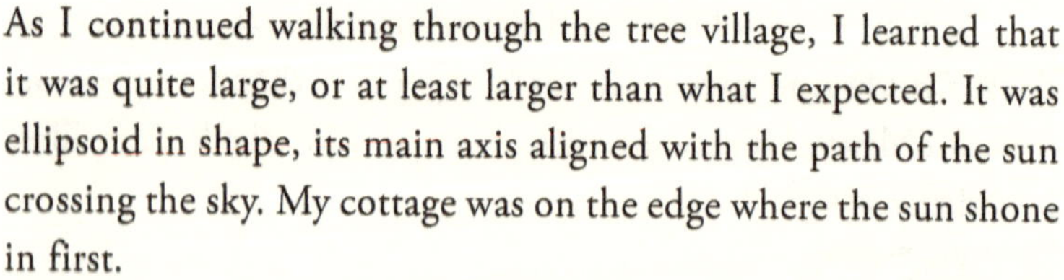

As I continued walking through the tree village, I learned that it was quite large, or at least larger than what I expected. It was ellipsoid in shape, its main axis aligned with the path of the sun crossing the sky. My cottage was on the edge where the sun shone in first.

A short distance away from the tree village, there was a clearing: a large, square-shaped field where the vegetation was very different from the rest. It looked like a matrix where different plants grew in different parcels. I saw many people walking along the paths between these wards or crouching in the midst of them. I realized these must have been specifically planted, and I wondered where the colony had gotten the seeds from.

I shielded my eyes with my hand to see better. Some of the field parcels held rigid green plants that grew taller than any of the Humans. They had green tube-shaped structures that people seemed to be harvesting. Some other plants had broad but short leaves, reaching not even up to one's knees. A few of them had been dug up, and I could see their round roots dirty with the dust and soil.

Thinking of food, I automatically touched my right thigh, the place where food bars were stored on my skinsuit. Instead, my hand touched the beige cotton material of the thin dress that flowed around my body, carried by the soft breeze. The top part of this dress had an uncomfortably wide neck opening, and long sleeves that almost reached my fingertips. The cut around my legs was so broad that I felt the fabric on the skin of my legs only while walking. Everybody was wearing something similar to me, but I still felt uncomfortable without my skinsuit: the sensory and tactile sensations from the Human clothes were truly distracting. The only thing I still had was my E-band. I had no real use of it because it lacked a connection to the mainframe, but in a strange way I needed the slight pressure the E-band strap made on my wrist. It was a link to the world I knew all my life. And it reminded me that this beautiful world was not just a dream.

"Are you Human?"

I heard a tiny voice on my right. I turned and looked down. A small girl—long brown hair, deep, dark eyes—looked at me intently.

"No, I am not."

"I am Lemony."

"I am Dora," I said. Then I smiled without any specific reason, simply to see this little girl looking at me and addressing me so directly.

"So what are you?"

"I am Senthien."

"Sentient? Does that mean you're smart?"

"No, this name was chosen many years ago for my specific Descendant species."

"In our world, sentient means smart... I think."

I didn't know how to respond to that.

"Why are your eyes green?" Lemony continued, deeply focused on my facial features.

"This feature appeared as a side effect of the genetic transformation used for the particular genetic coding in Senthiens."

"What is genetic trans... ration?"

"Genetic transformation?"

"Yes, that."

"It is a change in your own genetic code with different genetic material inserted into your cell structure to change your physical appearance and your mental state."

She was silent for a little bit, as if grasping what I just said.

"What is a genetic code?"

"A genetic code is a chemical structure in every cell of your body that determines how your body is developed, physically and mentally."

"I can see you two are having a real scientific discussion." I heard Tania's voice behind us. I turned around to face her.

"Mommy!" Lemony came close to Tania, hugged her around her waist, and looked up into her eyes. "Dora says that she is not smart and that this is because of the green color they put inside her body."

"Is that so?" Tania nodded and looked at me with a smile.

"This would not be an exact description of our conversation."

Tania's smile broadened, and she took Lemony by her shoulders and started guiding her back to the village.

"Lemony is seven years old," Tania said and started toward the village herself. "We start our school at the same time we remember from our lives before freezing, when children are five years old. They start with basics, which is reading and counting. I think genetic engineering comes only when they are around ten or so…" She winked at me.

I felt completely out of place. I had conversed with a seven-year-old child as if she was an adult. Lemony, seeing two of her friends standing at the edge of the tree village, started running to meet them.

"Dora, don't worry about it!" Tania said. "I'm sure Lemony is quite happy that someone finally talked to her as a grown-up and not as a child."

I looked at the ground. We stayed silent for a bit.

"What plants do you grow on those fields?" I asked to change the subject.

"Oh, all sorts of stuff. Potatoes, corn, carrots, tomatoes…"

"Do they naturally grow here?"

"They don't grow wild, if that's what you mean. They were planted. Compliments of the transfer manager."

"I do not understand."

"Ah… they were cryo-stored in the same installation we were transferred to."

I pondered that for a moment. Whoever had the authority to transfer them to the safe underground installation—whoever overrode the hundred-year wake-up plan—had also some hope that they might de-freeze in the far future. In that case, they would be in need of nutrients. Whoever this person was, he'd given them the best possible option for a food supply.

"Dora, there is something else I wanted to tell you. I just saw Stevanion. I think he's doing worse than this morning. He seems to have developed a cough. We'll keep him in the infirmary for a few more days."

"Can you show me where this infirmary is? I would like to see him."

"Yes, of course, Dora. Come with me."

The infirmary was a cottage one bridge away from Tania's. It was bit larger than other cottages, and it had six tightly aligned beds. All the beds were empty except the last one to the right.

"I'll be in my cottage," said Tania. She gave me a gentle smile and left.

I turned to face the room again but stayed where I was.

What should I say to him?

I didn't even know him that well. He just happened to be porting with me. And happened to get stranded on Earth.

I approached his bed, my leathery shoes soft against the wooden floor.

If he hadn't accompanied me on my port, he would still be in Uni. And he would not be ill.

I sat down on the neighboring bed. He was so still that for a moment I thought he wasn't breathing. Then all of a sudden he gave a throaty cough. My heart skipped a beat.

What should I do?

I turned around to see if Tania was there so she could help him, but the next moment he relaxed and continued sleeping.

I remembered my Vision of Stevanion—the first one I'd ever had in an awake state. If the Vision was true, then he was seriously ill. The only way I could help him would be to return him to Uni and take him to the Anas, who could cleanse his whole body. They could save him.

I took a deep breath and held it for a moment.

If we'd been ported here, it was feasible that porting would work in the other direction as well. Earth obviously didn't have porting chambers, but my E-band might be able to generate a hyperspace resonance field that could potentially connect to the same porting channel that brought us here.

I breathed out.

I needed to find some kind of power source for recharging, or a working computer system where I could load up my E-band. That was the only way I could at least start the process and then hope to enable the porting link.

It was late afternoon and I was strolling along bridges, not following any pattern, simply taking one turn at a time. I was mostly looking down, seeing the forest ground through the gaps in the branches of the bridges, or looking up, seeing the clear blue sky through the crowns of the trees.

Every now and then, I saw a bird flutter between the trees. The sounds of the forest were ever present. There was not one silent moment. And I enjoyed it immensely.

This world…

This world was perfect—full of colors, sounds, and smells—and I tried to record all I could on my nanoprobes. I needed to see it, to smell it, to remember it after I leave.

I took a deep breath and trapped the air in my lungs, savoring all the oxygen.

It was not my world, but would I want to leave it?

I closed my eyes.

If the Vision was true, if Stevanion was really so ill that he needed the help of the Anas, then I had no choice on the matter.

I need to leave.

I opened my eyes and continued walking, accessing the map of the bridges on my nanoprobes. Tania had said there would be a meeting in the evening, in the clearing on the south side of the village. She had said I should come to her cottage so we could go together, but I was in a new area, and my nano-map did not show a direct connection to Tania's place.

Around me, several people were coming out of their cottages and heading in the same direction. I assumed they were going to the meeting, so I followed.

"Hi! Are you hungry?"

I turned. "Hello, Patrick," I said, happy to see a face I knew. "Yes. Yes, I am."

"Good, because there's always a lot of food at the bonfire meetings. What have you been doing today?"

"Tania took me to a small lake pool in the morning. I took a bath."

"Did you like it?"

"Yes. A most unusual tactile experience. I would like to do it again."

"There'll be plenty of opportunities, don't worry." Patrick looked at me sideways and grinned. His skin was a lot darker than the other Humans I had seen, and his hair was threaded into thick shoulder-length strings. "This way," he said, pointing to the bridge on the right.

"Hey, Peter, Tania!" he shouted.

Peter and Tania turned. Peter had his arm over Tania's shoulder and their bodies touched sideways. They were very, very close.

I couldn't take my eyes off them. This, I remembered, was called a hug. And the memory induced such a strong emotional response in me that I could barely control it. I closed my eyes. The picture burned in my memory looked exactly the same. Only the faces were different. I exhaled slowly.

"You okay?" I heard Patrick ask.

"I am… fine." I attempted a smile.

He smiled back. Then he turned to Tania and Peter. "Where's your bunch?"

"Rick's here." Peter pointed to a young man in front of him. "But the others already went. They wanted to see the fire getting started."

Rick turned around and waved, but just as he started walking again, he stopped to look back at me. I stopped as well and so did others around me.

"Wow, you're the new one!" Rick said.

"Rick!" Tania said, her eyebrows folded, her fists bolted on her waist. "This is Dora," she continued in a softer tone. "Dora, this is Rick, my sixteen-year-old."

Patrick laughed. "When you explain it like that, it all makes sense."

"Yeah, funny!" said Rick, whose face didn't at all correspond to his words.

"Let's move, people, we're making a jam!" said Peter, and we all pushed along.

People were lining up near three different trees that each had a way down to the ground. I took the one in the middle, while Tania, Peter, Rick, and Patrick took the one on the right. My slow pace caused a delay on the tree I took, but no one behind me complained. However, this also meant that I lost track of my group. I continued to follow the stream of people, certain I would be able to find them at the bonfire. A few people looked at me, obviously captivated by the color of my eyes, but most of them didn't stare, and for the briefest of moments, I didn't feel like an outsider.

When I got to the clearing, some sixty people were already there, sitting in a large loose circle. The bonfire turned out to be a large pile of branches and planks of wood engulfed in a crackling fire. In diameter, it was broader than one IP, and the flames rose up high in the air, spurting sparks and weaving smoke into a braided river pattern against the dark sky.

It was magnificent.

For a while I just stood there, transfixed by the light, the warmth, and the smell of burning wood.

A few people passed close to me; one of them even lightly nudged me from behind. This brought me back to the present. Standing at the outer edge of the circle, I turned left and walked around until I found a wide spot between two groups of people engaged in animated discussions. The area was three IPs wide, and I hoped no one would sit too close to me. I took one more look around to make sure no one was standing and then sat down, folding my legs under my body, my knees touching the dry dusty soil.

Within the next ten passes, more people came to join the gathering, sitting in a random pattern but still forming a broad regular circle around the fire.

I found myself fascinated just by looking at the Humans' faces. The fine movements of facial muscles conveyed a whole additional layer to what was being communicated verbally, and I wondered if they realized how much of their information exchange went on through this body language. The Human Jumpers were similar in that way too, but I could still clearly recognize them by their pale appearance and relatively fine build, compared to the Old Earth Humans. Zema4 had a slightly weaker gravity than Old Earth, so they appeared more fragile than original Humans. In Uni, though, Zema4 Humans were considered one of the most physically robust species.

All of a sudden, I was ripped from my thoughts, my gaze drawn to the flickering flames of the fire in the center of the circle. At that moment, while my eyes were locked on the hypnotic orange movements, I had another Vision.

> A Vision of the man.
>
> The man in my dreams.
>
> I just see his face, part of it lit with a dim flickering light, the other in the dark.
>
> His eyes reflect the flicker of the orange glow coming from the nearby source.
>
> Then, he looks at me.
>
> And I gasp.

The Vision was gone. I looked up from the fire.

Everyone was still in the same relaxed positions they had been a moment ago.

I realized I was holding my breath, and I exhaled. I had all but forgotten about my recurring dream. So much had happened since the last time I had it. And with a sad weight on my shoulders, I realized I'd missed having this particular Vision—this particular dream.

I miss him, whoever he is.

I smiled very slightly and raised my gaze toward a new group of people just coming into the circle, only to lock onto a pair of dark eyes reflecting a flicker of fiery orange flames.

Those eyes were locked on mine, too.

And they belonged to a man.

The man from my Visions.

CHAPTER 10

My heart was racing. Breathing erratically, I tried to make sense of the flood of jumbled thoughts that rushed through my mind.

Of course—the Vision.

Old Earth.

He is here!

The very realization had panic, thrill, excitement, and pure joy woven through it.

He looked at me for a few moments, but then he turned his head and looked away. A moment later, he looked back at me again.

And he kept looking as he walked to the other side of the circle, surrounded by several people. They all sat near a group of elderly men. Everyone else was very loud, talking at the same time, but he remained silent, his eyes fixed on me.

And me?

I kept looking back at him, transfixed, unable to break my gaze.

Then, without taking his eyes off me, he must have said something to the man on his right, because that man turned to look at me. He said something to my Vision man, shrugged his shoulders, and then turned away again, focusing his attention back to the group engaged in discussion.

Another moment passed with both of us bluntly staring at each other across the fire, and then he smiled, raised one hand, and gave a barely noticeable wave.

Not sure what he was gesturing, I turned my head and looked away. I was dizzy from the combination of rapid breathing and wild heartbeat.

I used all my willpower to slow down my breathing again, and with the deliberate trained force of hundreds of years and a Senthien background, I gained control over my body again.

By this time, all were quiet, and one man was holding the attention of the entire gathering with his strong but clearly aged voice.

I raised my head toward the source of words, careful not to let my eyes slip sideways toward the man from my Vision.

"The first time we did this," he said, standing up and moving closer to the fire, "we were all afraid. Everybody was sitting a lot closer together than you are now." And he moved his wrinkly hand in a circle, pointing to all the people sitting around the fire. "We didn't know what had happened. It certainly wasn't the cool flying cars and kilometer-high buildings I was expecting to see one hundred years after my beauty sleep." He chuckled.

"It seemed as if we had gone several thousand years back from our present, to a time when Humans did not yet exist. Some of you"—he gave a slight nod to Patrick—"thought that this was in fact the future, but that it wasn't the Earth.

"Some thought it was one hundred years later, as it was supposed to be, but an environmental catastrophe had happened to Earth and we couldn't recognize it anymore.

"Some thought our cryo-sleep had lasted a very long time

indeed, and as we acquired more information about our new surroundings, we realized that this was in fact the case."

He turned away from the fire, the orange light drawing patterns on the beige shirt hanging down his bony structure. He walked back to his seat, turned to the circle, and sat, folding his legs underneath him.

"Every time we lit the bonfire, everyone would tell something new that they'd found out or discovered, and we would all work together to find out what that meant. We also talked about our fears, our wishes, and our sorrows. Although we were alive, for some people, this also meant sorrow." And with that he gave a sideways glance at the man from my Vision.

I looked at him then and realized he wasn't looking at the old man at all. He was looking at me.

"With time," the man continued, "we learned to live in our new wild world, far from any advanced standard of living we had known in our time. Cutting wood, building houses, making bridges, fishing, farming… everything we used to be able to buy, we now had to make ourselves. We were all fortunate that many of us had jobs or hobbies that weren't necessarily linked to electricity and technology, and we made use of that."

I was quite sure he wasn't telling this for the first time. This was for us—for the Jumpers. This was for me.

"A few months ago, we started getting visitors." He smiled, his cheeks folding into half-circles around the corners of his mouth. "We welcomed the Human teleporters—Jumpers, as we fondly call them—and in these few months we learned so much more than we had in the last nine years.

"We learned about the News and the first Evacuation flights of Humans who would become Descendants. And we also learned how long ago that was… and that was so much longer than any of us could have imagined."

He sighed as he spoke the last word.

"We learned a lot about the future, actually, about the present, and the people in this new time. And we learned where Humanity is placed in the Uni hierarchy."

His voice was cracked and low. He didn't look at me, but I still lowered my gaze to the ground. I was the only representative of the Descendants at this gathering, and there was a part of me that felt ashamed.

"There are still many mysteries," he continued in a new vibrant tone, "and we will discover them along the way. For now, something we, the Old Earth Humans, want to do—*need* to do—is to get some of our prehistoric technology back."

He smiled slightly at the thought of whatever he was about to say.

"There is a certain charm in living purely with nature—wooden houses, cotton clothing, bio-organic food—but some of us miss certain products of technology. Like… light bulbs."

There was an appreciative laughter all around.

"There is a… *was* a technical university a few days' journey south of this village." His voice changed again, becoming louder and more authoritative. I wondered who he had been before his *beauty sleep*.

"We went there, two years after our de-freeze, and though most of the buildings are ruined, one of them in particular is extremely well preserved. We think this might be a computer facility, perhaps even with its own self-contained power source. But – we couldn't get in, although Patrick here worked there before going cryo."

He lowered his gaze.

"However, it seems we got some high-tech support in the last teleportation jump, and I hope that with this new knowledge, we just might figure out how to get in and, if we're lucky, find something useful." He smiled again, radiating enthusiasm and hope.

"All right, enough talking! Let's eat whatever's been crisping in this fire. It smells delicious, and it shouldn't be ignored any longer."

And with that everyone laughed and started conversing again.

I glanced down, gathering the courage to look at my Vision man again. A few moments later, I looked up.

He wasn't there, though his group still was. I looked around to search for him and found him talking to the old person who had just spoken.

He was squatting, leaning his elbows on his knees, his hands hanging between his legs, and that's when I noticed he was only wearing shorts. He wore nothing on top.

Though his body was crouched, the fire in front illuminated his frame. My eyes followed the lines his muscles made under his skin, slowly sliding over them from his chest down to his stomach, ending up at the string that held his loose beige shorts. And that was…

—irrelevant!

Why am I doing this?

I had no reason to look at the suntanned skin stretching over his abdominal muscles at all! But I just couldn't detach my gaze. My nanoprobes promptly signaled an alert: my heartbeat was a bit faster than normal, and it did not correspond with the level of motion I was doing.

This did not make any sense. *I* did not make any sense!

I peeled my gaze from his body and looked up at his face again and saw him looking straight back at me and—*smirking?*

I closed my eyes and swallowed.

Moons of Senthia! He must have seen me staring.

I quickly stood up and made my way out of the circle, carefully avoiding people sitting in smaller groups and occupied with their own conversations. My head was bent down, and I made sure my eyes looked nowhere but the path beneath my feet on the way back to the village.

I had so many questions on my mind. Who was he? What was his name? What was he doing here? What did that old person have in mind when he mentioned a high-tech Jumper of the last port? Did he mean me? Did he expect me to help them? *Could* I help them at all?

On one hand, I wanted to turn around and get my questions answered right away. Senthiens immediately pursue answers to open questions they have. They need to know all the facts because facts help them project Visions.

But on the other hand, I just couldn't. My body did not respond at all as I was used to. I needed to calm down, I needed to gain control again.

"Dora!" I heard Rick's voice behind me.

I stopped and as I turned in the direction of Rick's voice, I found myself looking directly at the man from my Visions. Dazed by seeing his bare chest so close, I blinked a few times and then quickly looked up into his eyes.

And for one long moment, time stopped.

There were no people. There were no other sounds. It was just the two of us, our faces only a few inches apart, each and every rule of interpersonal space broken and forgotten.

My Visions did not do him justice, I realized, feeling the

weakness in my knees and trying hard to remain standing. His eyes were deep and dark, hidden in the shadows of his eyelashes. A few strands of his short dark hair fell to his forehead. He was so close to me I could almost feel the warmth of his body, radiating the heat of a day spent in a sun.

"Ah, Dora!" Rick caught up with us and was now standing beside us, seemingly oblivious to the transfixed looks we were exchanging in front of him. "It looks like you already know each other. Cool! Old Mike wants to talk to you because of the trip to the old city."

"Dora," said the man from my Visions. His voice was deep but soft.

"Um, I thought you guys knew each other," Rick said, looking at each of us in turn. As neither of us replied, Rick took a short impatient breath and continued. "J, this is Dora Dana Dasnan. She is our last Jumper, the one Old Mike was talking about. Dora, this is J."

J. His name is J.

"Nice to meet you, Dora." This might have been a good time to say something, but I just couldn't find the words.

"Guys, could you please come back with me?" insisted Rick.

J looked at Rick. "I don't understand. Why would Mike want to talk to Dora about the trip?"

"Well, she might be able to help us get in the computer facility. She's a Senthien."

"Senthien?" J seemed puzzled. He looked back at me.

"Yes," jumped in Rick. "That's why she had access to computer technology no one else had." Rick was glowing, a broad grin on his face.

The thick wall of interpersonal space finally kicked in, and I took a step backward.

"I will respond to Old Mike's request for the exchange of information, but I do not understand the urgency," I said calmly, my Senthien façade back on my face.

J's expression changed. He frowned just slightly, his eyes narrowing as he looked back at me.

"This is so exciting!" Rick was almost jumping up and down on the spot. "This really might be the breakthrough!"

I then turned to Rick and gave him a long stare, communicating that my question had not been answered. Rick's head slumped to his chest and he exhaled impatiently. Then raising his eyes to look at me, he said, "Look, I don't know all the details, but there is something important about the timing. So could you guys please come with me?"

J and I looked at each other for a moment, and then J said, "C'mon! Let's talk to Old Mike."

He made a quick sideways movement with his head in the direction we'd just come from and then started walking.

"Dora. Dana. Dasnan," he said looking back, a half-hidden smile appearing at the corner of his lips.

I looked up at his dark eyes, getting completely lost in them. A moment later I moved my gaze away, hoping my emotions did not show on my face.

"What do people in Uni call you?" he continued.

"Dana… people in Uni call me Dana."

"I like Dora. It sounds… warm."

I glanced back at him. He was looking forward and had a smile on his face.

We reached the other side of the circle where Mike was sitting.

"Dora." Mike slowly stood up to greet me. "Excuse my old

bones. Standing up takes more effort than it used to. I am Mike. It's a pleasure to meet you."

"I acknowledge your hospitality," was the only thing in my vocabulary that seemed appropriate.

"Please, Dora, J, sit with me a little bit." His old voice had a pleasant rumble to it.

J pointed to a wooden log. He waited for me to sit first, and then he sat on the log next to it.

"Dora," Mike said, "you heard me mention the building at the old university. Now, we fairly often go to the city… ah, ruins, to—I guess the best word is—*scavenge* useful items."

I looked at Mike, my expression flat, not understanding his words.

"It means," J said, sensing my confusion, "that we take stuff—different items—from the ruins that we might have a use for here in the tree village, like… let me think… metal, or sharp objects, or cables. You know, things to use when you don't have anything." He smiled.

I had the most peculiar need to smile back at him, but not understanding this urge, I refrained and turned back to Mike.

"Thanks, J," Mike said. "So, very early on, perhaps two years after we woke, we tried to enter the computer building, or what we think is a computer building… Patrick worked at this university before the cryo and he thinks it's very likely that this particular building is a computer facility.

"As I said, we didn't manage to get in. It just looked… impenetrable. So, what I am hoping, what we are all hoping"— he moved his hand in a circular motion—"is that you, coming from a society with more advanced technology, might be able to help us enter. Perhaps you've seen something like that before."

"Yes, I understand. I will be in a better position to tell you of my ability to help you when I see the entrance."

Mike nodded. "Of course, Dora, of course," he said and glanced at J. "And – this is also our question for you – would you, please, join the group going on this trip? Your help would be extremely useful."

I looked at all three of them in turn and then answered to Mike, in my usual Senthien voice, "Yes. I think this is advisable. I will go with the group."

Rick exhaled audibly.

"Thank you," Mike said. "Thank you, Dora. We very much appreciate it."

"Rick said the trip needs to happen soon," I said. "Why?"

"Yes, there is a certain urgency to leave. The reason is that the way there crosses a river," Mike said. "At certain times of the year, the water level rises dramatically, and when it does, we cannot cross it anymore for several months. It often happens that it overflows, flooding the area."

"This will happen soon," J continued. "We only have about two to three weeks."

"That's why it's important that the group leaves fairly soon," said Mike.

"I understand."

"If you do manage to get inside the facility," said Mike after a moment's break, "we were also hoping that you can help us to access the computer system, in case it's too advanced for us to understand."

"What is your need for a computer system?" I asked.

J answered my question. "Well, first of all, accessing information about... well, everything, would be really valuable to us. Until now, we only had the knowledge that someone had remembered or worked with. Before cryo, knowledge was available at our fingertips. We could find out things about health, medication, building, cooking—everything, really—by connecting to the Internet. We don't have that information. And now is the time when we really need it."

"I understand. I myself do not have great expertise in the area of computer technology. However"—I lifted my arm, showing the E-band—"there is a high probability that this interface will be able to connect to a computer once it is fully charged."

"That sounds great!" J said and nodded to the other two.

Mike continued enthusiastically, "What we are also hoping to find is some information that will help us figure out how to power up our underground installation."

"You want to go back and live underground?"

"Oh, for heaven's sake, no!" Mike said and laughed. "But there is a whole infrastructure down there, like fridge rooms and heating stations… but it's all out of juice."

Juice?

"Battery power," J said, answering my unspoken question. I looked at J, his lips curling into a half smile.

I lowered my gaze to the ground, distracted for a few moments.

"So," I said, after I gathered my thoughts again, "if your installation has no more electricity, why then were your cryo-crèches still functional?"

"Well, we think that low power actually initiated the de-freeze process. When it was clear that the crèche maintenance power was running out, the thaw program was initiated—and we woke up," J explained.

"I understand," I said.

"We will have a rundown of the trip at Mike's hut in two

days' time, an hour after sunset," said J. "Could you please come? Perhaps you can give us some valuable pointers even before we leave."

"I will, of course, help you to the best of my abilities. But I cannot guarantee the success of this expedition."

"We understand that, Dora," J said, looking at me with an enigmatic glow in his eyes. "But you are the best hope we've had in years."

CHAPTER 11

That night was full of dreams—dark, damp, suffocating—with broken harsh voices and hooded creatures. I woke up several times, each time cold and covered in sweat. I greeted the morning with relief, a bright and fresh dawn as the birds' songs echoed in the trees above my cottage.

With my clothes sticking to my skin, it was obvious I needed one of those baths again. I smiled within, looking forward to it.

People should be in baths at least half of their waking time.

I decided to search for the pool myself. Tania had showed me the way, and although I hadn't tracked it on my nano-map, I was confident I could retrace our steps.

I took the path across familiar bridges to the end of the village and climbed down the tree. Thick, green ferns reaching up to my hips completely covered the ground. As I walked, I kept brushing the ferns with my open hand, enjoying their soft and malleable leaves. Fifty steps into the forest, I slowed down, looking around. I started to wonder if I had taken the right way. The images I was receiving here did not correspond to the data saved by my ONC. I frowned.

"And where are you off to?" a deep voice called out behind me.

I turned around and saw J, holding some kind of tool in one hand and several beige textile bags in the other.

"I am going to have a bath," I said, trying to maintain the Senthien tone in my voice.

He chuckled quietly. "Perhaps you'd like to take the opposite direction then? This is a path into the forest. It's easy to get lost if you don't know the way."

I turned, looking at the densely intricate flora ahead, and then turned back to J. "All right. Could you then tell me which direction I should take?"

"With pleasure." He smiled broadly, his white teeth contrasting his tanned face.

My eyes were glued on his features. Bronzed, slightly rough skin, lines at the outer corners of his eyes where his skin creased when he laughed, and the most wonderful smile...

"Shall we go?" J raised his eyebrows.

I raised my gaze, looking back at his eyes. "O—of course."

Then I pressed my lips together and looked away.

For the Moons of Senthia, Dora! Connect to your brain, this is humiliating...

I tried hard not to look at him as we walked back.

"Do you know how to swim, Dora?"

"No." I quickly glanced at his face and then looked back at the path.

"Okay, well, someone should be there with you. You know," he said a bit more quietly, "so you don't go under the water and—stay there. Ahm...I could take you." Then he coughed once and said, "Or shall I rather get one of the girls to take you? Perhaps that's better."

His voice was low, and he sounded confused. I looked at him, trying to figure out the sudden change in his tone, but he wasn't looking at me. His gaze was unfocused as he looked into the distance.

"Yes, J. I think this is advisable. I thank you."

He nodded and continued walking. I was stealing glances at him, but stopped whenever I saw him looking back. There was so much I wanted to know about him, but none of the words actually came out. Here I was, the calm, collected and eloquent Senthien—and my tongue was tied. I frowned and bent my head lower to the ground.

We reached the tree I used to climb down.

"Let me get someone to take you, all right? And I guess you need a towel, too?"

"Yes, that would be helpful."

He climbed up quickly, jumping over two or three climbing steps at a time. I watched him, dazzled, my eyes following the tight muscles working on his arms and legs, intertwining and stretching as he effortlessly ascended to the top of the spiral ladder.

As soon as he disappeared above the platform, I had a moment to think about my incoherent behavior.

Is it because I'd seen him in my Visions? Because I feel like I know him and yet I don't?

Or is it only because he's a Human and I can finally observe one up close?

I was lost in my thoughts and couldn't seem to find a rational answer to any of my questions.

Then I heard the sounds of two people walking on the wooden bridge that connected Tania's hut to the climbing tree platform. J and Tania were talking, but their voices were so quiet I couldn't hear anything. I gave a command to my tympanic audio enhancers to boost the volume.

"…were tempted, weren't you?" I heard the ending of Tania's sentence as she started climbing down.

"Tania, seriously, you're being ridiculous!" J said with a defensive tone in his voice.

"Am I?" Tania's voice was so quiet that J, still standing on the platform, couldn't have heard it, but I could see in her smile and the tone of her voice that she was having fun for reasons unclear to me.

She stepped on the ground, a thick beige towel over her shoulder.

"Good morning, Dora! You should have fetched me. Why did you go by yourself?"

I watched J while answering Tania, "You already guided me to this bath area. I assumed I would be able to find the way myself this time." My eyes were fixed on J swiftly climbing down the tree. There was something…primal in the smoothness of his movements. I kept looking.

"Shall we go, or do you want to stay a bit and enjoy the view?" she asked.

I quickly looked at her. Her head was tilted sideways and she had a crooked smile on her face.

"What? No! We can go." And I dashed off in front of her.

"Ah, you're both such pearls," Tania said quietly.

"What pearls? What are you talking about?" I heard J's voice call out to Tania as he reached the ground.

"Never mind…never mind," she said, laughing, and followed me. "Bye, J! See you later."

The path we now took looked a lot more familiar, and although

I felt embarrassed to have to be guided again, I was happy Tania was here.

"Dora, could I please ask you to tell me or J, or anyone else you feel comfortable with, if you're going somewhere? It's not at all that we don't think you could do it, but... there are so many new and different things for you here that you're not aware of yet. And also some dangers, like drowning."

She lifted her arm as if about to touch my shoulder, then dropped it down again, remembering the IP space.

"Just for a little while longer until you get used to everything here, okay?" she continued.

"Yes, Tania. I am in agreement with you."

"Stevanion is in the same condition as yesterday," she said after a few moments.

I nodded. That was good. My Vision had shown Stevanion getting sick. Perhaps what it didn't show me was Stevanion getting better again.

And if that was the case, that would mean that... that I wouldn't need to take Stevanion back to Uni. I could stay here, on Earth, hidden from the Zlathars.

And stay where J is.

I would like that.

I would very much like that.

Tania and I walked in silence for several passes while I juggled my thoughts. I wanted to know more about J, but I was afraid to ask so bluntly. So I asked another question that I'd had on my mind ever since I met Old Earth Humans.

"Tania?"

"Yes?"

"I have an inquiry about a certain aspect of your previous lives."

"Inquiry…?" She looked at me, her eyebrows raised. Something in her expression told me there might have been a better way to ask the question.

"I was wondering about cryo-preservation."

"Yes?"

"Why did the people do it? Why did *you* do it?"

She looked down, clutching a thin metal pendant on her leather necklace. "I guess it's an obvious question to ask…Well, people had very different reasons to go into hibernation. Some of them were simply curious to see how the world would look in one hundred years. Some were hoping for a cure for an illness. Some tried to escape from a tragedy they experienced in their life."

She let go of her pendant and looked at me sadly. "I was one of those."

After a few moments of silence, she continued, "My husband died."

"Your husband? I thought Peter is your husband."

"Yes, you're right. Peter is my husband. Well, second husband. Before cryo, I was married to Harry. He was a scientist—a molecular biologist. He worked on… I'm not even sure, some kind of neural-computing… something like that. His lab was at the University of Neurotechnology and Innovation."

Her gaze was absent, as if she was seeing something far away. "At any rate, there was an accident, an explosion in the laboratory, and… the whole team died." She shook her head slowly, deep in her thoughts.

She was silent for a few passes. I let her take her time, avoiding her eyes, waiting until she was ready to continue again.

"His project," she said at last, "was apparently cutting edge, new frontier and all that. No one else ever managed to reach the level they had."

There was an instant blank veil around my mind, and I realized I was about to see a Vision in real time. Then, abruptly, it stopped.

Nothing else came.

Suddenly, I realized what I needed to ask. "Do you know the status of the project at the time of the accident?"

She was a bit surprised by my interrogating tone but answered nevertheless. "I'm not really sure… he wasn't supposed to talk about it at all. It was top secret. I know they managed to do something groundbreaking, but officially I wasn't supposed to know that either."

All of a sudden, a dim light blurred my sight, like a fog blinding me from the images of reality, and the Vision scene appeared in front of me in full force.

A large room.

Eight malte-glass desks arranged in two rows.

Above each desk, shelves full of glass bottles, reagents, and kits.

Two walls with old-looking automation systems, blue light below the machines indicating they were operational.

The next moment, the explosion starts in slow motion.

Volatile fire bubbles, bursting in several places in the room at the same time, then expanding with enormous speed to the rest of the room, breaking windows, walls, floors, ceiling...

The Vision was gone. I was kneeling on the ground, my gaze empty.

Did I just see the past?

"Dora, are you all right?" Tania was now crouching next to me, touching my shoulder.

"Yes, Tania. I am all right. I am sorry, I was… sidetracked," I said, looking at her, the powerful image of the exploding laboratory dominating all my thoughts.

The one where her husband had worked.

The one that had been *empty* at the time of the explosion.

I needed more information. This Vision raised too many questions to be left unanswered.

I stood up and moved one IP away from her.

"What happened after that?" I said, my classical Senthien tone back.

"You make me feel like I am at a trial." She smiled, then stood up and continued walking.

"A trial of what?" I followed her.

"Never mind, Dora, I will explain later," she said, then took a few moments before continuing. "My children and I were devastated. None of us had a grip on reality anymore. That was probably my fault." She looked away. "If I'd been stronger, my kids would have managed better.

"At any rate, we decided to cryo-preserve, hoping time would heal the wounds… Unfortunately, this wasn't the case."

And again, she had that sad smile on her face.

"Being frozen for more than five thousand years turned out to be just a blink of an eye. When we de-froze, I was still suffering the same way as before the sleep.

"I think, however, that the shock of finding out what had happened to us forced me to recover faster. There were so many other things to worry and think about, I finally managed to stand on my feet again.

"And then, a few months ago, we started getting Jumpers. Humans. From Uni," she continued. "You would not believe what a blow it was to find out what had happened to the Earth. About the News, the Evacuation, and the solar storms." She raised her eyebrows, shaking her head as she looked at the ground. "And— about Descendants. And what they did to humanity."

"I am sorry for that, Tania," I said and lowered my gaze.

"It seems to be in the fabric of our beings, doesn't it? People have always found someone to abuse, someone to discriminate against. It was probably inevitable. The only question was who would get which end."

The black hooded figure of the High Zlathar Priest appeared in my mind. It wasn't a Vision. It was a very tangible fear of what he would do if he knew there were original Humans on Old Earth.

But the electromagnetic and radio silence of this world made it invisible to the universe.

After a few passes we reached the pool. She stopped a few IPs away from the water's edge and handed me the towel. "I'll stay here. Don't do any diving like yesterday— -nothing interesting to see down there."

"Diving?" A new word needed explanation.

"Sightseeing under the water...?" Tania raised her eyebrows and smiled.

"No... I will omit it. This time," I said.

She laughed sweetly. "Good, you are learning! There's some Human in you after all."

CHAPTER 12

I was going back to my cottage, careful not to miss the turns I took on the way there.

On one bridge, a few people were walking my way. They moved to one side, still deep in their conversation. I squeezed my fists, clenched my jaws, and braced myself as several people brushed past my arm.

"You are the Senthien?" I heard a female voice right next to me. I opened my eyes and looked at the last woman in the group.

She was way too close. I stepped backward until I had one clear IP between us, then started breathing again.

Now that I had some space and could focus better on them, I recognized them: They were the Zema4 women from the Boolean Institute.

"I saw you a few days ago," she said, clearly recognizing me as well.

"Yes." I nodded. "I remember you. What were you doing there? Zamnan Second told me that they did not have any Humans in their institute."

She smiled a thin smile. "I guess he lied."

The rest of the group quietly laughed, and I realized that all of these women must have been at the Boolean Institute too, though I never clearly saw the others.

"Why are you here?" said a person to the left of the woman I talked to.

"I had been on my port to the Zlathar planet, and there was an error in the porting coordinates. I got ported here."

"All porters that came here were Humans, *Senthien*," said the person on the right. "You don't belong here."

"The Mind made an error in the porting procedure. I had not planned to come here," I said in a very calm and neutral Senthien voice.

"Go back to where you belong!" said a woman in the back, and the others echoed their agreement. "This is our world."

I looked at this group of women and for the first time understood how the malice the Descendants felt for Uni Humans had affected them. I wanted to respond, but I was distracted by footsteps approaching from behind.

I turned and saw J walking toward us. My heart skipped a beat, but my expression remained aloof. He stopped between me and the women, making sure he was one IP away. "Is there a problem?"

"No, there is no problem, J," said the woman in front. Then she looked at me and said, "We were just saying that Earth is for Humans."

"And not Descendants!" called out the woman in the back.

"Well, Andrea, Julie"—he nodded toward them as he said their names—"the Old Earth Humans welcome everybody who ports to Earth and brings no harm. That includes Descendants. And the new Humans had better remember that."

While still looking at the women, he said, "Dora, there is something I would like to discuss with you." He then turned toward me. "Would you please walk with me?"

I nodded.

He walked past them, and I quickly followed. We crossed two bridges before he asked, "Are you okay?"

"Yes, J, I am fine. What would you like to discuss with me?"

He stopped for a moment to look at me and then grinned. "That was just an excuse to get you out."

"Get me out?"

"From the ladies with the pitchforks."

I frowned, not understanding at all what he was talking about.

"So, what's this issue about, anyway?" he said.

"Humans are treated badly in Uni. This is simply their response to Descendants in general."

He shook his head slightly. "That's a very mature way to look at it. I think their attitude, although justified, would get me pissed."

"Would get you what?"

"Pissed," he said and continued walking.

"I do not understand."

"Uh, the word? It means upset, angry. Aren't you angry?"

"For what?"

"For how they talked to you."

"It is they who should be angry. Zlathars pushed Humans down to the bottom of the hierarchy of the Uni society. I would react the same way if I were them."

J stopped again, looking at me and narrowing his eyes. "I don't get it."

"Shall I explain it again?"

"No, I mean: if you have such a noble way of looking at it, how come Humans are put in such a bad position in the first place? Aren't all the Descendants like you?"

I held my breath, staring at him for a few moments. *Relax,*

Dora. It's the most logical question. Answer in the most logical way. "No, there are several different species of Descendants."

I moved on, hoping he wouldn't press the subject.

"But," he said, catching up with me, "they don't all think like you, do they?"

My eyes were glued to the floor patterns of the wooden bridge. "Descendant species were developed by targeted genetic manipulation and are, therefore, very different in their physical and mental states."

He stopped in the middle of the bridge. I stopped as well and turned around to look at him.

"You are not answering my question," he said, crossing his arms. "Okay, so which ones are the rulers?"

"There are no rulers. It is a homogenous society."

J laughed out loud. "No. Not if Humans are treated the way they are, it's not. So, who holds the strings?"

Strings?

"Who tells everyone else what to think?"

I understood now what he meant, and amazingly enough, he was more right then he could have imagined.

"Zlathars."

"Zlathars. Okay. So, how come they didn't tell you what to think?"

I took a deep breath. *Time to leave.*

"This discussion is not of interest to me," I said with my best Senthien intonation. "I would like to retreat to my living quarters."

He opened his eyes wide, and for a few moments, he was just looking at me. Then his face changed into an expression I could not decipher.

He shrugged and said, "Yeah. Fine. Whatever."

And he left in the direction we'd come from. The bridge shook from his heavy steps until he reached the other side. He walked over several other bridges and then he was gone.

I bowed my head low and walked back to my hut, sat on a wooden chair, my gaze empty on the floor.

Why did I say that?

I actually *didn't* want to retreat to my living quarters. And *I didn't* want him to leave, either. I wanted to be near him, I wanted to look at him, I wanted to talk to him. But instead—I pushed him away.

No. No, this can't be. I'm doing things the wrong way. I need to go back. I need to find him.

Just as I was about to stand up, I heard footsteps over the wooden bridge leading to my hut.

"Dora!" It was Tania's voice. "Dora," she said again as she opened the leaf curtain. "It's Stevanion. He's not doing well. I think you should see him."

Stevanion. Oh, no!

I got up swiftly and followed Tania until we reached the infirmary.

Tania moved the curtain away. I walked in, but then stopped. I stared at Stevanion in the bed. His face was white, unmoving, his eyes closed. Drops of sweat were shining on his forehead.

Oh, no! I have seen this.

I shivered from within.

The next moment, Stevanion coughed a heavy, throaty cough as his face grimaced in pain. I walked quickly to him, supporting his shoulders until his coughing frenzy ceased, and then helped him gently lay back on the bed. He resumed his corpselike posture, not moving, barely breathing.

"What is wrong with him?" I asked, though I knew the answer, but voicing it as a memory about to happen.

"I'm sorry, Dora. I don't know. It seems he has a flu. Just a regular flu. It normally lasts for a few days only, but it's as if his body doesn't have the means to fight it."

I closed my eyes with sorrow, defeat, and guilt.

Sorrow, because he was my only link to the world I had known all my life.

Defeat, because I had seen it. I knew what was going to happen.

Guilt, because he had accompanied me on my port in the first place. If he hadn't, he would never have come to Earth. And he would still be healthy.

"Dora, how do you feel? Are you all right?"

"Yes."

"I mean… do you feel healthy?"

"Yes, my health is optimal, Tania. I thank you." My eyes were still closed.

"I am afraid for you, Dora. This is a classic Human disease, and it's usually not life-threatening. But for him—and for you—it could be. Here, could you please drink this? It's a specific herbal tea that might prevent you getting ill."

I opened my eyes as she handed me a cup of warm green liquid.

"There is no need, Tania, I feel perfectly healthy." My voice was strong, but inside I felt weak and uncertain.

She lowered the cup to her lap and looked at Stevanion.

"If he has any Human immunity left in him, he might survive."

And if he doesn't?

I looked back at Stevanion.

Then—then he will die.

I dropped my gaze to the floor.

What am I to feel for a dying person from a highly advanced world where disease doesn't exist anymore?

"It's difficult…" she said, as if she knew my thoughts.

"Yes."

I stood up and walked slowly to the door. Then I turned back. "I need to… I have to… go. I need to think."

"That's all right, Dora. I understand. I'll watch over him, you can go. But please, stay near the village, okay?"

"Near the village. Yes…" I said distractedly, and left.

CHAPTER 13

I walked across a few bridges, not really caring where I was going. I passed some people, but at this time of the day most were on the ground, working in the fields, so my time on the tree bridges was solitary. And that's exactly what I needed. I spent more than a hundred passes walking around the village, thinking of the last few days.

What had happened? How did we port here? Was this really a mistake? Would the Mind really make a mistake? Or was it sabotage?

By who?

Certainly not by Uni Humans. I would have seen it. My Visions would have shown me something so drastic, I was sure of it.

My gaze was unfocused and empty on the bridge planks, but my thoughts were crowded.

The Mind.

Zlathars.

Visions.

Disease.

Death.

Death? Will Stevanion die?

I didn't know how to deal with death. Not many in Uni did. We were not used to it.

But death exists here. These people were used to that. They know how to cope with it. With that thought, I turned and walked back to the infirmary.

Tania was still there, wringing out a soft white cloth over a bowl of cool water and placing it back on Stevanion's forehead. She looked at me as I walked in.

"How do you feel?" she asked.

"Better," I mumbled.

I looked at Stevanion, his face seemingly more relaxed than before.

"Tania," I said quietly, "do you think he will die?"

Tania quickly glanced back at Stevanion. His face remained calm and unmoving.

She then stood up and said, "Let's get some fresh air, shall we?"

I tilted my head, not understanding. The glassless windows and open door enabled plenty of fresh air in the infirmary. Tania passed me by with less than one IP and then walked to the outside platform. I followed her.

She leaned with her elbows on the fence rope, laced her fingers, and looked down to the green undergrowth below.

"Death is never easy… regardless of who it happens to, it's never easy," she said in a quiet voice.

We were silent for a few moments.

I looked at her sad features. She must have been thinking of her own past.

"What do you... how do you... with... persons not alive anymore?" I stumbled upon words in a very un-Senthien way.

"You mean, the funeral?"

"The funeral?"

"How do we say goodbye to dead people?"

"Yes."

She lowered her head and closed her eyes, pulling her eyebrows together so that the bridge of her nose wrinkled. She wiped both of her hands over her face and then brought them back to the fence.

"We burn them." She opened her eyes and looked at me. "What do you do in your world?"

"I don't know. There aren't many deaths there."

"People used to bury their dead in the ground long time ago." Tania's eyes were empty as she gazed into the distance. "But with the Earth's overpopulation, it became almost impossible to keep the ground space—any ground space—for the dead... so cremation became mandatory. No space for graves."

After a few moments of silence, she turned to me and said, "Sometimes, it is difficult, not to be able to visit the place where your loved ones are buried."

I was sure she was now talking about herself.

"But don't worry about funerals now, Dora. It might not come to that at all."

I gave a brief nod. With no clear Vision, I had no idea of how it would end.

As if reading my mind, Tania smiled softly. "It's difficult for you now, Dora, isn't it? There are so many new, unusual, and strange things for you to live through... to process, to absorb. All of this just takes time."

She bent forward, leaning over the fence, looking down to

the greenery underneath, as the setting sun drew long shadows on the ground underneath us. "I still think you should do the trip. It will do you good. It will take your mind off things… it was the same for me."

Then she looked at me and said, "And if you feel unwell in any way, health-wise, please, tell me right away, okay?"

"I will, Tania. And I thank you for your assistance with Stevanion."

"Of course, Dora. You're welcome."

The night embraced me in a deep, dreamless sleep, and although I felt rested, I was glad to be woken by the early rays of sunlight passing through my window. The night felt like *nothing*.

It felt like death.

I sat up on my bed and shivered once. I needed to see Stevanion. I needed to make sure he was still alive.

I dressed quickly and walked through the sleeping village to get to the infirmary. Once I reached the thick dark green leaves at the entrance of the cabin, I stopped. My heart was pounding.

I was afraid.

I didn't know what to expect, which was a real irony, coming from a Visionaire Senthien.

I swallowed and moved the leaves to the side. Stevanion was still lying in the same bed. His head was turned away from me, but I could tell he was breathing.

I sat on the bed next to him and then got a fright as he turned toward me. His skin was a lot less pale than before.

"Dana." His voice was harsh as he spoke. "I acknowledge your presence."

"Stevanion," I said, nodding slightly. "How do you feel?"

"My health condition is better. I appreciate your concern."

He tried to lift himself up but wasn't able to. I reached down and pushed another pillow under his back. Only when I sat down again, did I realize he was looking at me with wide-open eyes.

I clearly broke the IP border without even thinking about it. He needed assistance, and there was no doubt in my mind of what I should do.

"We are on Old Earth," I said to break his stare.

"Yes. A person named Tania told me that," he said, then stopped for a moment to catch some breath. "I have some reservations regarding its truthfulness."

"Are you doubting that we are on Earth?"

"Earth is dead, Dana. We have seen the videos. And the only people who say that we are on Earth are Humans."

"Does this automatically mean that they are lying?"

"It means… that it is difficult to believe them."

"They are taking care of you, Stevanion."

"They are not doing a good job. I want to port back."

I looked at him, not knowing how to respond. After a few moments of silence, I said, "There is a group of Humans who will try and access the computer systems in the old city."

"Is there a porting chamber there?"

"I do not think so, Stevanion. We are on Old Earth. There were no porting chambers pre-Ev. But what I am hoping is to fully charge my E-band at the power source of the computer facility. If I manage, the E-band will have enough power to create an HSR field."

"A hyperspace resonance field? You want to connect to the porting channels?"

"Yes."

"The process only works on specific planets, Dana, and only on specific locations."

"I understand that. But it is our best chance to bring us home, and… to take you to the Anas."

He looked at me for a long moment and then turned his head away from me.

"Just get us out of here."

I looked at the back of his head and then dropped my gaze to the floor.

What did I expect? That he would blindly trust the Humans, when from the very beginning he was taught not to? He's reacting like any other Senthien would. Like any other Descendant would.

I wanted to sigh, but I stopped myself. I got up and said, "I wish that your health continues to improve, Stevanion. I will see you again once I am back from this trip, so we can discuss our departure."

He turned back to me and said, "I thank you, Dana. May Torquemada Joseph Nadraque watch over you."

I nodded and turned around.

It's going to be something completely different keeping me safe. And definitely not the High Zlathar Priest.

CHAPTER 14

I wandered inconspicuously around the tree village during the morning hours, scanning the ground and fields trying to find J. It was funny of me, really, because if I did find him, I would probably hide, not knowing what to say to him or how to act.

I definitely wasn't showing qualities of exquisite genetic manipulation here. But here on Earth, with J, I found it difficult to be the calm, wise Senthien. Neither my brain nor my body responded in the way I was used to.

I kept thinking about him. It felt as if he was always there, right behind me, and I just needed to turn around and he would be standing less than one IP away, smiling, lifting his arm and opening his hand to take mine, as I'd seen him doing in my Visions.

How was it possible for one person to be so ever-present in another's thoughts? My higher brain centers seemed incapacitated, and that was truly distracting. The most disturbing thing of all was that none of these symptoms were recorded on my nanoprobe encyclopedia, so I couldn't even find out what this was all about.

Annoying!

I had just left the fields, happy to be in the forest and away from the heat of the sun, when I saw a group of men talking a few IPs from the climbing tree. J was standing at the edge, and I could see him from the side. None of them noticed me, so they continued talking. I stopped and moved slightly sideways behind a thick tree. Like this, I could look at him unobserved. Perhaps it would give me a better understanding of why he was constantly on my mind.

His scruffy hair was falling on his forehead, and his shoulders and broad back made a shadow over the rest of his body. I leaned with my hands on the tree to bend further sideways while my eyes glided down his tall frame. The thin shirt was tucked inside his beige trousers, which hung loosely on his hips and fell down all the way to his bare feet.

My mouth felt dry and I needed to swallow. I wiped the sweat from my palms on the tree bark and continued looking. He ran his fingers through his hair, and then crossed his arms on his chest. I could see him breathing, his chest moving slowly, as he listened to the person in the front. He moved his weight from one leg to another, and that made his buttock muscles shift.

I licked my lips, trying to moisten my dry mouth.

"*What* are you doing here?" I heard a loud voice coming from the side. I pushed away from the tree and looked at her. It was Julie, the woman I had seen at the Boolean Institute, again. She walked toward me, stopping less than one IP away. "Why are you sneaking around? What are you looking at?"

She looked at the men and they all turned toward us.

"I... I wasn't sneaking."

She narrowed her eyes, then looked at J and then back at me. And then she laughed in a most unnatural way. "You were looking at J, weren't you?"

"No! I wasn't."

By this time, J was coming toward us. He stopped one IP away from me, then touched Julie's shoulder with his hand and gently pushed her away from me so that she was more than one IP away as well.

"So, ladies," he said looking at her and then at me, "is there a problem?"

Julie snorted. "She—" She raised a finger toward me. "She was watching you. She was *eyeing* you!"

Oh, no, no, no, this is not good! I wanted to say something, I wanted to defend myself, but my voice was gone.

"Really?" J looked at me, surprised, his confident composure gone.

My breath was locked in and I could not say anything. I had completely lost control over my body.

"What do you mean, 'really'? Yes, really," Julie said and moved forward, but J instantly raised his arm to stop her from moving closer to me. "And I can't even imagine why! *They*"—she pushed her chin toward me in a disgusted way—"can't even *do* anything! They are completely incapable of it."

I clenched my hands into fists and brought back the Senthien. Though my heartbeat was loud under my rib cage, I said in the calmest of voices, "Humans are an interesting species to observe."

"Bloody hell! *Observing*. She was looking at your butt!" Julie spit out.

"Hmmm, game-spotting, ey?" J said, arching his eyebrow. My Senthien was gone yet again and I was speechless.

His head tilted, a mischievous smile on his lips, he was looking at my eyes. Then he shifted his gaze to my lips. And this did something unexplainable to me. My heartbeat sped up instantly and a new indescribable craving rose deep, deep inside my belly. All of a sudden, I was lacking air.

I need to get out of here.

I let out a shaky breath and said weakly, "I'd... better leave."

And I walked in between J and Julie to the climbing tree, hoping I still had the strength to climb up and get back to my hut.

I looked outside. Night had fallen, and it was soon time to go to the meeting at Mike's hut. I folded my day clothes in a cupboard as Tania had showed me and then put on an evening dress. I had started to like it, the new clothes. Though somewhat distracting on a sensory level, it made me feel *free*.

I looked at the dimming light of the fading day with a contented smile on my lips. I felt serene now, though it had taken me a long time to reach this level of calmness after the small disaster this afternoon. I understood now what had happened. It was very clear to me: I was simply gathering information. It is a basic Senthien feature—we need to observe in order to project accurate Visions. And that's all there was to it.

I stood and walked to the door, but just as I moved the curtain aside, I froze in place. The breath I took in a moment ago stayed locked in.

J was standing right in front of me, slightly taken off guard himself.

"Dora."

"J."

"Ahem, I was… I was just about to get you. The meeting started."

"Oh," I muttered as I finally exhaled, lowering my gaze.

He was wearing his shorts again and his chest was bare, the muscles underneath his skin tight from a hard day's work.

My serenity was gone as if it was never there to begin with. I closed my eyes for an instant and then opened them, focusing on his eyes, but his eyes were not on mine. Instead, he was looking at my lips.

Oh.

My heart was beating frantically, and I started feeling dizzy again. I was afraid my knees would let go.

And then he took a step backward, coughed once in his fist, and looked me in the eyes. "Are you ready? Shall we go?"

I nodded, not trusting my voice.

He smiled an awkward smile and then turned and walked over the bridge. I didn't move; my feet were glued to the floor. It took me a few moments to engage my automotive brain centers and start walking. My knees were shaking, my heart was pounding, and my stomach felt queasy.

He turned his head slightly and looked at me sideways. "So, did you have a good afternoon?"

After the embarrassing episode that happened earlier, you mean? "Yes."

"Do anything special?"

"I filed and categorized the images and recordings of Earth's flora that I have collected so far." I sighed in relief. It felt good to talk about something rational. I was calm, and my train of thoughts was once again organized and methodical. *Back on track.*

"Ah… yes… interesting," he said.

"No. Not really. But it needs to be done to keep order in the storage space."

"Storage space? Of?"

"Nanoprobes, of course."

"Of course."

I frowned. If it was clear to him, why did he ask in the first place? I shook my head, dismissing the thought.

"And nanoprobes are... ?" He raised his eyebrows in a question.

"You do not know?"

"No. At least not under that name."

"They are inbuilt storage and data processing chips."

"Okay, so I don't know it under any name," he said under his breath. "And they are inbuilt—where?"

"Most of them are in the brain. Some nanoprobes circulate the bloodstream, but their role is more related to health homeostasis. One of the most useful attributes of these devices is that the data are not modified in any way upon retrieval. They always stay the same."

"As opposed to... ?"

"Real memories. Every time we access a real memory saved in the brain, we change it at the same time."

J looked at the floor, his face turning serious. He didn't say anything.

I glanced at him from the corner of my eye. *Did I say something wrong?*

I tried to rewind the conversation, wondering what had changed his mood all of a sudden.

Then he lifted his head and took a deep breath. "So, I spoke to Tania today. She said Stevanion is getting better." He turned his head to me.

"Yes, I know. I went to the infirmary in the morning." I didn't mention the conversation I had with Stevanion, though. J didn't need to hear Stevanion's opinion of Humans.

When we arrived at Mike's hut, J opened the leaf curtain, but then he stood next to it, waiting for me to pass. There was less than a quarter of an IP between him and me. It made a very narrow gap.

I looked at the door and then back at him again. *He's not expecting me to walk past him so narrowly, is he?*

J tilted his head with a subtle smile on his lips. "The IP space, I know. But you're on a new planet now. New rules. It's slowly time to get used to it. After you," he said and motioned with his head for me to go first.

Realizing that he wouldn't change his mind, I swallowed and quickly stepped forward. Though I was fast, I could see from the corner of my eye that he was looking at me. I felt his breath on my shoulders and my neck as I passed him by. And that had such an effect on me that, once I was inside the hut, I sat on the closest chair I could find, just as my knees gave in.

Mike's cottage seemed crowded. Everyone else was already here, standing in small groups, engaged in discussions. In an IP area suitable for four people, eight chairs were arranged in a circle. Several candles lit the room, giving it a warm feel with soft shadows dancing on the wooden walls.

Mike took a seat opposite me and J sat on an empty chair just next to him. "Shall we start?" J asked.

In a few moments, everybody found a seat and quieted down.

"I think everyone knows Dora by now," Mike said to the others.

Everybody looked at me and nodded their heads. I felt self-conscious but kept my trained calm Senthien pose.

"I'm not sure you know everyone here, Dora, so let me quickly introduce them for you. J and Peter you know already. Rick you've met, right?"

I nodded.

"Patrick and Simon were in the party that found you. And—Frank, I don't think you've met yet."

"Correct," I said.

Frank waved.

"All right, let's get started."

Mike took out two parchments of paper: one that looked like a map, another that had a blueprint of a compound drawn on it.

"J drew the route of the trip during the previous expeditions," Mike said, pointing to one piece of paper. "J?"

"All right, so this is mainly for Dora, Frank and Rick, who weren't with us on our previous scavenging trips. The route hasn't changed much, so I don't expect we'll find anything out of the ordinary now. The path over the river," J said as he touched the map with the stick, "should still be accessible, so I don't see a problem there either."

"Thanks, J. Patrick, you want to explain about the blueprint of the complex?"

"Sure, Mike," Patrick said and turned to me. "Dora, before the cryo, I worked at South Cape University of Technology. This is the place where we are going. I made a map of all the buildings at the time. This building here was the IT department." He pointed to a square in the middle of the compound. "Servers, storage, and mainframe devices for the whole institute, but also some groups doing IT research. I was in one of the research groups. I was working with Dr. Janfeld. He was the leading scientist on a—"

Mike coughed.

"Ahem. Never mind," said Patrick. "Anyhow, the first time we came there after we woke up, this building was gone. Completely."

"Where are the computers, then?" I asked.

"My best guess is that they are here," he said, pointing to another square near the original IT building. "This building didn't exist when I was working there."

I nodded. "And was this the place you could not enter?"

"Aye," said Peter. "We forgot the key."

"A key? Like a password?" I said.

"No, he meant a real key," Simon said, grinning. "A piece of metal with a specific pattern that fits a specific lock."

I nodded. "All right. So, will you bring the key now?"

They all laughed.

"Sorry, Dora, that was just a joke," explained Peter.

I nodded, slightly embarrassed.

"No lock there, I'm afraid," continued Patrick. "Just a sliding metal door."

There was a brief moment of silence when I felt people were expecting me to say something more, but when I didn't, Mike said, "Frank, do you have everything you might need?"

As Frank started to answer Mike's question, my eyes returned to the compound blueprint. The sides of my sight blurred just slightly, the level of conversation in the room dipped as if I was hearing it from another room, and then—it was gone.

A Vision?

I bent down and slid the blueprint closer to me with my fingers.

The very next moment, all the talk muted completely and the orange light of my surroundings vanished behind the white veil.

Three large screens.

OLED.

Not an AI—an older system.

Then I see a map. I can't interpret it, but the people around me are happy.

I don't know what the map means, but I know that we will be able to access the computer system. Somehow.

"Dora, are you okay?" J was looking at me with interest. The others turned as well.

"I was… just interested in the drawing." I looked at them, hoping my lie would hold up.

"All right." J nodded, holding my gaze for a while longer, but then turning to the group and the discussion.

They continued talking and I kept observing them, once again I was intrigued by how subtle facial expressions and certain voice intonations influenced the meaning of the content. I felt inadequate to pick up all the details of communication these Old Earth Humans used. All face-to-face communication in Uni, and particularly on Senthia, was exclusively verbal. If a word was not said, it wasn't meant, either.

"…which would then make it easy for us to find it," said Peter, and everyone else nodded.

And—I just missed some of the verbal communication as well. I tried to pick up what they were talking about.

"And if that's the case, then let's just hope it still works," said Simon. "Otherwise, we'll stay in the Stone Age forever."

"I thought this was the Middle Ages," said Peter and smiled.

Simon smiled back. "You know what I mean."

Everyone else laughed as well.

I looked at J. His teeth contrasted his tanned skin, and he had small dimples in his cheeks when smiling. I couldn't take my eyes off him.

Then he looked at me, and the dimples slowly disappeared.

We kept looking at each other. And neither of us could stop it.

Peter coughed and said, "May I interrupt?"

J blinked and then turned to Peter. "Sorry—what?"

Everyone laughed, and I had the strangest feeling it was about us.

"Peter, J, all fine?" Mike turned to them.

"Mmm." Peter nodded. "Food's ready. Tents are already packed. We're good to go."

"Simon?"

"I'll have everything ready by the time we leave."

"What's still missing?" asked Peter.

"Plantain and comfrey. We used the last one for Carmen."

"Aye, I remember. Was a tough call," said Peter, shaking his head.

"Ended well, though," said Simon.

"Thanks to you, buddy!" Peter inclined his head in an emphatic nod in Simon's direction. Simon smiled.

"All right. We are basically set for the trip. Dora?" said Mike.

I turned to look at him.

"We need to talk about the expansion of the village now. You're welcome to stay, if you want to, but we're not going to discuss the hike anymore. Do you have any questions?"

"No, Mike, I think everything is clear. I thank you."

"No worries. If you do have questions, just bug any one of the team to help you, okay?" he said. Then he turned to the group. "Rick, could I please ask you to fetch Sandra and Tony?" He turned to me and said in a lower voice, "They are our architects, you see."

"Right away, Mike, right away," said Rick, already on his way out.

"I wish he listened to me like that!" said Peter once Rick was out of the doors.

Mike laughed. "It never works on your own children, you know."

"You should feel lucky," said Patrick turning to Peter. "This means he really accepts you as his father."

"Aye. I feel better already." Peter shook his head again.

And everyone laughed.

While waiting for their architects, they spontaneously formed three groups based on discussion topics. J, Patrick, and Peter were standing while talking, and J was facing in my direction. Every now and then I peeked at J, and every so often, I saw him looking back at me. Then Peter moved closer to Patrick and J's window between them was gone.

I closed my eyes for a moment, trying to make order in the messy clutter of my confused thoughts.

What did all this mean? Why was he looking at me? And why was I looking at him so much?

I opened my eyes and exhaled. There has to be a logical interpretation. There is one for everything. All I need to do is find the premise, and the solution will appear, as it always does.

Good.

I felt content with my plan.

I said good night to everyone and just before stepping out, I peeked one more time in J's direction. He was talking to Patrick but then saw me looking. He stopped then, tilted his head, and smiled just slightly. Patrick turned to see what had caught J's attention, then grinned and turned back to him.

I quickly stepped out before there was time for me to misunderstand yet another nonverbal communication.

I stopped outside Mike's door. The fresh evening air washed over my face. It helped me to relax, and to focus again.

There were too many unknowns for me to extrapolate the solution. The only pattern I could detect was my increased heartbeat and—I exhaled a breath I didn't know I was holding in—my breathing problems, combined with the strangest instinctive, almost visceral feeling somewhere deep inside me, so deep I could not even locate it.

I sighed and closed my eyes.

The next moment, I heard footsteps on the bridge. I opened my eyes and saw Tania approaching quickly. She stopped in front of me and said in a low voice, "Dora, Stevanion is dead."

CHAPTER 15

I looked at her with my mouth opened, but no words came out.
"My condolences," she said. "I am so sorry. Would you like to come and see him?"

There was a silence in my mind.

After a while, I said, shakily, "N—no…"

I was confused, and none of my higher intelligence brain centers told me how to behave in this situation. I simply didn't know how to react.

"We will prepare the funeral tomorrow. It will be in the clearing a bit farther away from the village. Downwind. I will come to pick you up, all right?"

I nodded.

"If you need anything—anything at all—let me know." She lowered her head, still looking at me, making sure I understood.

"Yes." My voice was nothing but a whisper.

She looked at me for a few moments. Her body language told me she wanted to come closer, but she restrained herself.

"I'll go and tell Mike," she said, then looped around me and entered Mike's hut.

It was late evening. I felt tired and exhausted, but I could not sleep. I was looking at the wooden wall of my hut, almost white from the bright moonlight, with a few dark leaf-shaped shadows from the trees outside.

I didn't feel sad.

I felt empty.

Stevanion didn't mean much to me. I didn't really know him. I had almost never seen him back on Senthia. But now that he was gone, I realized I did miss him. Or, to be more precise, I missed the place in my life where he used to be. And although this was a very small hole, it reminded me of a much larger hole that I had sealed inside me, a long time ago.

I sighed.

It was connected, all of it. Stevanion came with me. And he died.

And I lived.

And I knew why.

I shook my head, trying to chase away these thoughts and place logical barriers around my feelings.

I was too late to bring him back to the Anas. I had failed.

He shouldn't have come on the port with me. I should have gone alone, and he would have still been alive.

I pressed the heels of my palms to my closed eyes.

It was my fault we'd been ported here. This was clear to me. And then I'd brought him to the Humans—and he got the flu.

My throat felt tighter, my eyes stung.

It was my fault.

It was my fault that he died. I shouldn't have brought him to the Humans. But how could I have—

I took a deep breath and held it in. Then I slowly exhaled, placed my arms next to my body, and tried to relax. Using a trained pattern of breathing techniques and focused relaxation of all my muscles, one at a time, I calmed myself down.

It took more than fifteen passes to completely relax my body, and by then I was starting to fall asleep.

Right then, I heard footsteps on the wooden bridge leading to my hut, and a moment later on the outside platform as well. There was a knock on the side of the door.

"Dora?" I heard J's whisper. "Dora, are you awake?"

My heart rate picked up immediately. I stood and walked to the door, moving the heavy curtain away. "J?"

"I'm sorry, I didn't want to wake you…"

"No, no, I wasn't asleep, it's okay. Do you… do you want to come in?"

He smiled but shook his head. "No, that's fine, you need to get some sleep. I just came here to tell you that… that I'm very sorry. About Stevanion."

He looked down at the floor between us.

"Thank you, J. I appreciate it."

"How do you feel?" he said, looking back at me. "Are you okay? Do you feel… ill?"

With this strange feeling I had in my stomach I almost said that I did, but I knew what he was asking, so I shook my head. "No, J. I feel healthy."

He exhaled loudly. "Ah, good!"

One side of his face was lit by moonlight; the other was in shadow. He opened his mouth to say something but paused for a moment, thinking.

Then he closed his mouth, obviously deciding not to voice what he had in mind. Instead, he said, "I should let you get some sleep. Good night, Dora. Sleep well."

I nodded. "Good night, J."

He turned and walked back to the bridge. I let the curtain drop, then moved a leaf just slightly with my finger so I could still look at him through the narrow gap. Scruffy black hair, thin shirt over his broad shoulders, trousers hanging loosely over his hips, the buttock muscles moving as he walked—and I was doing it again! I was *eyeing* him just as Julie had said. And I had no idea why!

After he stepped off the bridge, he turned in my direction one more time.

I froze in place, stopped breathing, and hoped he didn't realize I was hiding behind the curtain, watching him. He then turned and stepped on the neighboring bridge.

I finally let out the breath I had been holding in and turned to face the room.

But I didn't see it. I didn't see the wooden floor, the table or the cupboard. I didn't notice the intricate moonlight patterns anymore. I saw J, half of his face in the dark and half lit by silvery light, eyebrows casting a shadow over his eyes.

Beautiful…

With my back against the wall, I slid to the floor. Then I did something unthinkable, something no Senthien would do. I imagined I touched his face, and I could almost feel his skin, warm under my palm.

I closed my eyes and sighed.

About two hundred people gathered around the clearing, even more than at the bonfire. I was standing close to Old Mike. Next to him were Tania and Peter. J was standing just behind me. Although all of them were careful not to stand too close to me, with so many people it was impossible to give me my needed IP space. I was entering their interpersonal space, and they were entering mine. But somehow, at this very moment, I did not mind.

It was strange, being at Stevanion's funeral. I didn't know what to feel or how to act. The only person linking me to my Uni world was now white and rigid, lying on a platform of wood and branches, in his skinsuit once again. His hands were crossed on his chest, and underneath them was a small branch with thick succulent leaves. This, I assumed, meant something, but I didn't want to ask. Not now.

I felt empty and I felt lost. I felt like running with no direction, but I also felt like falling, deep, deep underground.

And somehow, having all these people around me, surrounding me, entering my IP space, actually helped me in the strangest way.

Their personal spaces acted like bubbles, and they pressed against me from all sides.

They supported me.

And kept me from falling.

Mike stepped forward and then turned around to face the crowd. Everyone fell silent.

"Friends. We are here to say goodbye to Barka Stevanion Narth. Although he belongs to the Senthien species of the Descendants, we will give him a Human funeral, because he is—a Human," he said it in a low tone, his eyes flickering to the group of Jumpers to his right.

I looked at them as well. In the front were Julie, Sarah, and three others, probably the women from the Boolean Institute. Most of the other Jumpers looked down, but Julie's eyes were on me. She narrowed them to thin slits and kept her gaze. I did not know what this nonverbal communication meant, but it gave me shivers nevertheless. Whatever it meant, it definitely wasn't friendly.

I turned back to Mike and realized I missed what he was saying. I deliberately let go of my thoughts of Julie and paid attention.

"His path led him somewhere he didn't plan to go. And because of it, he is now gone. Let him have peaceful rest."

Peaceful rest? I looked at Mike, not understanding. He's not going to wake up.

Perhaps it's one of those Human expressions again…

"Dora?"

I snapped out of my thoughts.

"Would you like to say a few words, as you are the one who knew him best?"

For a moment, I stopped breathing, surprised by Mike's question. Then I stepped out next to him, leaving a few IPs between us. I did not turn to the crowd. Instead, I looked at the corpse.

This wasn't Stevanion anymore.

It wasn't anyone.

It was just a body.

"I did not know him," I said, not having any idea what to say next. "There are people who knew him a lot better than I did… they are the ones who should be standing in my place."

I paused for a long while.

"He was not supposed to be here. He should have stayed in Uni. He should not have come… he should not have come…"

My next words came in a whisper.

"And it is my fault that he's dead. The port mistake happened – because of me."

Mike took a step toward me and said in a gentle voice, "It was an accident, Dora. It's no one's fault."

I looked at the ground in front of me, my gaze empty.

"Dora, do you want to light the fire?" asked Peter from behind me.

I turned to him and looked at him for a moment, incredulous at the question he just posed. Then I shook my head. "I can't."

"Do you mind if I do it?" he asked.

"No… please do," I whispered and took a step backward.

Peter walked to the wooden platform and took a torch, which was already burning next to it.

He bent down and held the torch between the branches for some time. Then, they caught fire, and it spread through the whole pyre with surprising speed. One person in the crowd started singing and a few other people joined her. I didn't understand the language they used, but I couldn't have imagined a more graceful farewell for anyone.

Dark smoke clouds bulged up into the sky, spiraling above the fire. A sickening smell reached my nostrils. My throat tightened and my stomach cramped to the size of a small stone. I pressed my lips together, closed my eyes, and used all my willpower not to vomit.

The next moment, the wind changed, and I could breathe again. I shivered.

I looked at Peter.

"The smell?" I said through my teeth. "Is it because he's Senthien?"

Peter shook his head. "Nah. It's the same for Humans. It's just the Human body being burned."

I shivered again.

When the song finished, people started leaving.

"Do you want to stay longer? A few people need to be here until the end, to make sure the fire doesn't spread. You can stay with them, if you wish," said Peter.

I took a moment to answer.

"Yes, I'll stay."

I turned around to see J behind me. He didn't say anything. He just looked at me, gave me a sad smile, and then bowed his head low.

After forty passes, there were only a few people left. Mike was to my left, Peter to my right. J was behind me and so was Tania.

The fire was dying out.

"Dora," Mike said, looking at the coals, burned wood, and ashes, "the trip we've planned to the city is scheduled for tomorrow. We would still like to go, because of the river." He turned to look at me. "You remember?"

"Yes, Mike. I remember."

"I know it is difficult for you right now, but we would still like you to join the expedition. Could you, please, still go with them?"

"Yes, Mike," I looked at him. "I have agreed to it. I will go."

I was standing on the bridge leading to Tania's hut, leaning on the rail and looking down at the green vegetation below me.

Tania stepped out of her hut and walked toward me. She leaned on the rail too, making sure she left enough space between us.

"The dinner will be ready soon."

"Thank you," I said and attempted a smile. "I... I am sorry... I do not know how to make food." I looked at her. "At Uni, there is a machine that does that for me. But it is far less tasty than what you make."

Tania smiled gently. "Thank you. I'm glad you like it."

There were a few moments of silence while we both gazed at the sun setting behind the horizon of the rainforest.

"How do you feel?"

"I feel healthy, Tania. Thank you."

"Yes, but how do you feel—inside?"

I took a few moments to reflect. "I do not know. I thought Stevanion would recover. I thought he was getting better."

She nodded. "I understand, but I know that sometimes people appear to be getting better just before death strikes. I don't know why," she said and shook her head. "I just know it happens like this sometimes."

I was silent.

"Dora, there was nothing you could have done. You know this, don't you?"

I still stayed silent. I was not sure.

"Mommy, Dora, the dinner is on the table," said Lemony from the entrance of the cottage.

"Thank you, sweetie, we're coming," said Tania.

I pushed away from the rail and started walking toward Tania and Peter's hut.

"Dora?" Tania said.

I turned to look at her.

"There is something I think you should know. I don't know if it will make sense to you or if it was just the fever kicking in, but…"

"I do not understand what you mean," I said.

"I'll just tell you what Stevanion said and you can decide what to make of it, okay?"

"What did he say?"

"Half an hour before he died, Stevanion had a really high fever, and he was talking in his sleep. I couldn't understand any of it," she said and shook her head. "I went to get fresh towels, but when I came back he was awake. And alert. He looked at me and... and he said, 'Tell her I have seen it. Everything. I understand it now. Thank her for choosing my name.' And then—he died."

My eyes were wide open.

Stevanion had a Vision.

"Did he say anything else?"

She shook her head. "No, I'm sorry, that was it."

I nodded and looked toward the forest. This bridge was a bit higher than the rest of the forest, and through the gaps between trees, I could see the tops of the tree crowns, like stormy waves, a turbulent surface of a forest ocean. It looked beautiful with the setting sun.

I have seen it. Everything, he said.

Everything—what?

Everything about the Humans? About me? Or something only related to his life?

"Does this mean anything to you?" Tania asked.

"No."

"Do you think he meant you, when he said 'tell her'?"

"I do not know. As I said, I did not know him all that well. Perhaps he meant someone from his own life." My gaze was still far above the forest. "But I do not know anyone from his life, so I can not tell."

I looked at her, and then shrugged and looked back to the forest. "Maybe he was not all that lucid..."

"Yeah, that could be. Well, anyhow, I just thought you should know."

"Thank you for telling me, Tania."

She smiled, then stepped forward and entered her hut.

I closed my eyes and silently recorded Stevanion's Vision on my nanoprobes for the future.

I wish I knew what he'd seen.

I opened my eyes. The sun had just disappeared behind the horizon, and the air immediately became cooler. The soft orange hue of the last sun rays on the trees changed into a dark green, almost black, and it covered the forest like a carpet of soot.

I pushed myself away from the fence and walked toward the hut.

I wish I knew…

CHAPTER 16

There was a lot of commotion around us while we were getting ready. Children were laughing and people were talking about what this trip might bring. Some of them even brought a few small items to the group, like bracelets or lucky charms. They hugged, shook hands, kissed. Everybody was excited. And somehow among all this commotion, all the good wishes, I felt alone. This was for the Humans in the group. This wasn't for me.

I pushed another small bag of medicinal herbs into my backpack and paused. I closed my eyes. In my mind, I could still smell it: the burned flesh, as if the stench still lingered in the air. I shivered.

"Dora, you're coming?" asked Patrick.

I opened my eyes as I pulled my hand out of the bag, then picked up my backpack, and joined them.

We walked for more than three hundred passes with only short breaks in between, and my legs were beginning to hurt, but I didn't say anything. I pressed on with the others, trying to stay close but still making sure I was at the very end. J and Frank were just in front of me, carrying large backpacks. They were talking to each other, but every now and then I saw J looking back. I guess he was making sure I was keeping up. I was curious what they were saying, so I raised the level of my tympanic audio enhancers.

"Do you think we might find some reptile delicacy on our road?" I heard Frank say.

"I doubt it. Unless we make an extra trip up the Falls River."

"But you went upriver a few times, didn't you, J? You caught a few, right?"

"Yeah, I did. Twice. Once with Peter and once with Lars."

"So, how did you catch them?"

"We sat up a trap, made a tight passageway out of wooden stakes, put the bait in it, and waited. Once the beast was in, it's very difficult for it to reverse backward fast enough. We got both of them with spears. You don't want to go any nearer than that," J said. "It was a wild fight, though. Strong animals—they don't give up."

"I bet! Well, I only enjoyed the fruits of your labor. They do taste mighty fine, don't they?" Frank said and nodded at the same time.

J grinned. "All right then, we can go on a hunt on our way back. That way we can also bring some for the village."

"And what shall we use as bait?" Frank said more quietly, turning his head in my direction.

J stopped in his tracks and pushed his index finger into Frank's chest, growling, "Don't you ever say anything like that!"

"Hey, J! It was just a joke, just a joke! Take it easy, man!"

"It's not funny, Frank." J moved on, perhaps realizing he might have slightly overreacted.

"She's not bad bait, you know," Frank said in a mischievous tone and continued walking.

"Stop talking!" J hissed.

"Hey guys, what was that about?" Peter said, hiding his laughter. "Seems like some stag fight."

J narrowed his eyes and picked up his pace, lengthening his stride.

I fell backward a bit, realizing there must have been some double meaning in their talk, but I wasn't able to interpret half of it. I didn't know what the bait was, nor what would make a good one.

Stupid. Such great powers of deduction, if only I knew what the premises were.

After another one hundred passes, we stopped.

"Let's camp here," J called out. "We still have about an hour until nightfall, but we are coming close to the gorge and I don't want to miss the edge in the dusk."

He rolled his backpack from his shoulders and it slumped on the ground with a thud. Everyone else followed the suit, starting to unpack their tents.

"Do you need help in setting up your tent?" J placed a large bag next to my feet.

I looked at him, a sudden thrilling jolt somewhere deep in my chest. I had dreamed of him so many times, but I never really grasped that my dreams would turn out to be Visions, that I was seeing the future, and that he was actually here.

"I appreciate your offer to help, J, but I am certain I will be able to do what the rest of your team does to the same extent," I heard myself answer, my tone cold and flat—and so different from what I felt inside.

His shoulders dropped.

"Yeah… okay… whatever." He waved his hand once, then turned around and walked away.

Oh, why did I say that? Why couldn't I say what I really thought? I was furious at my Senthien voice and my Senthien behavior. *Yes, I want help. And no, I don't know how to set up my own tent, thank you.*

But three hundred and ninety two years of persistent and relentless conditioning created behavior patterns that could not so easily be erased.

I knelt on the ground and pulled the tent out of the bag, checking the numerous folds and layers of thick beige fabric. I opened it, and folded it, and opened it again, then sighed, looking at the others. They already had their tents upright.

I sighed once more and bowed my head low.

"Hey!"

I looked up.

J was back.

I smiled within.

"You'll need to use these." He knelt down next to me and took out several straight wooden poles that were wrapped inside the folded tent.

"There are small nodes on top of these poles, see…" He pointed to the end of the wooden pole and stretched the material over it until the node found a little hole. "Like this."

He pulled harder on the fabric and continued, "It holds well, and you can stretch your tent upward."

Then he looked at me, his dark eyes fixed on my green, and for a moment, I didn't see anyone around us anymore. We looked at each other for what could have been an eternity. Then his gaze fell to my lips, and my heartbeat inevitably quickened.

He swallowed and then quickly stood up. "Ahem… I'll set

up the other side, all right?" he said, then walked to the other end looking at the ground.

My thoughts were a mess; I couldn't make any sense of them at all. Looking back in his direction, I only managed to say, "Thank you, J."

He looked back at me and smiled.

It was *the* smile. The one I saw in my dream. It was warm and gentle, and—as in my dream—it made me happy.

"You're very welcome, Dora."

Peter and Rick collected the firewood, and by the time it started getting darker, we were all sitting in a circle around a pile of coals and a few remaining flames. The potatoes and meat, covered in large-grained salt, were cooking under the burning coals.

I was starving. Food made in a food processor was highly nutritious and gave me all the necessary ingredients for healthy survival, but the taste the Old Earth Humans had in their cuisine was simply out of this world—which, when I really thought about it, it really was. It was out of *my* world.

I needed to continuously swallow as I looked at the mesmerizing patterns of red veins glowing on the coals, thinking of the food underneath. How embarrassing, I thought, to succumb to such a basic instinct. And yet how could I not, when it was so delicious?

Once the meat was done, Frank cut it into slices and handed it over to the others. J gave me a fork and a knife, and I copied the others as they peeled off the salt from the meat.

I inhaled the aroma.

Fabulous!

I took the first hot bite.

"Good?" Peter called out over the fire.

"Mmm, yes, wery," I responded with the food in my mouth. Everybody laughed. This, I realized, was my first spontaneous answer that did not sound so typically Senthien.

I smiled.

"J, how long to the city?" Frank asked as he stabbed another potato.

"I reckon we need a day and a half, so not much longer. However, I would like to check one of the side paths I saw last time we were here. I'm not sure what's up there, but it looked like an old road. Could have been a large paved road before, but most of it is gone now. Perhaps it's only an animal path, who knows. But I'd like two or three of us to go, see if there is anything of interest to us."

He stopped for a moment as he bit into a cooked potato crust.

"I didn't get to check it last time," he continued. "And I think we are making good time and have enough food with us to do the detour. So, to your question, Frank, we should get to the city in two, two and half days."

"Mmm. Good," Frank acknowledged as he munched on his meat.

"I'm really curious about the computer system! Must be awesome!" said Rick.

"We'll find out…" said Frank.

"*If* we manage to enter the building in the first place," said Simon.

"Aye," said Peter. "And, *if* that awesome computer has an equally awesome power source."

"I do wonder what type of power source that would be,"

Patrick continued. "It might be something very different from what we used to know."

"Dora," Peter said, turning to me. "How do you produce energy in Uni?"

Still finishing my last bites of meat, I now resumed my Senthien front. I was communicating knowledge: finally something I was good at.

"There are several ways of producing power in Uni. It depends on the planet. For example, on Senthia, we mainly use solar power. The solar cells are embedded as very small chips on the branches and leaves of engineered trees. There is a very specific pattern of chips, so these trees are highly symmetrical and identical to one another."

I put the meat skewer on the floor, deciding that I'd had enough.

"This kind of solar cell was developed by the Descendants, though. I do not think you will find anything like this on Old Earth."

All eyes were fixed on me. They were all silent, their faces a mixture of surprise and wonder. This was probably the longest talk they ever heard from me. As soon as I realized that, I looked down, deciding to eat some more.

"Wow, something different." Simon was the first to snap out of his silent awe. "What about other Descendant worlds, then?"

"Geothermal power is used on almost all worlds. Some worlds also use the bulk movement of gasses on a large scale."

"Movement of gasses?" asked Peter.

"Bah! Can you imagine the smell?" said Frank and all of them burst out laughing.

I looked at the group in confusion. I did not understand their reaction at all.

Once they calmed down, J asked, "What gasses are you talking about?"

"That depends on the home planet. Usually it is the breathing air with hydrogen, nitrogen, and oxygen."

"Ah, you mean the wind!" exclaimed Rick.

I looked at him. "Yes, wind, but also gusts, squalls, or gales. All of these are bulk movements of gasses, and they are all used for power production."

"Sorry, Dora. Our Old Earth terminology is coming back," said J. "So, what other energy sources are there in Uni worlds?"

"The thermal energy of organisms is used as well. My skinsuit, as well as my E-band," I said, raising my left arm up for them to see it, "can be partially powered by my body heat. But that is usually done on a small scale."

"Can you imagine how much energy Jessica Donovan's skinsuit would generate?" said Frank with a sly smile.

"Oh, Frank, get a grip," Patrick said and shook his head.

"Come on, she's hot! Or… was hot."

"Perhaps she got a ticket to space—who knows? Maybe there's an entire Descendant species that all look exactly like her," said Simon.

J shook his head, and then turned to me. "What power did people use just before the Evacuation? Were there big changes, do you know?"

"From what I remember from my history recap classes, they mostly used fossil fuels and biomass, but gas movement, solar power, and hydropower were growing in significance."

"What about nuclear power? Still in use?"

"During the twenty-first century, large-scale nuclear power plants were used less and less, and instead were being replaced by nuclear microgenerators, which were developed to be portable."

"Portable? Really? How big are they?" asked Peter.

"Fairly small. They are cube-shaped, about a quarter of an IP in length. Newer versions are even smaller."

"Aren't you guys afraid?" asked J.

"Of what?"

"Of radiation? Or nuclear waste that takes ages to decay?"

"Nuclear microgenerators are highly stable and clean," I said, almost surprised by their questions. "And used-up generators that do not produce anymore are ported to waste planets and moons. There is no danger."

They all nodded slowly, accepting this new concept.

"What about fusion power?" asked Patrick. "I know there were a lot of successful trials and experiments in that direction, but none of this was being used for real before our cryo-time."

"You are correct. Fusion power was used too, but the large-scale production was perfected on Descendant worlds. However, the most used power source in Uni is bioenergy."

"Bioenergy? What kind of bioenergy?" asked Patrick.

"KCFC," I said.

They all looked at me without saying a word.

"Should we… know what this means?"

I looked at them and then checked my nanoprobes to see when the research for KCFC started. *Ah, yes—not in their time.*

"Krebs Cycle Fuel Cell," I said. "It is the ultimate fusion power cell that makes energy by joining hydrogen and oxygen without producing waste."

"Krebs cycle?" said Simon. "Isn't that the energy production in living cells?"

"Yes. The principle is taken from a living organism, but then transferred to a synthetic environment."

"What kind of synthetic environment?" asked Patrick.

"I am sorry, Patrick. I do not have all the details. It is proprietary information developed by Loreans and Booleans."

"Hmm, pity. That would be interesting to know…"

"I know that the initial research happened in the late pre-Ev period, but the final technology was developed only on the new planets. For this reason, I doubt that you would find this technology here."

"Basically, we don't really know what power source we'll find out here, do we?" asked Simon, looking around at everyone.

Patrick and J shrugged.

"See and be surprised, aye?" said Peter.

After a few moments of silence, Rick said, "Does anyone want the last piece of meat?"

Everyone shook their heads.

"Great! I'll volunteer then," Rick said and stabbed the last piece.

Once everyone was finished, they put their plates and cutlery into a washing bag, and I did the same.

"Who's youngest?" asked Simon.

"I am. I know," mumbled Rick with a full mouth and grabbed the bag as soon as all the plates were in. Recognizing the pattern, I smiled. It would take a while until it was my turn to wash the utensils.

Frank and Simon headed off to their tents, and Peter picked up an empty leather bag and followed Rick to the small stream to fetch water so he could put out the fire.

J and I were the only ones left.

I looked at him but immediately dropped my gaze when I saw him glancing at me. I so much wanted to talk to him. There were so many things about him that I wanted to know, but every time I had an opportunity, there was a heavy weight on my chest, as if my heart was being squeezed into a sphere smaller than its volume.

And, like always, I dealt with this confusing feeling the only way I could: by placing a calm Senthien façade over my mixed emotions.

"Good night, J," I said in a monotonous voice, knowing my face looked like I'd seen it on the holos: calm and cold.

He took a few moments to respond, puzzled by my quick departure.

"Um… okay. Good night, Dora. Sleep well."

"I shall."

The moment I turned away, my façade dropped and a deep pressure pushed painfully against my solar plexus.

I closed my eyes. The Senthien in me made it impossible to do what I wanted to do the most. I wanted to be Human—for him—but I simply didn't know how.

CHAPTER 17

Peter woke us up early the next morning. We had a short morning meal, where I sat in the outer circle around the remains of the last night's fire, hoping no one would notice me. I was still fenced in by my self-made Senthien wall, though I could not stop glancing at J whenever I thought he wasn't looking. Every now and then, he caught me and his face relaxed into a barely noticeable smile.

We packed our gear and were soon on our way. The vegetation was just slightly different here than at the village. I wouldn't have even noticed the difference myself, but my nanoprobes automatically compared the images on my ONC and communicated this information. The soil was drier and darker. The grass layer was almost gone, and the majority of the trees in these woods had needlelike leaves. And they smelled *fabulous*.

We walked for almost sixty passes when J lifted his hand to slow us down.

"I think we're approaching the gorge," he said.

Within a few passes we reached the end of the forest that opened up into a narrow clearing, which disappeared four IPs from where we stood.

"Slowly now," J said and came to the edge of the cliff.

Several IPs below the steep rocks, a clear blue river was

rushing past. The gorge wasn't very wide, but the rocks leading to the river were so steep it was virtually impossible to climb down.

I swallowed involuntarily and then looked at J. He looked back and smiled. "We're not climbing down, don't worry."

Then he looked upstream, shielding his eyes with his hand.

"Do you see it?" asked Peter.

"No, not yet…" He was scanning the other side of the river. And then he stopped. "There it is, I see it!"

"I don't," said Rick, frowning.

"You can't see the cable: it's too thin to see it from this distance," said J. "But look at the river's edge. Last time we marked it with red rope. On the tree. See it?"

"Ah, yeah, I see it. Cool! I'm so looking forward to trying it out!" said Rick, hopping from one leg to the other.

"Let's go!" J said and started walking along the edge of the gorge. "Just be careful, everyone," he said but looked at me.

It only took us a few passes to reach the tree where the rope cable was attached on this side of the river.

"Are we sure it works?" asked Peter.

"Yeah, I checked it," said Patrick. "Fynn and I did a perimeter check two weeks ago. Tried it out. Runs smoothly."

"So, who's going first?" asked J, looking around.

"I'll do it," said Patrick, stepping to the large tree a few IPs away from the edge. The thick metal cable was attached to a small mechanism on the tree, and it stretched over the river to the tree on the other side. On our side, the cable could be positioned higher or lower on the mechanism, making the attachment site either higher or lower than the cable attachment on the other side of the river.

Patrick pulled few small ropes on the mechanism to raise the cable higher. Then he reached down to his bag and took out a leather harness with a metal wheel and multiple belts. He hooked the wheel of the harness on the cable and sat in the leather sling while J checked all the bindings.

"Peter, could you please have a look too?" said J and stepped back.

Rick, standing close to me, explained, "They always do double or triple checks with things like that."

I nodded, not looking at Rick, my eyes fixed on the cable system. *This just seems life-threatening.*

"Good to go," said Peter.

Patrick swung away from the edge. There was a high zipping sound as he slid down the rope, shouting over the noise of the river rushing through the gorge.

"Why is he shouting?" I asked out loud.

"It's fun!" answered J and smiled. Once we could see Patrick on the other side, J pulled the ropes of the mechanism to bring the cable attachment to the lowest position.

"You want to go next?" he asked me.

I shook my head.

J tilted his head, looking at me. "Dora, why don't you? If you stay here and keep looking at people sliding down, you'll get more and more nervous. Come, I'll help you in."

"In where? There's no seat!"

"There is now." He smiled as the leather sling slid back along the cable. He knelt down with one knee and held the sling open for me. I came closer.

"You need to put both feet here..." He looked up at me. "I'll hold the sling."

I lifted one foot and aimed for the gap in the leather seat, but I lost my balance and stood on both feet again.

"Hold onto my shoulder," he said.

I blinked at him twice. *He wants me to touch him?*

I stood still.

"What?" he asked.

"The IP, mate," said Peter.

"Ah, the IP…" He nodded to Peter and then looked back at me. "Okay, can you just try and forget about the IP distance for a moment… or two, or three?"

He gave me an encouraging smile.

"Okay," I said in a low voice, as he positioned the sling again.

I squeezed my jaw and carefully put my palm on his shoulder. His shirt was thin, and I could feel his skin stretching over his shoulder muscles.

His eyes then moved away from the sling and shifted up my body until he was looking at me in the eyes.

I swallowed. My heat started racing; I could feel it in the veins of my neck. My legs all of a sudden became very weak, and once again, I felt this yearning somewhere deep inside me.

What was that?

I moved my hips slightly and voluntarily squeezed my pelvic muscles to release the pressure. He tensed his jaw muscles and swallowed, then lowered his gaze to the sling he held open for me. I put one foot in and then the other. J stood up, not looking me in the eyes. My hand was still on his shoulder. I somehow… forgot to move it away. He arranged the harness so it reached my hips and tightened the band at the front. As he did that, he also pulled me closer to him, and then—he looked at me and I looked at him. For a moment, time stood still, our eyes glued to each other's.

My heart was beating wildly from him being so close, from feeling his skin under my palm through his thin shirt. I had the feeling that my stomach was filled with a thousand bubbles, hundreds of them bursting at the same time. Little black dots started appearing at the edges of my vision, and I was afraid I would soon lose consciousness if we stayed close like this.

"Guys, you're all cute, but we don't have all day!" said Simon.

We both dropped our gaze. J took a deep breath, and then he moved behind me to fasten one more strap. I looked down at my hand that had touched him, still dazzled by this tactile experience.

How can the body have such an influence on the mind?

I lifted my head, closed my eyes, and relaxed the tense muscles in my body.

J moved around to my front again.

"You're set," he said in a low voice. "Peter," he turned and called with a stronger voice, "could you please check the straps?"

I opened my eyes just as J stepped back to give Peter space.

Peter circled around me, touching and pulling a few straps to check the hold. "Aye, good to go," he said and moved away.

J came closer and gave me the smile. The one I'd seen him do in my Visions, the one no one else did quite like him.

I wanted to sigh, but I refrained.

"Are you ready?" he asked.

I nodded. "I think so."

"You don't need to hold on, the straps work fine. But you can hold them if it gives you comfort."

I grabbed both straps attached to the cable and nodded.

"It starts slow, but then picks up speed halfway down," he explained. "Don't worry about it; it will slow down again before you reach the other end."

I nodded again and looked down the cliff one more time.

"And—you need to jump to get going."

"Jump?" I repeated, disbelieving.

"Yeah, jump. Would you like me to help you?"

"Help? Me?"

"Yes—would you like me to give you a little push?"

"No! Thank you. I will manage," I said as I looked down to the rushing water.

"And it doesn't help if you look down. Just look straight to the other side."

"Yes," I said, half automatically. "Just straight."

"You'll be fine," he said and smiled again. "See you on the other side."

I attempted a smile, probably failing miserably.

I looked to the other side where Patrick was waiting and then jumped, the sling swinging into empty space. At first the speed was slow, but then quickly accelerated. The wind picked up, blowing the hair off my face.

I held my breath in one silent, exhilarating moment, with the adrenaline raising my heartbeat and the sweat moistening my skin. The air rushing past me made my eyes teary and my throat dry. The whistling sound of the sliding mechanism just above my head mixed with the wind blowing rapidly next to my ears. Just when I thought it was too much and the adrenaline would make me faint, the leather sling decelerated and came to a stop on the other side of the gorge.

My feet touched the ground, and at the same time Patrick grabbed hold of my harness straps and brought me to a complete stop.

"You seem to have enjoyed that," he said, with a smile.

"It was… unbelievable!" I could hardly catch my breath. My heart was racing and my palms were sweating. "Do we take the same route back?"

"What, you'd like to try it again?"

I nodded.

"Yeah, we're coming back the same way. You'll get another ride, don't worry," he said. As I stepped out, Patrick let go of the sling and it rolled back along the cable to the other side, where the rest of the group waited.

Once everyone was across, we continued on. I was at the back as usual, my eyes on the ground, listening to the conversations of the others, but I was mainly interested in hearing J.

He was quiet for the last few passes, and I looked up to see him. At the same moment, he turned around and saw me looking, so he stopped walking and waited for me to catch up.

"Patrick said you enjoyed the cable slide," he said, falling into pace with me.

"Yes," I said in my usual neutral tone.

"Mmm."

We were silent for a while, and I wondered if I should have said something more in answer to his question.

"I guess Earth is very different than your own world?" he tried again.

"Yes."

He sighed, obviously not content with my answer.

I didn't understand. I'd told him the truth; what else would he want to know?

"So, where do you live? I mean, where did you live, before the… teleportation error?"

"I lived on Senthia," I said, and looked at him. He met my gaze, and I looked down again.

"Senthia has two moons," I said and glanced at him again.

"Do they look like our moon?"

"No."

He arched his eyebrows. "What do they look like?"

"They are a lot smaller than Earth's moon. They are both white, but one has a wonderful purple hue. It is one of my favorite wall images."

"Wall images? Like paintings?"

"No. Like walls. Only it is an image."

He sighed again.

I lowered my head. *I must be doing something wrong.*

I looked to the front, observing the other members of the group. They were talking in a lively fashion and their conversation flowed easily, melting from one sentence to another.

But our dialog seemed so disjointed.

I am not like that. I could converse without any difficulty at all, but—I glanced at J—not with him.

I looked at the ground below my feet.

I do want to talk to him.

And I want to know everything about him.

I can't just let it slip like this!

I took a deep breath, then turned my head to him and said, "J?"

"Yes?" he said so suddenly I almost jumped. "Ah, sorry... I didn't expect you to... say my name," he said, his beautiful smile appearing on his face. I looked at him, and then I forgot what I wanted to ask him.

He took a quick breath, looking in front to the others for a moment and then back at me.

"What did you want to say?" he asked.

"You..." I closed my eyes for a moment, then looked at him again. "You are close to breaking the IP border."

He looked at the space between us and moved a little bit away while still walking.

"I'm sorry. Is this better?"

"Yes. Thank you."

"No problem."

"How come Earth Humans know about IP distances?"

"I heard the Jumpers joking about it."

I nodded. "And when you first encountered Jumpers, did you know who they were?"

"We didn't." He shook his head. "At first, we thought they were other Humans that had been cryo-preserved as well, but at some other location. Of course, we soon found out where they came from. And more kept coming."

"How did you know where to find them? And when to find them? Peter said you always know when portation occurs."

"That's right. Whenever a teleportation happens, it leaves a bright shining light in the sky, like half a rainbow, only it's pure white. And it touches the Earth just at the drop point, and for some reason it always happens in the same location."

"Must be a natural porting field resonator," I said to myself.

"Sorry?"

"Porting field resonator," I said, turning to him. "In Uni, all the porting channels connect to porting chambers. Here on Earth, however, it seems the porting can be established without a chamber."

He looked at me uneasily and said, "You think you could use the same place to teleport back to Uni?"

"The data I have now is inconclusive, but I think this possibility exists."

"Would you… want to go back?"

I thought again about my imminent port to the Zlathar planet, and my immense relief when I realized that I had accidently managed to escape.

And then I looked at J.

I was so happy that I'd found him, that my dreams were in fact Visions, and that I was here, right now, talking to him.

I don't know what would make me want to port back. Ever.

"Ah," he said and waved his hand once. "You don't need to answer that. It's your business, I guess. So, Uni... is that a solar system?"

"No. Uni is a network of planets and moons where Descendants terraformed their environment."

"And how many Descendant worlds are there?"

"Currently inhabitable, two hundred and three. But"—I checked my nanoprobes—"there are three more in the making."

"Okay. Does that mean there are two hundred and three Descendant species?"

"No. Each Descendant species inhabits many worlds."

"So how many Descendant species are there?"

"Seventeen."

"What about the name, Uni? Where does the word come from?" He looked at me. "Is it like universe? Uni?"

"No," I said and looked at him, surprised the Jumpers hadn't explained it. "Uni comes from the old university where the foundation for Descendant evolution was created."

"Okay. Was that on one of your new planets, this university?"

"No, that was still on Old Earth. It was the University of Neurotechnology and Innovation."

Peter, who was walking just a few IPs in front of us, suddenly stopped and turned around. "University of Neurotechnology and Innovation? That's where the lab of Tania's husband was."

"Deceased husband," said Patrick, joining the conversation.

Peter looked at him. "Aye, deceased husband. He seemed to have worked in a really important place..."

And in a really important lab, I thought to myself. "Yes, that is correct."

"Whatever was made there must have been really important to name the whole galactic community after it," J said, raising his eyebrows. "So, what was it?"

I hesitated for a moment. Simon looked back and also slowed down to join the group. I looked at all of them and then said, "The first Mind prototype was built there."

"Really?" Simon shook his head in surprise. "I didn't know we had that type of technology in our time."

"The prototype was very simple back then," I explained. "The computational power was minimal. But the foundations were there."

"What is the Mind again?" asked Rick.

"It's just a computer," said Frank, waving his hand dismissively.

"It is not *just* a computer," I turned to him, feeling the strong unexpected urge to defend the most unique artificial intelligence system ever created. "The Mind controls all the portations at any given moment, across a network that spans several hundred light years of space. It connects to all the AIs in the Uni at the same time. Its power is inconceivable for a Human brain."

"You make it sound like God," said Patrick, grinning.

"God?" I said, not understanding.

"But unlike God," J jumped in, "it still makes mistakes." He tilted his head toward me and arched his eyebrows.

"Don't we all?" laughed Peter.

"We do!" said J, pointing a finger at Peter as if to make a point. "But *it* can't. It's not a Human, it's a machine. It shouldn't make any mistake. Or am I wrong?" He looked back at me, a mysterious smile on his face.

I looked at him without responding: I was completely distracted. *Dark eyes, dark hair, bronze skin and... lips...*

His smile broadened, and I completely lost my train of thought.

I dropped my gaze, and then after a few moments I said, still looking at the ground, "I do not know. As I said, the proprietary details of the Mind are unknown to me."

"Your bunch is really good at keeping secrets," said Patrick. "Back in our time, something so big would spread like a fire on a trail of gunpowder."

"But it did happen in our time, didn't it?" J said, looking at Patrick. "At least the start of it..." Then he lowered his gaze and shook his head, looking puzzled. "Still, I would think people would find out about something like that."

I remembered seeing the evacuated lab just before the explosion started. Someone had made sure it wasn't revealed. *Someone took drastic measures to keep it a secret.*

"I guess the Mind was perfected on the new Uni planets?" asked Simon.

I tapped into my nanoprobes to access additional information on the topic. "The technology was perfected on one of the Seedships. This is how all the different Seedships had instantaneous contact. It was crucial to establishing the network of colonies and a unified society."

"But wait a minute—didn't you say that for all teleportations, you need a chamber? Even if they set up a teleportation chamber on one Seedship, how did they reach any other ship?" asked J.

"Each of the Seedships had one portation chamber built before it left the Earth, so that when porting technology became available, the Seedships had an automatic connection to one another."

"Wow, clever… but how could they build the chambers before they had the technology ready?" asked Patrick.

"Well, the theory was already there. They just needed to put it into practice."

J nodded and said, "I guess with the successful prototype they built here at the University of Neurotechnology and Innovation, they knew it was possible. It was just a matter of time, no?"

I looked at him and nodded. Then I looked at the rest. They all seemed crowded around me as we walked, deep in their thoughts. All of a sudden, I became aware of their close proximity, and my IP sensitivity kicked back in.

I deliberately slowed down to drop to the back of the group. Realizing I needed space, they all moved on ahead.

CHAPTER 18

Three men are walking.

Their step is light; they haven't been walking for very long.

They are talking, laughing at the jokes from the person in the front.

They come to a fork in the path and must decide which road will get them to their destination faster.

The person in the front decides the right path is better. The left path, he explains, would take longer.

They take the path to the right.

Not long after, they are on steep terrain, walking on a rocky path, watchful of their steps, on the narrow, winding trail. They come to a section where the path is only half an IP wide: a steep cliff on their left, a deep abyss on the right. One moment, all three are silent, slowly moving forward. The next, a side of the hill breaks off and slides down into the abyss, taking the first two men with it. The last person scrambles to safety. After several moments, he turns around and retreats.

I sat up straight, gasping for air as if I'd been under water for too long. My heart was pounding under my rib cage as I tried to inhale enough air into my lungs. With shaky hands, I wiped drops of sweat off my forehead and tried to swallow.

A dream Vision!

I leaned my head on my hands, resting my elbows on my bent knees, eyes wide open.

Simon was the second in the group, and J…

J was the first.

I wanted to walk to J's tent and tell him about my Vision. Tell him that he shouldn't take the right path. He should take the left. And if he does, I will see him again.

But I couldn't.

He was still asleep.

Everyone was.

It was still early morning. The air was fresh and the birds had just given their first musical performance of the day.

I had to wait.

Patience, I discovered, had an interesting twist for me here on Earth.

Senthiens were never impatient. There was no need to want something done before it was feasibly possible. In Uni, that was never a problem for me. Here, however, I found that being patient was a lot harder.

I simply had to wait.

And I didn't like it.

Breakfast was just getting started as J explained the detour he wanted to take. Simon and Patrick volunteered to go with him.

I was silent.

I didn't know how to bring it up.

What should I say? *Good luck with your detour, and by the*

way, I can also see the future, so please take the left path so you survive this little excursion?

For most of the time during the breakfast, I just looked at my plate, avoiding J's gaze, not knowing how to act.

When the meal was finished, Peter, Rick and Frank took the plates and utensils to a nearby stream, and Simon and Patrick put on their backpacks and started walking into the forest. J crouched down, picking up a few more flasks of water and placing them in his bag. Then he stood up and looked at me, an undecipherable expression on his face. He nodded slightly without saying anything and turned to leave.

I had to tell him.

I had to tell him *now*!

"On your way..." I started saying and then paused.

J stopped and turned around to face me.

I lowered my gaze to the ground and forced my voice to be calmer. "On your way, you will come to a fork in the path. The left one leads straight uphill and does not seem like the fastest path to take. The right one seems more comfortable at first, but it becomes very narrow later on and it will lead you to a narrow path next to a cliff."

Clearly puzzled, he studied me as I spoke. "Yes?"

"Do not take the right path," I said, looking up, realizing my green Senthien stare must have been as clear as the Vision I had the night before, "or only one of your group of three will return. Take the left path. It is a bit longer... but you will come back." I looked at the ground again, hiding whatever emotions he might see underneath my eyelashes.

He silently looked at me for half a pass, his mind clearly full of questions as my eyes constantly moved between his face and the ground.

"All right," he said quietly. "We'll take the left path."

I sighed in relief.

"And then, you and I need to talk. For real."

Oh…

He smiled at the expression on my face, then turned and left to join the others waiting for him a few IPs away.

It was a calm day. Frank, Rick, and Peter were discussing various subjects: whether we would be able to find a way into the computer facility, what we might find there, what else we might be able to scavenge in the ruins, and so on.

I couldn't talk to any of them. I constantly walked in a large circle around them, too anxious to be still. And the more I walked, the more I thought about it, and the stronger one thought became: *I shouldn't have let him go.*

All of my Visions came to be. They shouldn't have gone at all. He should have stayed here. He should have stayed with me.

But he didn't.

Because I let him go.

I closed my eyes, stopping for a moment to try to calm myself. Then I opened them again and continued walking.

My father told me that the Visions are only a possibility of what might come, and that the future could change if decisions changed.

I kept repeating this to myself as if it was a mantra.

I hoped that he was right: that Visions only showed possible paths of the future, but that they could change.

I hoped J would save himself, knowing what could happen on the wrong path—and thus save me as well.

It was one of the most difficult days for me. Every moment

crept by as I waited for the group to come back. And as ashamed as I was for having the thought, the only thing I really wanted was for J to come back. Even if something happened to the others, I needed J to come back. Selfish and mean these thoughts were, but I simply could not change them.

The moon appeared in the dimming afternoon sky. It was quiet. Everyone was occupied with something and no one talked. By now, I thought, everyone was expecting them to come back. And they didn't.

I sat on a rock, my palms pressed together between my knees. I sat still, as if a part of the rock itself. I barely breathed. And then I heard the sounds. I looked to the right. Voices. Grass and leaves being moved by footsteps.

They're back.

Oh, the Moons of Senthia—they are back!

We all stood up to greet them. Simon came first, then Patrick. J was the last. They were all in great spirits. Lots of laughter, shouts, and engaged talking. Still grinning about a recent joke, J looked around the campground until he found me. He smiled to me and mouthed: *Alive.*

I had to smile back.

J turned to the rest of our group and said, "So, who wants a rabbit?"

"Rabbit? You caught one?"

"Patrick did. Two of them," J said and swung from his shoulder a rope with two dangling rabbits.

They seemed very large. I checked the available information on my nanoprobes. The database described the long ears and elongated bodies, but their size seemed unusual.

"They are big!" I said.

"Yup. We still call them rabbits because they—" J lifted one up and looked at it.

"—most likely originated from the rabbit," interrupted Frank. "But time and some intense solar radiation made some changes to its blueprint."

"And they taste like rabbits, too," said J.

"You mean they mutated?"

"Yup," said J, who sat down, placed one rabbit on the ground in front of him, and sliced through its skin with a sharp knife. "Like many other species who managed to survive the apocalypse."

He stripped the fur off the rabbit, then cut through the belly and opened it up. Several dark red and off-white baggy organs spilled out. He dipped his hand in the rabbit's insides and removed all the organs from the abdomen cavity with a calm efficiency that told me he had done it many times before. I watched him in a trance, amazed at this true survival drive. Put any Descendant in an environment like this, without technology, and in a few days he would starve. But these people know how to survive.

Humans.

Why did the Zlathars force them to the bottom of Uni society when they are such great survivors?

"Dora?"

Hearing my name snapped me from my thoughts, and I turned to Patrick.

"Yes?"

"Could you please help me put these sticks on the side of the firewood?"

I walked to Patrick and took one of the branches he was talking about. "What do you need them for?"

"These will be holders for the spit. Into these forks," he said, pointing to the V-shaped ends of the branches, "you put the spit with the rabbit and then keep turning it over the fire."

"Well, actually, it's next to the fire," said Peter. "We don't want it burned."

J walked over to Patrick and handed him the spit, all four limbs of the rabbit wrapped around the wooden rod. Pink, smooth, with no fur on, it looked repulsive. I shivered slightly and turned away.

I moved a few IPs back and sat on a log.

Once both rabbits were cleaned and skewered on spits they were placed next to the fire and we all sat in a circle around it.

"Did you see anything interesting on your little off-road trip?" asked Peter.

"Yes," said Patrick.

"And... ?" asked Peter, when there was no continuation.

"We don't know," said J.

"What do you mean you don't know?"

"Well, we found a building. Actually, we found quite a large complex, but most of the buildings were destroyed—"

"Except one," jumped in Simon.

And then none of them continued.

"Bloody Mary, you're keeping us in suspense here!" said Peter.

"No, sorry, it's just that we don't know what it was," said J. "The building was sealed by a massive steel door."

"No door handle, I presume," said Frank.

"No, actually, there was. But it was like... a wheel."

"Come to think of it, you know what it reminded me of?" said Patrick.

"What?"

"A nuclear shelter entrance."

"Lovely," said Peter, rolling his eyes.

"Couldn't you get in?" asked Rick.

Patrick shook his head. "Nope. We tried. Couldn't open it."

"Dead end, then?" asked Peter.

"I guess so," said Simon.

"I reckon it really was a shelter, Patrick," said J.

"Well, no big loss then," said Peter, looking back at the fire.

After several more passes, he rose from his log to kneel next to the roasting meat. He cut one small part from the side and then, holding the piece between knife and thumb, he put it in his mouth.

"Mmm." He nodded. "Ready!"

Then he sliced the meat for everyone and handed over the plates. The conversation was replaced by silence, and all that was heard was the soft chewing of food and leaves rustling in the wind high above us. Every now and then I stole a glance at J, and every time, I saw him looking back. I ate a lot less than I really wanted to because I was unsure my stomach would keep the meal inside.

I knew that once the dinner was finished, he would want to talk to me.

And I was so afraid of that.

My heart was in my throat, and my palms were shaking. I was afraid of being close to him, of us talking without the buffer of the group where I could hide whenever I needed to.

J put the plate down next to his feet, and after a few passes, so did Simon, Patrick, and Peter.

"Here, give me those," said Patrick and reached out his hand to take the used plates. "I'll do the washing up."

"Thanks, buddy, for taking my place," said J and then winked at me.

Patrick looked back, his face confused. "It's—no, it's my turn… ah!" he said and waved at him dismissively. "I know what you're trying to do. Don't you trust him, Dora. He's older than he looks!"

"It's all about how you feel," said J. "And I feel young."

They all laughed, and although I understood the joke, I couldn't join the laughter. My stomach was in knots.

"All right, I'm ready for bed," said Peter, who then looked at J and gave him a barely noticeable nod. "C'mon, guys. I think we all need a good rest for the trip tomorrow."

Patrick left with the dishes, and Simon, Rick, and Peter stood up and left for their tents.

"Actually, I'll stay by the fire for a little bit," said Frank to Peter, then turned to J. "You know, to warm up for the night."

J rubbed his forehead and sighed. Then he looked at me and asked with a smile, "Dora, want to walk with me?"

Walk?

I nodded and rose from my seat, not saying a word.

We walked a few dozen IPs away from the campground in silence until we came to an uprooted tree. It had six or seven thick roots spreading in different directions. J chose a thick horizontal root and sat down, as if it was a bench.

"Come, Dora, sit with me." His voice was amused but mysterious at the same time.

I chose a root on the other side, a few IPs away, and sat down, masking my face under Senthien calmness and looking at him with a pretense of disinterest. He laughed quietly and lowered his gaze. Then he shook his head slightly, stood up, and sat down on the root I was sitting on.

I swallowed.

This was definitely less than one IP, and I felt like a heavy weight was pushing on my chest.

"What do you want to talk about?" With my best Senthien intonation, I clearly indicated that there was nothing to discuss. So far, it had always worked.

So far.

"Tell me," he said.

"Tell you what?"

"The future. You see the future, don't you?"

"No."

He shook his head. "I saw it. The fork in the path? It was exactly as you said it would be. And my first instinct was to take the right path, as you said I would. And I would have done that, if you hadn't warned me."

I listened to him without saying a word.

"And on the way back, when we came to the fork again, I went and checked the right path quickly. I was just curious. And do you know what I found?"

I shook my head, not trusting my voice.

"A fresh mudslide. The path was completely gone."

He took a short break before continuing. "I reckon if we took the path in the morning, we would have been dead. *You* saw the future."

I lowered my gaze and said, "But you are still alive."

"So?"

"So, it is not the future," I looked back at him, trying to keep my voice calm. "It is one possible and most likely probability, depending on the current course of events. This is what Senthiens do. This is our ability."

He leaned back a bit. "Why didn't the Jumpers tell us about it?"

"They don't know."

"What about other Descendant species? Do they also have some… abilities?"

"Yes, most of them do. These were targeted DNA changes to express or inhibit certain phenotypes and characteristics. And our society is built on the diversity of our different abilities."

"Like?"

"Each Descendant species has a role in the society. Booleans do science, Loreans develop technology, Zlathars… keep order, and Senthiens process information and—predict."

"The future?"

"The possible future paths, yes."

"What else have you seen?"

"What do you mean?"

He leaned in toward me, almost touching my knees with his. My breathing instantly sped up.

"Did you see yourself coming to Earth?"

I lowered my gaze. My Visions had showed me something else.

"I… didn't know it was Earth."

"But you saw something. What was it?"

I closed my eyes for the briefest of moments, remembering J's touch, his hand holding mine, his kiss…

"They were… they were just predictions, J." I looked back at him.

He leaned in closer and tilted his head. "Did you see *me*?"

How does he know?

I swallowed.

"You did, didn't you?" He leaned in even closer.

I took a deep breath and held it in for a few moments.

"What did you see?" he said quietly.

I breathed out. My heart was racing, and I saw little black dots that told me I wasn't far from losing my consciousness.

"Dora?" He was whispering. "Tell me. Please."

My head was spinning and my thoughts were a blur.

"I… saw you," I said, the Senthien intonation gone, my voice showing true emotions for the very first time. "I saw you, before I ported to Earth. And I didn't know if it was the future or simply a possible prediction that might never take place."

He was patient, trying not to push me. After a few moments of silence, he said, "So you were right, you did see me." And he smiled, encouraging me to continue.

"No," I said.

"No?" He was puzzled. "You didn't see me?"

"I… I didn't see you as I thought I would see you," I said.

"What do you mean? How did you see me?"

I looked at him, my heart racing. "In my Vision, you were very… very close to me… and…"

There was a long break.

"And you kissed me."

I don't remember ever hearing my heart beating so loudly in my ears. I stopped breathing altogether.

At first, he was just astonished. But then his expression changed, and I could see resolve and a clear intention in his eyes. He knelt next to my feet, cupped my face, looked down at my lips and—kissed me.

Whatever the Human heart was meant to do in this situation, it was not what a Senthien's body was ever supposed to experience. His lips on mine, triggering the most amazing sensation I ever felt, my mind went blank, and I lost consciousness.

CHAPTER 19

"You know, I've been told I make an impression on women, but I don't think anyone ever fainted when I kissed her," he said as soon as I opened my eyes. "I know it must be the IP space you're used to, but I just like to think it was because of me." He smiled widely.

"It is you." My voice broke.

I looked around. "It's… this is not my tent," I said.

"No. It's mine." He smiled again and said, "Sorry, I just can't believe it. It's what people in black and white movies used to do!"

"Black and white movies?"

"Don't worry, I'll explain another time. So, you said you saw me, right? What happened after that—after I kissed you?"

"I do not know. I woke up. Every time."

"Ah… okay… I thought… Never mind."

I realized then that he had a specific thing in mind when asking about the rest of my Vision.

"You thought… you thought that there was… a… a continuation?" I didn't even know how to phrase it.

"No, no, I didn't—really!" He raised his eyebrows in defense.

I gave a burst of resonating laughter but a second later I stopped it, both of my hands pressing against my lips. *I can't believe I just did that!*

He touched my hair and said, "You have a beautiful laugh. I've never heard you do that before."

"I don't think I ever have." I was confused but also happy. I liked what it did, the laughter. I smiled at him.

He let a few moments pass.

"So… you saw me, before you came to Earth?"

"Yes."

"And you knew it already when we met at the bonfire?"

"Yes."

"And you didn't tell me?"

I laughed again. I enjoyed it and let it last longer this time. "What was I supposed to say?" I said.

"Oh, I don't know—something like, 'I know we've never met before, but we should kiss. Soon.'"

I laughed again. When I calmed down, I said, "You know the Vision I had of you falling down the abyss? It was a prediction. I was hoping, wanting—needing—it not to happen." I lowered my eyes now as I thought of it, and shivered slightly from the sudden chill I felt. "And seeing you in my Vision was a prediction, too. I didn't know if it would happen."

"I know," he said in a serious tone now, "and I realize it was very difficult for you to tell me any of that. It's not the Senthien way. And I am happy you did."

We were silent for a moment, hearing only snoring from the neighboring tents.

"Come, I'll take you to your tent. It's late." He opened the door of his tent. Then he stopped and looked back. "Listen, do you mind if I tell the guys about your… future-seeing ability? Or would you like to keep it a secret, since Humans aren't supposed to know?" His lips twisted into a crooked smile.

I had to smile back. "I think we've passed the Human–Descendant barrier, don't you?"

He looked at my lips for a moment, then back at my eyes. "Yeah. Yeah, I do."

Breakfast was awkward. Everybody was sitting in a circle, and they all talked except J and me. We were both silent. We kept looking at each other, smiling when we saw the other looking back.

For the whole time, no one really noticed it until the plates were being cleared away, and Peter looked at J and then at me, pulling his eyebrows together.

"What's with you two? You seem… different."

J looked at me for a moment and then smiled the most wonderful smile. I was left speechless. J turned to Peter and shrugged. "Nothing that wasn't there yesterday. Nothing that won't be there tomorrow."

Peter narrowed his eyes. "Huh? Should I even try to understand that?"

"No," J said, laughing. Then he turned to me. "Dora, do you want to join me to wash the dishes?"

I nodded and got up. I still wasn't sure if my vocal cords were functional, and I didn't want to try them out in front of everyone.

As soon as we moved away from the group, J looked at me sideways. Then he moved the dishes to one hand and stretched the other one toward me. "Can I hold your hand?"

I looked at his hand and back at his eyes. My heartbeat accelerated in a second, and I had a feeling like someone was holding me by my throat.

I swallowed and then shook my head. "I'm sorry… I can't."

"No. I am sorry. I am being too pushy. Let me know when you feel comfortable crossing the IP distance, okay?"

I nodded.

In reality, it wasn't the IP distance. It was coming closer to him that made my heart go wild, my breathing erratic, and my thoughts a mess. And I wasn't sure if it would ever go away.

We continued on our trek. J and I were the last in the group, several IPs behind the rest, but J made sure we didn't lag too far.

"J, how did you all start living again after being de-frozen?"

"What do you mean?"

"I am curious: how do people rebuild the society when they have nothing? No power, no clothes, no food, no living quarters… not being where or when you thought you'd be."

J gave a half smile that didn't reach his eyes.

"It was difficult. Really difficult. Some people had real issues adjusting to reality. Psychologically, it was very challenging. We lost some people then…

"Also, there were several dozen people who went into cryo because they had a terminal disease. And so they died soon after we woke up… "

There was silence for a few moments. All I heard were leaves cracking under our feet, birds chirping in the trees, and faint talking a few IPs up ahead.

"We had to pool all the knowledge from each and every one of us, figuring out how to build stuff, how to hunt, how to grow crops without any power. You would not believe it"—he smiled now—"but a lot of information came from the books people had read in their lives before the freezing. And luckily, in a lot of the fiction literature, a lot of the information was accurate. Like, one of the girls read some cheesy love-story books before the freeze, and apparently the story happened in a prehistoric time—a time before power, when people lived… well, I guess they lived like us now. Anyway, in that book, a lot of the stuff was described really well. It was really lucky that she read it, and also that she loved it enough to remember it so well."

Without a pause, he continued.

"But some people also had direct knowledge either from their hobbies or remembering stories from their parents or grandparents. Patrick, for example, was a world-class archer. I think he was even at the last held Olympic Games." He looked down, slowly shaking his head to remember. "I'm not sure, I need to ask him. At any rate, he knew how to make the first weapons for us.

"Frances had a jewelry shop. Not just selling the jewelry, but actually welding and making the jewelry pieces. Spoons and forks—and knives, for that matter—we have thanks to her. She did an amazing job at teaching us, although I'm sure she didn't enjoy it as much as making jewelry." He smiled at the thought.

"All of this hands-on knowledge was important; in fact, it was essential to a society," J continued. "But what I think really pulled people together was Mike's bonfire sessions. He is a real leader, although you wouldn't think it the first time you see him."

J was looking at the ground now, almost talking to himself. "He really showed us the incredible lottery we all won. The fact that we'd actually survived after all that had happened to Earth, and what a real adventure it was to start a new life, the way we actually wanted it, because most of us were not very happy before cryo…that's why we all decided to freeze in the first place." He turned to look at me with a half smile.

"So… what made you not very happy?"

His smile broadened. "Curious, aren't you?"

"Yes. Senthiens always are."

"Let me tell you about it some other time."

"But I would like to hear it now."

He moved his gaze away from me, his smile fading. He sighed and said, "It's just… not the happiest part of my life, and I don't want to dig out those feelings again. They're past, that's all."

"Does it have to do with a woman?" I surprised myself with this question.

J looked at me, the side of his lips twitching slightly upward. "Hmm, this doesn't sound like Senthien curiosity. It sounds more like Human curiosity."

I looked down.

"Yes, there was a woman. Monica. She was my wife… but she is gone now."

"I am sorry."

I didn't ask him for more details, but he told me anyway. "We… we froze together, but when we woke up, she wasn't here. And it wasn't just her. There were hundreds of other people that went cryo, but…" He shrugged his shoulders. "I don't know, something went wrong, and they were not with us anymore when we woke up."

"It… must have been very difficult for you," I said.

"It was, for a few years. But it's all right now. Time heals all wounds." He tried to smile, but his eyes were still sad.

"Do you miss her?"

"I did miss her… a lot. I loved her very much."

There was a moment of silence again, and I wished I hadn't brought up the subject.

"But, she is in my past," he continued. "You are my present.

And my future, if you want to be," he said, glancing at me sideways, weighing my reaction.

My lips parted into a huge smile. I was speechless. And overwhelmed.

He mirrored me, broadening his lips to the limit, until there was almost no more space for the cheek between his lips and ears.

He made a step forward, then turned toward me and offered me his hand to take it. I looked at it for a moment, and then reached out with my own, sliding it into his rough, warm palm.

We walked, holding hands, not talking, every now and then sneaking a look at each other and smiling whenever we caught each other's eyes.

I was happy.

And I don't think I have ever been as happy as right now.

CHAPTER 20

In the middle of the day, we reached a wide-open space where the grass grew thick, completely covering the ground. Peter called out for a break, and we sat down in a circle. Simon handed over plates and Patrick sliced bread and dry meat. We were all hungry and ate in silence.

I was sitting next to J, and I didn't mind the silence at all. I had all the sensual input I could wish for: his warmth, his scent, his closeness.

Rick finished first. He left his plate on the ground.

"Dora," Rick said, still chewing his last bite, "I wanted to ask you about the News. I've heard several things from our Jumpers, but I can't really make a story out of it."

He looked at the others for approval, then looked at me and continued, "What do you know about it?"

"What would you like to hear?"

"Well, what was the News about? I've heard something about solar storms. Was that it?"

"Not entirely. Sometime in the early twenty-third century, scientists discovered that the magnetic poles of the Earth were destabilizing and likely to change polarity within the next two to three decades."

"I've heard about that. I think it normally happens every four hundred thousand years, something like that?" said Patrick.

I quickly checked the information on my nanoprobes, then said, "Yes, about four hundred and fifty thousand, you're right. However the polarity switch in the middle of the twenty-third century happened a lot sooner than expected. The last occurrence was only fifty thousand years ago."

"All right. And then?" Rick's eyes were wide open.

"So during this period, the Earth would completely lose its polarity. At some point, there would be no North or South Pole anymore."

"So?" Rick frowned.

"So, the magnetic field protection around the Earth would not exist at that time," said J before I could answer.

Rick's shoulders dropped and he shook his head. "I don't get it."

"Me neither," said Peter. "What was the big deal? I mean, you said yourself, the last switch, before the twenty-third century, happened fifty thousand years ago. And – mind you my memory is a bit rusty – but I think that was during the last ice age. Humans were already here. They must have survived changes in magnetic poles before."

I again accessed the data on my nanoprobes. "You are correct. Humans already existed at that time. And they survived."

"So what was different about the magnetic change in the twenty-third century?" asked J.

"The solar storms. In 2232 scientists studying the solar cycle progression forecast an upcoming period of frequent solar storms that would likely hit Earth. This was the year of the News."

"So if these storms happened during the absence of polarity," said J, "the Earth would have no protection against the sun's flares."

"Precisely," I said. "And they predicted that these storms would be among the strongest and most violent the solar system had ever experienced."

"This would cause the Earth's global power grid to fail," said J.

"Not only that. If a solar storm hit the Earth directly at the same time the magnetic field protection was missing, it would not only cause a shutdown of all electronic equipment; it would simply burn the Earth. Nothing would survive."

There was a moment of silence. Everyone must have been imagining how devastating the whole event was.

"So, people decided to leave Earth?" asked Rick.

"There were two options, really," I continued. "One would be to hide deep under the ground. But no one really knew how long the solar storms would last, and once it was over, if there would be anything left on the surface to enable life to continue. The second option was a much greater technological challenge, but also more promising. It was to build spaceships and colonize other planets. If these Seedships didn't find any planet that they could adapt, the alternative was to return to Earth after several generations, hoping the planet's surface was habitable again."

"And they chose ships," said Simon, who had been quiet throughout the conversation.

"Yes."

They were all in their thoughts again, silent for several moments.

"But," Simon asked, turning to me, "they wouldn't have had all the ships needed to evacuate eleven billion people. Right?"

I knew that sooner or later they would come to this conclusion. I took a moment before I answered.

"No, they didn't. Only a small fraction got to go." I looked down and continued, "Many scientists, doctors, engineers, and other highly educated people were chosen, but also many rich people who paid for the huge technological investment needed at this time. In this way, they bought their ticket off the planet."

I looked at all of them, wondering how they would react.

"That means that we," said Peter in a different tone, "being underground, cryo-preserved, were actually saved in this way, right?"

I nodded. I was happy that no one insisted on the utter unfairness of it all.

"But why didn't the Descendants come back? The Earth is"—Peter looked around while talking—"a very livable place. Why didn't they return?"

"From the information I am aware of, the Earth was considered dead, not viable for any organism. The last images taken before the ships left the solar system showed a dead planet. That's why they never thought to come back."

"But this total annihilation did not happen, otherwise we'd be sitting in sand… or, in fact, we would not be sitting here at all," said Simon.

"Well, the fact is that all electronic equipment we found so far was dead. That must have been the EMP. But the solar storm wasn't long enough or strong enough to eradicate all life," said J.

Patrick leaned his elbows on his knees, pressing his lips with two fingers. Then he took a stick and moved the bits of fallen dry leaves until he reached the soil underneath.

"Okay, let's say this is the sun… and this is Earth." He drew two circles half an IP from each other. "Now, Earth has an axial tilt of twenty-three degrees. Let's draw it like that, okay?"

"Yeah," responded others.

"In the moment of no magnetic field protection, when the sun's flare is greatest, it would reach the planet like this." He drew arrows from the sun to the Earth. "If this side here is the west side of North America"—he re-drew the line in the circle that faced the sun to make it thicker—"then this part here would hypothetically be protected, to a certain extent." He pointed to a circle on the opposite side of the sun. "The southern part of Africa," he said and nodded, looking at the others. "Could work…"

The others looked at the drawing and nodded.

I looked at Patrick. "Is this where we are?"

"That's right. Formally known as South Africa."

"So, Patrick, if your theory holds, that means that the majority of the rest of the world is really a desert?" asked J.

"If it holds, then, yes."

"It also depends on how long the solar storm lasted," I said. "The Earth takes a day for full rotation, and from the astronomical information available to me, the solar flares of the sun that could reach Earth lasted several hours."

"Which means only the opposite side of the Earth was burned," said Frank.

"If it was only one solar outbreak," J added. "Could have been more. Potentially, we could be the only viable part of this planet."

"Aye, very optimistic. Thank you, J," said Peter.

J laughed out loud. "I thought we were just hypothesizing."

"We are," said Patrick. "We're not going to find out more until we reach farther north and see for ourselves."

"How about reaching the computer facility first?" said Peter. "Let's get going."

Everyone laughed and then slowly stood up.

Simon collected the plates and cutlery and put them in his backpack and J packed the remaining food. We picked up our gear and were on our way again.

CHAPTER 21

It was late afternoon when J called it a day, pronouncing this the last stop before we reached the city the following day. As soon as all the tents were up, J came to me. "Hey!"

"Hey!" I stood up from a squatting position. Just as I did, he planted a soft kiss on my lips. My breath locked in my lungs for a moment.

"Wanna see something beautiful?" he asked.

Beside you? "Yes, J, I'd like to."

"Come," he said, smiling, offering me his hand.

I took his hand. He gently squeezed it once and it felt like the most natural thing in the world. It felt wonderful.

Peter and Simon were at the camping grounds, the others were nearby.

"Bye, guys! We'll be back in an hour or so!" shouted J.

"Where are you off to?" asked Simon.

"Can't tell you!" said J. Then, looking at me, he continued, "It's a surprise!"

"Maybe she already knows, did ya think about that?" Peter grinned.

J looked at me, serious now. "Do you know? Have you... seen it?"

I shook my head, a big smile on my lips. I had no idea what

he was talking about, but I thought it was amazing, the way he saw me: just like another Human, able to be surprised.

He smiled back and said, "Good!" And he pushed on.

After several passes, I realized my sight was starting to get blurry—it was a Vision, wanting to present itself. J's intentions were so determined that there was only one possible projection of the future. The Vision was pushing its way in.

And I kept blocking it. I focused on the sounds of our feet, on the plants we were passing, on J's arm and shoulder, on the subtle movements of the muscles under his skin.

He stopped and turned to me. "Now, close your eyes! I will guide you."

"Mmm… okay…" I said and did what he asked.

This made it harder for me to push the Vision away. There was nothing to distract my thoughts.

Excitement. Amazement. And—blue…

No! I don't want to see it—I want to be surprised!

In my mind, I pushed away the blue that appeared in front of my eyes and focused on black. Black room, black floors, black walls, black—under my eyelids.

The Vision disappeared and I sighed in relief.

J continued walking, guiding me forward, unaware of my inner battle.

With no visual input, I started focusing on different senses. I could hear the pine needles cracking under my feet and the birds singing high above us in the branches. And a sound. A new sound I couldn't place. It was a very regular, deep, background noise, so calm and soothing that I could almost ignore it. But, of course, I didn't. It was new. And I could not find any reference on my nanoprobes.

What is that?

And with the sound came—a scent. It was different, refreshing, and it came carried by the wind.

I'd never smelled anything like this before. I moved my head to follow it, opening my nostrils to take all of it in.

The deep rolling sound was now getting louder. It never stopped and the rhythm never changed. I was getting even more curious, and my Vision started seeping through.

No! Black!

And it was gone again.

I realized we must have come out of the forest, because through my closed eyelids, more brightness shone through. Whatever was before me had that intriguing smell I was sensing before, and it was carried by the wind in a fine spray, like miniature drops of rain.

"Now can I open them?" I asked.

"Yes. Now," he said, standing beside me, still holding my hand.

I opened my eyes and saw something I had never seen in real life before.

As far as my eyes could reach, I saw deep blue water, with many white foamy lines parallel to the horizon.

"Oh, the Moons of Senthia! Is that... is that the ocean?" I turned to him, realizing he wasn't looking at the water but at me.

"That's the ocean," he said with a huge smile plastered across his face. "I knew you'd like it."

This was an amazing moment for me. For some indefinable reason, I felt like crying. Not because I was sad, but because the sight touched me so deeply that this emotion needed to have some kind of physical release.

I tried hard to fight it, not letting it show. Senthiens would never cry at such a majestic creation of nature.

Senthiens wouldn't cry at all.

I looked at J. He was watching me intently, his expression serious, his head tilted to one side.

"Why do you think you didn't get the flu?" he asked abruptly.

I looked at him, startled. "I don't know. I guess I was lucky."

"Luck has nothing to do with it. And I think you know it, too."

"I do not understand what you mean, J."

"Look, I don't know what happened to you in your past to make you so… so closed up. But I would bet that whatever it is, it's not present here on Earth."

"I still do not understand. What are you suggesting?" Automatically, I hid behind my invisible but unmistakable Senthien wall.

"Just tell me—how do you think you evaded the flu?"

"Why are you making such a big deal out of it? You didn't get the flu either!"

"Yes," he said, his voice deeper with a slight sense of victory behind it, "but I'm *Human*." He stressed the last word intently, looking at me. "I have an innate immunity against it. Humanity has had it for millennia."

My eyes were wide open now, my heart racing, my throat closed shut.

How does he know? How can he possibly know?

In all of my years of disguise, no one had even come close to discovering my secret.

J came closer and took both of my hands in his. Warm orange sunlight drew the most beautiful shadows over his neck and shoulders. And for a moment, I forgot what we were talking about.

"Your eyes are green. Bright green. I've never seen anything like that. Your hair is thick and straight and dark gray. I've never seen anything like that, either. But you can cry. You can even smile when you want to."

He smiled, trying to make me smile and confirm his statement.

I remained serious, though. My whole body was geared to preserve the secret and tell no one—*no one*—about my true origins.

"Tell me, Dora. How come you evaded the flu?"

I lowered my gaze to my hands, then sat on the sand, pulled my knees up, and hugged my legs, looking at the place where the sky meets the ocean.

"My father… my father had green eyes, even greener than mine. He was respected in the Council of Senthiens. He had what others thought were true Visions of the future, but he always said that he only saw glimpses of probability.

"He was one hundred and ninety-five when he met my mother. She was twenty-six. They wouldn't have been able to meet normally, but my father had a certain project where he was ported to… the planet where my mother lived. My father said she was stunning, which I think was the primary reason he wanted to get to know her better… although he was not supposed to.

"He said they were immediately attracted to each other, like magnets bearing opposite charges. They kept looking at each other from a distance, because they did not move in the same circles. I never asked him, really… I wonder if he had a Vision then, if it was clear for him that they would be together."

"How old are you?"

"Excuse me?" I was surprised by this interruption of my story, which I was now willing to share.

"It's just that you said your father was one hundred and ninety-five when he met your mom. That's very old, in Human terms."

"Ah, that, yes… well, um… I am three hundred and ninety-two standard years old." I looked at him, half expecting to see a hint of repulsion behind his eyes. But I saw nothing else than calm and inviting depths of ebony.

"Mature woman. I like that." His lips spread in a crooked smile.

I smiled in return and continued, "Anyway, they fell in love. A Senthien and a…"

I stopped. My heart was racing, my palms sweating and my breathing uneven.

"And a…"

I took a deep breath.

I had to laugh at myself, realizing the absurdity of the situation: I was afraid, almost paranoid to tell him the truth, but I couldn't have picked a better listener. I looked at him and said, "A Senthien and a…"

"Human," he finished. He smiled gently and reached to take my hand again. "And so you could fight the most common virus on Earth."

"How did—how did you know?"

"You might have had an easy time hiding it from your other fellow Descendants who never saw a Human up close, but here most of us can recognize a Human, even when she's undercover."

"Under what?"

He let out a hearty laugh and said, "It means in disguise."

"Ah."

"Don't worry, it's an old term. So… do you think that the mistake of this teleporting computer—"

"The Mind."

"Yes, the Mind—happened because you are half Human?"

I lowered my gaze and said nothing.

"I mean, all the other Jumpers were Humans," J continued. "It's a pattern."

"I know." I nodded and then looked at him. "Yes, I think the error happens only to Humans. I don't know why, but I am here because I'm half Human… and Stevanion is dead because he ported with me."

I lowered my gaze again. It was my fault that Stevanion died. I knew this. And now it was obvious to others. It was obvious to J.

J tilted his head and lifted my chin with the tips of his fingers.

"That was not your fault, Dora. You know this, don't you?"

I didn't respond.

He sighed. Then, changing the subject, he said, "Tell me more about your parents. How did *you* happen?"

"They didn't exactly go into detail," I said. "I do know it was the old-fashioned way."

"The old-fashioned way?" He arched his eyebrows.

"At Uni, most progeny creation is done extracorporeally."

"You mean *tube babies*?"

"Tube?"

"Like, in a laboratory?"

"Yes, that's correct. But of course, my parents couldn't have something like that go through official venues, and frankly, I think they liked the old-fashioned way, for some reason."

"Surprising indeed." His crooked smile was back, and he

studied me. "You've never tried the 'old-fashioned way'?" he asked.

"Not for the purposes of making offspring, no," I said calmly.

"Not for the purposes of making offspring..." he repeated bluntly. "Okay, I am confused now. You haven't had sex to have kids, but you did have sex not to have kids, and... you have kids but without sex? Did I miss anything?"

"What is 'sex'?"

"The old-fashioned way."

"Oh, okay. The first two are correct. The last one is not."

"Sorry, I'm not following you. What's not correct?"

"Your last point. I do not have an offspring. I did not contribute to the Office of Progeny."

He was looking at me, slowly shaking his head. "Office of Progeny?"

"Okay, let me try to explain." I poised myself as if I was about to start a lecture on Visionaire studies. "In Uni, there is no urgent need for progeny because many Descendant species live several hundred, sometimes thousands of years. However, there is a need for some inflow of new individuals, and those are made at the Office of Progeny. Women donate eggs cells and men sperm cells, and the rest is done by technicians."

"Voyeurs." He grinned.

"Voyeurs?"

"Never mind. So what about parenting and upbringing?"

"There are professionals who take that responsibility."

"So children never meet their parents?"

"They never meet their biological parents, no. I was... I consider myself lucky to have spent a part of my youth with my parents."

He smiled, looked down at our laced hands, and stroked the

back of my hand with his thumbs. Then he looked up and said, "And what about the second point?"

"Which second point?"

"Where you have sex but no babies?"

"Ah, that. Well, for most species, the time right after rejuvenation is the time they have several physical encounters."

"Several?" he repeated. "With the same person?"

"No, usually not," I said, not knowing his reason for this question.

"Oh." His face fell.

"You see, the virus that enables rejuvenation also causes a rise of hormone levels, and the post-rejuvenation interaction is simply the way of releasing the tension."

"You make it sound as if it's completely devoid of joy."

"Joy? Well, it does release the tension, so that's pleasant—but, you see, the IP inhibition in Uni citizens is so strong that even while the encounters are taking place, people have this mental barrier which makes them feel extremely uncomfortable when they touch each other."

"But you're half Human. Didn't you enjoy it?"

I looked at the ground, pondering the question. "I think I probably enjoyed it more than my partners, despite the flexile IP skin protectors. But I always had a feeling that there was more, as if I was just at the beginning of something, and then it would be over." I looked up at him to explain. "Most encounters don't last more than eleven seconds."

"What?!" He almost jumped from his seat in the sand.

I looked at him, bewildered. "Why is that so shocking to you?"

"Dora, Dora, Dora, Dora." He was shaking his head. "They really didn't feed your Human side there at Uni, did they?"

"I am still a little bit confused."

"Sex—or 'making love,' as it's called when it's with someone you love—should, in my humble opinion, be measured in minutes… I mean, passes… at least."

He then lowered his gaze, a mischievous smile on his lips as he came closer, holding a thought I could not decipher.

"Perhaps… we should do something about that."

My heartbeat picked up immediately. I bit my lip and looked down. I wanted to withdraw, but at the same time, I wanted him to come even closer.

"You do that, when you're unsure," he said, "biting your lip like this." He placed his finger on my lower lip and gently pushed it down, releasing it from my teeth.

I held my breath, my heart was thrumming, and I saw little tinkling spots blurring my vision.

He came closer then, his lips just an inch from mine.

"Before you fall unconscious," he said, his hand gently touching the side of my neck, "you should at least have a reason…"

I inhaled. My mind was racing with a million thoughts and at the same time empty as a blank page. Still holding my breath, I felt it—his warm lips on mine—and a feeling like an electric shock zipped through my body.

And then everything went dark.

I lost consciousness.

Again.

CHAPTER 22

"You know, there's more to it than that. You should really stay awake," he said as I opened my eyes. I was lying with my head on his chest, looking sideways at the ocean.

"I'm sorry," I said and lifted myself up to sit.

"Don't be. I'm still enjoying the ego boost when I cause such a reaction. By the way, I was wondering if you still want to keep it a secret, your origin, I mean, or is it all right that I share it with the others?"

My heart skipped a beat just from a thought that everyone else here will now know my deeply kept secret. I swallowed a lump in my throat, trying to calm my racing heart. *This is a good thing, Dora. This is how life should be, free and unrestrained.* I took a deep breath and said, "You can… share it with the others. It's okay."

"Good." He stood up and offered his hand. "Come, I still want to show you something."

We walked on the very edge of the water where small waves washed over a shore, building tiny sand dunes. I stopped for a moment, looking at the ground.

I watched my feet on the sand as the salty water washed over them. It was mesmerizing. Every little wave brought some sand on my feet, and as it retreated, the grains found their way between my toes. With every wave, I was also sliding deeper into the sand, the water washing away some of the sand under my feet.

I stepped forward and pressed one foot on the wet sand. The small area of sand around my foot dried out, like a temporary drought at the rim of my sole. When I moved my foot, the dry sand flooded with water.

I kept walking, looking at my feet, drying and flooding the little islands of sand underneath. As we walked parallel to the water, the waves every now and then washed the collected sand off my toes. J didn't talk, but he held my hand and kept looking at me.

"I love the ocean, J. It's amazing!"

He smiled. "I thought you would like it!"

He brought our laced hands to his lips and kissed the back of my hand. "But there is something else I want to show you." Then he looked forward and narrowed his eyes to see better. "We're getting close."

"Close to what?"

"Well, since you're enjoying our vegetation so much, I thought you should see the forest around the river."

In front of us, I saw the ocean entering deeper into the beach, making a small bay. I could not see the end of it - it was hidden behind the trees. As we walked toward it, I realized that it wasn't really a bay. The water just continued into the land. And the forest around it was—*ah!*—simply breathtaking.

"We call this the Falls River," he said, answering my unspoken question as we reached the river's shore. "This is the sweet water, and it runs into the sea. Up there," he said, letting go of my hand and pointing with his finger to the top of the small hill, "is a beautiful waterfall, hence the name, and it comes crashing down over a cave system." He looked at me sideways and smiled. Then he walked a few IPs ahead of me while I stopped to view the hill, which was completely covered in trees with dense and lush foliage.

I looked back at him. J was about four IPs away when, all of a sudden, I shivered. I was somehow… too far from him. I didn't understand why this was a problem, but something seemed very wrong. I started walking toward him. He turned and stretched his arm to me. "Come," he said and smiled. "We can't walk there now, it's a bit late, but we'll do it on our way ba—"

At that moment, several things happened at once. J's jaw dropped, his eyes open wide in a shocked stare. The next second, his expression hardened into something I could only define as ready for combat. His mouth shut tight, his eyes narrow slits and his head thrust forward, he started to sprint toward me.

I could not hear anything. I knew there was something very wrong, and I should do something to help myself. It was clear I was in danger, but all I could see was him running toward me, his legs flexing and bending in uniform motion, skin stretched over muscles, using his arms to gain speed. His chest was packed tight with muscles tugging against one another, stomach muscles forming a solid wall around his abdomen. I knew I should be scared, but all I could think was how beautiful he was.

Two IPs away, he stretched his legs as he leaped forward, stretching his arms and folding his hands in a double fist as he flew through the air like an arrow, aiming at something very close to me. As I turned my head to follow his motion, I saw a large jaw with pointy fangs open to grab my body from the side. As it lunged, the animal twisted its head to clasp its jaws around my waist. In this position, the animal's belly was turned toward J, and it met his double fist with a dull thud.

The sound was back on.

The animal was roaring, falling backward from the hit. Its closing jaws scratched my arm and stomach, and I fell sideways away from where J had landed on the animal. The sand cushioned my fall, and I looked backward to J. The animal was on its back, but it quickly turned itself around.

J's arm was grabbing something from the other side of his hip, and with the next quick movement, I saw him stabbing a sharp metal piece into the animal's chest right between the front legs. The animal was struggling violently, but its movements now were not of a predator, but of prey, afraid for its life.

As J kept the knife deep in the animal's chest, its violent movements abated, then gradually stopped completely. J was holding the animal, keeping the body still with his legs bent over its belly and hind limbs.

They stayed like this for what seemed like a long time.

The animal did not move.

J pushed himself away in a quick movement and grabbed me by my arms, and we fell back several IPs away, his arms around me. We were both still, lying sideways on the sand, looking at the beast. Once J was certain that it wouldn't move again, he looked at me, worry on his face.

"Are you okay?" he said.

"Am I okay? Are *you* okay!"

"Dora, I'm fine. But—oh, no!" His gaze fell on the bloody tooth marks on the side of my waist. "You're bleeding!"

"I'm okay, it's not that bad," I said, trying to calm him down.

"Have you ever been injured this badly?" he said as he effortlessly lifted me up in his arms. "You're in shock, Dora. The body doesn't register an injury when in shock. We need to get some help back at camp."

I held onto his shoulders, but suddenly felt so weak I let my arms drop to my side. He looked at me, and his face softened as he said, "We'll get some of the guys to fetch it. Crocodiles are quite tasty." He winked at me and squeezed me in a stronger hold. "Seems you really are a good bait."

Ah, so that's bait…

I smiled weakly and then leaned my head on J's chest.

CHAPTER 23

"What happened?"

I heard the alarmed voices of several people shouting at once. I must have fallen asleep in his arms, because I didn't remember the walk back to the camp.

"A crocodile attacked her!" J said as he laid me down on a mattress of leaves. I heard several sharp gasps, but no one said anything.

"I was at the mouth of the Falls River. Right near the beach. The beach!" I could tell from his voice that he was angry, but I didn't understand why.

"That's impossible! A crocodile wouldn't go that far down the river," Frank said.

"We've only ever seen them farther upstream, miles before the waterfall," Peter continued.

"Yeah, well, this one decided to stray. Rick, could you get me some water and some bandages? Thanks," J said. Then he turned to me and said in a much quieter voice, "Dora, how do you feel?"

"I'm… fine. A little… dizzy…"

"I know, honey."

Honey? I wanted to ask him about it but I simply didn't have the energy to voice the question.

"Perhaps it's the loss of blood." His voice was still low.

Someone knelt next to me and whispered to J, "Could be just shock. Here's some prunella. This should help with the bleeding." I heard some rustling from a bag. "I'll put it under the bandages."

"Thanks, Simon," J said.

Although my eyes were closed, I realized Rick must have returned, as he loudly dropped to his knees.

"Did it hit an artery?" Rick said with a hushed voice, handing bandages and a water bottle to J.

"If it did, she'd be dead," Simon responded.

I heard J take in a heavy breath, hold it in, and then exhale again.

"She was lucky." I heard Patrick's voice as he lifted my head a bit to place a rolled up blanket underneath. There was silence for a few moments.

"How could I have been so stupid?" J whispered, his voice broken.

I realized then that J was angry at himself. I wanted to open my eyes, tell him it was okay, that he saved me, but my words stayed silent under layers of physical shock and exhaustion.

"It's gonna be okay, J. She didn't lose a lot of blood. She's just in shock." Peter placed his large hand on J's shoulder.

"J, you saved her." I could sense in Peter's voice that he was smiling. "As impossible as this is, she is alive because of you."

"I shouldn't have tak—"

"J, just stop it! You couldn't have known. Now, you tell me where the animal is, and we'll go and fetch it. I'm starving." Peter gave a short, gurgling laugh.

J said something about a beachside and a riverbed, but I couldn't follow. I fell asleep again.

I opened my eyes. Pine needles high on the top of the tree were dancing with the wind, colored by orange flickering light from below, sharply contrasted against the black night above. I took a deep breath. Something smelled nice.

I inhaled again.

A delicious smell instantly made my mouth water. I turned my head toward the fire. Blinded for one moment from the light, I closed my eyes again.

I inhaled deeper. Burned wood, smoke, and meat. *Deliciously smelling meat.*

Slowly, I opened my eyes again. Most of our group was gathered close to the fire, holding long wooden sticks with meat stabbed on the top and folded in a spiral. They were all talking in low voices. I didn't understand them, but I *did* want to try some of that meat.

I tried to sit.

"Dora!" J, sitting next to me, gently supported my shoulders then moved next to me so I could lean on him.

"How are you?"

"Better," I said, looking down on the bandage. I moved my hands toward it to remove it, but J stopped me.

"No!" he shouted.

"J, it's fine. Look." I took the bandage off. "One of the benefits of Descendant heritage. Faster healing."

J kept looking at the cuts, which were already closed and appeared to be healing nicely. "Wow. Why… why would you need such… healing powers? I mean, it's not like you go fighting wild Uni animals… do you?"

I started laughing but stopped, realizing that hurt. "No… no wrestling with beasts. It's just one of the nanoprobe tasks, that's all."

He gave a sigh of relief and then looked into my eyes. "Are you hungry?"

"No, I'm not hungry," I said and instantly saw his face fall. "I'm starving!" I continued with exaggerated enthusiasm.

His lips spread into a brilliant white smile, and he laughed a happy, hearty laugh. I looked at his lips, momentarily distracted, and forgot what I was saying. He hugged me even tighter to himself and kissed my forehead.

"All right, Human, let's eat! Looks like our predator's very tasty."

He helped me get up, and we walked slowly to the fire, though I wanted to run to get to the food sooner.

"Good evening, sleeping beauty! Feeling better?" said Patrick loudly and moved to a side to leave space on the log for J and me.

"Much better, Patrick. Thank you." I smiled as J gently helped me sit down on the log, and then sat behind me so I could lean against him. Both of his legs were resting on the outer side of my thighs. I was acutely aware of his body wrapped around me, but I tried hard to stay focused.

"Here, Dora," said Rick as he handed me a stick with nicely cooked meat, "I've been saving this for you."

I took it and smiled at him, "Thank you, Rick. This smells so nice I don't know how much longer I could have waited."

There was a short moment of silence, and all that was heard was soft, chewy munching, crackling firewood, and gentle wind sounds coming from the pine needles above.

"Why aren't you eating?" I turned to J, mumbling a bit with my mouth half full.

"I want to see you have enough. I'll eat later."

"I'm not going to eat the whole animal! There's plenty. Please, eat."

J smiled but didn't move.

"Ah!" Peter sighed theatrically as he stabbed raw meat onto a new empty stick and walked toward us. "Here you go. Just so you don't need to move away from Dora for a few seconds." And he winked at me as he handed the stick to J.

"Thanks, Pete." J smiled, lifting his hand to bring the meat over the fire.

The evening soon turned out to be very cheerful. I didn't feel any pain, and I was ready to sit by myself, although J never let me go. I enjoyed his undivided attention immensely.

At the end of the evening, everybody went to their tents. Only Rick, J, and I stayed by the fire, still talking.

"Dora," Rick said, looking straight into my eyes, "why are your eyes so green? I mean, the color is just amazing," he said, not realizing I was a bit embarrassed by his words. "And the whites in your eyes are… not really white either." He leaned a bit closer to me. "There is this same shade of green."

I looked away. "It's the fluorescence."

"What fluorescence?"

"It's a green fluorescent protein, and its gene is connected to the gene of interest in the Descendant species of Senthien."

Rick shook his head. "I have no idea what you're talking about."

I braced myself for an explanation, but J was faster. "If you have a feature that you want to introduce into an organism using genetic engineering, and this feature is difficult to measure or see, you need to link it to another gene that you'll be able to see more easily. So in our time, and this is probably what they did with you," J said, looking at me, "was to link this gene of interest which causes a specific feature, to a green fluorescent protein, a GFP gene. The GFP lights up fluorescent green when excited by a wavelength of UV light. So if a cell, or organ, or the entire organism lights up green, you know your gene of interest is there as well. Right?"

"Yes, thanks." I was amazed by the simplicity of J's explanation.

"All right… but we don't have UV light here. Why do I still see it as green?" Rick persisted.

"During the day, the sun emits UV light and excites the GFP. This excitation is so strong that the fluorescence lasts for many hours, even when the sun is down. Additionally, the concentration of the GFP is so high that you see the color simply because of its density," I explained.

"So the protein of interest is important for this future-seeing stuff, right? So, why isn't it expressed only in the brain?" asked J.

"Mainly it is, but there are some random areas where the gene was inserted by mistake during the genetic engineering, in some specific epithelial cells and connective tissues like eyes, bones, and cartilage, as well as nails." I lifted my hand and showed the backside of it to Rick so he could see my green tinted nails.

Rick raised his eyebrows. "Cool!"

"Now, a question for you," said J, his left eyebrow arched inquisitively. "Why did Descendant researchers still use basic molecular biology techniques when they made such a perfect Descendant species?"

His query triggered further questions in my mind.

Are Senthiens perfect?

Are any of the Descendants perfect?

Was Zamnan cleverer than nature itself?

I answered J without mentioning my thoughts. "The gene of interest that led to the Visionaire feature was meant to do something else. This gene was linked to GFP—"

"Green fluorescent protein," J quickly repeated for Rick's understanding.

"—and incorporated into random places in the genome and ultimately manifested itself as a new trait, which was to be able to predict future outcomes based on the current course of events. The protein was expressed mainly in the brain, and more precisely in the primary motor cortex."

Rick frowned. "I don't understand—what's that?"

"It's the brain center where body movements are controlled, and it processes a huge amount of data extremely fast," explained J. "Even in a Human."

I nodded. "But it took some time before the changes in the brain stabilized and the new ability was understood."

"So," Rick asked, "were your Visions ever wrong?"

"If I didn't interfere in the process of the decision," I said, looking at J, "then no, all my Visions came to be."

"And for other Senthiens? Were they always right as well?"

"No. Senthiens do make mistakes. The Visions are only possible projections of the future. I cannot guarantee I will always be correct in my Visions. I can also make mistakes like any other Senthien."

"Theoretically, yes," Rick pressed on, "but in reality, no. Your other Senthiens have already made mistakes. But you haven't!"

"This is true, but I am less than four hundred years old. I am sure I would have had some inaccurate Visions if I was older."

"But don't you think there is something else?" J asked,

obviously heading in the same direction as Rick. "Don't you think that this gene acts differently because you're half Human?"

"Genes mutate over several generations, not in one person," I said.

"But what if we're not talking about gene mutation?" J continued. "What if your genes are still the same, but the genetic environment is different? Basically, what I want to ask: what if your Human genes improved the function of your Senthien genes?"

I was silent. I didn't know the answer to that. I looked at the dying fire and glowing embers radiating light and heat.

Epigenetic influence... this could be possible...

And then somewhere, deep in my mind, a new thought started to form: an insight about Humans and Zlathars.

Why did the Zlathars push Humans to the bottom of the Uni society under all other Descendants? *It's all linked, somehow, somewhere...*

"I don't know," I said, looking at them. "But from all the current premises, I assume this is a possible answer."

We stayed silent for a few passes longer, and then J squeezed my shoulder and whispered, "Time to go to bed."

I started to get up, but J stopped me. "Let me carry you! You need to rest as much as you can."

"But I feel good, J."

"Okay, then do it for me."

I smiled. "All right."

I didn't mind being in J's arms. Not at all.

CHAPTER 24

It was late morning and we were on the road for about two hundred passes. Although I got used to the captivating greenery of this world, every now and then I was swept away by yet another tree, yet another plant.

I stopped in front of one such fascinating tree and looked at it for a moment. J stopped, realizing that I wasn't following, and returned to stand next to me. He followed my gaze with his eyes.

"What are you looking at?"

"This! Isn't this just amazing?"

"Hmm." He pressed his lips together, looking at the plant. "I guess so. What do you think makes it so amazing?" J turned to me.

I shook my head a bit, still looking at the tree. "I can't really explain it, but... look!" I raised my arm, finger pointing to the tree trunk. "This one is different. I saw a similar type of a tree before, and normally these long leaves start only at the top of the tree, and the trunk is just bare, brown, and woody. But look at this one! This one has the leaves all around the trunk too, it's just that they are light brown, and those on top are green. But it didn't lose any leaves, you see?" I kept looking at the tree, and J continued looking at me. I turned to him, "J, you're not looking at the tree!"

He laughed. "I've been seeing this type of a tree for more than nine years now. It's not amazing to me. You are!" And he bent down to kiss me. My heart skipped a beat, and I momentarily stopped breathing.

"Hmm…" J gave a crooked smile as our lips parted. "It's a real shame I have to shorten my kiss every time. I keep worrying how long you can last without a breath!"

At first I thought he was serious, but then I smiled, realizing his joke. "Ha! You're being so funny!"

"I know." J laughed. "And I'm so happy you released your Human side so you can get my jokes."

I frowned. "I kept my Human side hidden because it saved my life!" I let go of his hand and continued walking, following the others a few dozen IPs ahead.

"Dora, I'm sorry." He sped up to catch up with me. "That was really meant to be a joke."

He gently held my elbow to stop me. "I'm sorry. I can only imagine how your life must have been before. And I think I understand it, I guess, the best I can without actually having to disguise my ancestry and being afraid for my life if my secret were uncovered."

He leaned his head to a side, looking into my eyes, but I looked away.

"Dora, look at me." He lifted my chin with his finger. "What I really wanted to say is that I am really *happy* that you brought out the Human in you, that you didn't lose it, and that you can react to me like a Human can. Because… I understand that. I understand Human reactions, and it was difficult for me to understand Senthien ones."

I looked at him, green eyes fixed on black.

"But the truth is… " He lowered his gaze for a few moments

and then looked back. "It's the half-Human, half-Senthien that…
I fell in love with." He gently tucked a strand of hair behind my
ear and moved closer, his lips just about to touch mine. "You do
know what falling in love means, don't you?" he whispered.

My heart was beating madly. I'd heard the term before, from
my mom. And now, I finally knew what that feeling was. The one
that made my heart race, the one that induced uncontrollable
desire deep inside me; the one that was nowhere to be found on
my nanoprobes data.

Falling. In. Love.

"Yes…" I whispered back.

"Good." He still did not touch my lips. "Now, kiss me," he
said softly.

I looked at him, startled, my breaths shallow.

"Kiss me and stay conscious," he whispered again.

I understood what he wanted me to do.

For the longest moment, I gathered my courage, and then
very slowly I came closer. Lifting up on my toes, I softly pressed
my lips to his.

His lips were warmer than mine, and I felt as if they were
molding perfectly into mine. I realized then that I would not
lose consciousness. The intense feeling of excitement and
anticipation, like a strong pressure in my chest, I now felt I could
hold and enjoy.

He slid his arm around my waist, and with the other he
gently circled my neck, bringing me closer to him. He leaned
forward and with his lips he opened mine, reaching out with his
tongue to find mine. As our tongues met, my passion burned
with a new flame; wanting, needing, craving… him.

He held me tight, our tongues exploring each other, my
body reacting by itself with no input; yet, feeling such immense

sensations, I realized I was only a few moments away from fainting. I held my hands against his chest to tell him we should part, but I could not stop kissing him.

He realized it and released his tight embrace, but still holding my arms as our lips parted.

We were both breathing heavily, taking a moment before we could speak.

"Wow," he said, looking at the ground. Then he looked up at me. "Are you okay?" His voice was hoarse and broken.

"Yes… yes." That was the only thing I could muster. "I… needed, you know—space… before I…"

"Yeah, I know. Me too."

I heard footsteps coming back down the path.

"Boring, boring!" Peter laughed from a few IPs ahead. "Don't you get tired of that?" he asked, folding his arms on his chest.

"Pity you're so old, Peter. You forget what youth does to you," responded J, his arms still around me.

"Yeah, yeah!" Peter muttered, still loud enough so we could hear him. "Let's go, guys, we should be at our destination by early afternoon…if you don't stall us all the time!" And he winked at us as he turned to follow the group up ahead.

J looked at me and smiled. He released me from his embrace but still kept my hand in his.

We walked without a word for a while, hearing the others talk in front of us. I didn't know what to say. This was so unexpected, so strong, so primal, I couldn't do anything but obey my body's needs.

My Human rejoiced; my Senthien was out of her mind.

I looked at him, but he was looking away.

"What is it?" I asked.

He shook his head. "Nothing."

"You don't… seem very happy," I said, feeling the anticipated pain of his answer. "You don't like what we just did?"

He looked at me. "No, no, it's not that. It's just…"

"What?"

He exhaled.

What?

"The last time I kissed someone like that was… my wife. And, it… it just brings memories back, that's all."

I looked to the front and let go of his hand.

How can I compete with a dead person?

"Dora!" He took my hand again and stopped. I stopped as well but didn't turn toward him. I had a lump in my throat and I didn't want him to look at my eyes.

Then he embraced me in a hug, wrapping both of his arms around me. I leaned my face on his chest, feeling weak and vulnerable.

"I'm such a fool! What am I saying? Don't listen to me! You are… you are a gift from heaven, you really are. I was just… I was certain that I wouldn't *want* anyone else anymore, that I wouldn't *need* anyone else… that I wouldn't *love* anyone else… and then, you came. Ha! You literally dropped out of the sky!" He laughed at that. "And I don't even know why you want to be with me—"

I moved my head back to look at him. "It was meant to be, J. Before there was any indication of this probability, of this possible future, I saw it, I saw *you*, I saw *us* so many times in my Visions, that—it couldn't go any other way… I was *yours* before I even came here."

He looked down at me, then cupped my face with his hands. "You are such an amazing woman, Dora. And I am so lucky you're with me." And he bent down and kissed me again.

CHAPTER 25

We reached the edge of the forest.

In front of us spread the ruins of a forgotten city. Blocks of concrete that used to be buildings, walls, and houses were overgrown with crawlers, moss, bushes, and trees.

I continued walking, and then realized I was the only one. I turned around. The others were standing still, their gaze empty and sad as they stared at what used to be a vibrant place.

Peter lowered his head. Simon walked over and put his arm around his shoulder. No one said anything for a long while.

I looked back to the city, then up at the sky.

The dark gray clouds hovering over the ruins threatened rain. Even the green of the plants looked gray under the thick layer of vaporized water blocking the clear sky.

I lowered my gaze to the city again and waited. It seemed to me the clouds only emphasized the history and tragedy of the place, and I wondered what it would look like in the bright daylight.

Rick, who'd spent more of his life in the untouched nature than in the high-tech world of the past, started walking forward. He came to stand next to me, then turned around and said, "Let's go, guys. It's easier to see things in daylight."

Several heavy sighs came from the group as they continued

walking, but I was focused on J. He was still standing, looking far away to the left side of the city. I looked in the same direction: several sharply broken skyscrapers and the collapsed remains of a large building, oval in its footprint.

"That's a…" J pointed to the oval building but then dropped his hand. "That *was* a rugby stadium."

He looked at me and then took my hand in his. Smiling sadly, he said, "Time flies."

I smiled back, although I knew that his eyes carried a high degree of sadness.

"Let's find some computers," he said, winked at me, and tugged me forward.

We walked on the road. The only way I knew it had once been a road was because there were several patches of flat concrete spread in roughly one direction. In between them, grass, bushes, and vines poked out. The road was surrounded by bits and pieces of what were once building walls, but most of them were no higher than a few IPs. The rest of the buildings were crumbled on the ground, tangled among the dense vegetation.

We all walked a lot slower than we had in the forest, even though the path was a lot clearer. After passing under some kind of arch that amazingly still stood, we turned right and walked uphill. At the top, we entered what looked like ancient remains made out of stone rather than concrete.

"This was the South Cape University of Technology," said Patrick as he turned to me. "This is where I worked."

The group continued, but I stopped for a moment. I was in the middle of the field bordered by large square-shaped blocks of stone neatly set into the high grass. Unlike the concrete, the stones were not so densely covered in moss, and it made the distinct color contrast between the stone and grass even greater.

These must have been the remains of a large hall of some kind—an auditorium, perhaps. I turned around in a circle, looking at this structure that once held a roof, potentially even a few floors, imagining what it would feel like to be listening to the lecturer, closely—too closely probably—surrounded by so many determined and knowledge-driven people.

Would I fit in there?

Would I fit in the life that J had before his cryo-time?

Would he even notice me then?

"Hey."

I turned to see J coming.

"Kingdom for your thoughts," he said and stopped really, really close to me.

Even if I knew what he was asking of me, I wouldn't have been able to answer with him being so close.

This was not the broken IP.

This was him—his face so close to mine, feeling his warmth, inhaling his scent.

I dropped my gaze and thought about his words again.

"I do not understand you," I said, still looking at the high grass next to his feet.

He bent forward until our foreheads touched. "I knew you wouldn't," he said. "But I like to teach you our ways, our language."

Then he lifted his head and kissed my forehead. "What it means is that I would give up something very valuable simply to be able to know what you are thinking, because it is that important for me to know."

I nodded, thinking of his original phrase. "Yes. I understand it now."

He smiled. "So?"

"So what?"

"So what were you thinking?"

"Ah," I had to laugh, "I don't really remember anymore. I got distracted."

He tilted his head sideways and gave me a mischievous smile. "I don't really believe that, you know. Not a Senthien."

"How about a Human?"

"Mmm," he said, his lips twitching. "Okay. Fair point. C'mon, let's go. I think your expertise will be needed soon."

He took my hand in his, and we followed the rest.

The area we entered didn't have a wall around it, but some thin poles still stood around the complex, indicating that a fence was once there. There were several fairly well-preserved low buildings, only two floors high. Others had only a ground floor. They were all covered in green.

"Over here!" Patrick called. "This is the entrance."

J squeezed my hand just a little bit and then let it go to walk over to Patrick. They were standing in front of a one-story building, which appeared to be almost entirely intact. It must have been built to far more rigorous structural standards. The entrance to the building was blocked by a solid metal door hiding behind a dense mat of creepers. On the side, just visible was a once-white access control panel with a number pad.

"All the doors opened automatically after entering the correct access codes, or at least they did in my time," Patrick said, following the rim of the entrance with his gaze.

"That requires power," said J.

"Which we don't have," Patrick responded.

"In Uni, these kind of systems work on multiple power

sources," I said. "On the newly terraformed planets and moons, all critical computer hosting centers had to have standard disaster recovery infrastructure. This included independent and self-contained power sources, with multiple redundancies, also including renewable energy. I would assume this is the case here too."

Patrick nodded. "All right, what are we looking for?"

I raised my forearm to look at my E-band. It could override the access control circuitry, but it didn't have enough of an energy charge to open the gates themselves. So I needed to find a local power source from which my E-band could draw energy.

I swiped the screen of the E-band. "I'm initiating a scan of the proximal area… I can override the access codes but I need power to open the gate… So I'm looking for a power sou—there, solar."

"Solar power?" asked Rick.

"It's not gonna work. All the electronics were fried, including solar panels," said Frank.

"Aye, but remember, this part of the planet was protected," said Peter, nodding. "Like us, saved in the crèches, this was on the other side of the planet when the solar storm hit the surface."

Peter looked at me and said, "I think it might work."

"As soon as there's some electricity available, I can get the doors to open," I said, nodding at my E-band.

"All right," Patrick said and then looked up. "Let's check the roof, shall we?"

J leaned on the wall with one shoulder and laced the fingers from his hands into a small stepping platform, which Patrick used to climb onto the flat roof. We watched him as he scrutinized the area around him, trying to decipher on his face what it was that he was seeing. Then he walked to the center of the roof, and we lost sight of him.

"Anything?" Peter called up to him.

"It's all green here, guys. I don't... I don't see anything that *looks* like solar panels."

J turned to me. "What do you think he should be seeing?"

"They might not look as you expect them. There were large technological advances in design and functionality in the years before the Evacuation, so the new cells looked nothing like the large dark panels you would have known. But they probably won't look like ours either, the small solar chambers engraved into leaflets. That wasn't pre-Ev technology, so I wouldn't expect to see it here."

"So what *am* I looking for?" said Patrick, standing at the edge of the roof, lifting his arms in a question.

I turned my face up to look at him and said, "I think you are looking for something in between the two. Smaller surface area. Might not even cover the whole roof, only an area of it."

He scanned the roof surface again and then shook his head. "No... I just don't see it."

"J, can you help me up?"

As an answer, he leaned against the wall again and made a stepping platform with his hands.

I took off my leather shoes and stepped onto his palms with my bare foot, holding onto his shoulders. He gently closed his hands around my foot. It felt warm and intimate, and it inevitably raised my heartbeat. We looked at each other for a long moment, oblivious to the others surrounding us.

"Today still?" asked Peter behind me.

"Sorry," I said and lowered my gaze. Then I leaned on J's shoulders and pushed myself up.

Patrick reached out with his hand and helped me onto the roof. It was like stepping onto a soft green carpet. The roof was layered with moss.

It was beautiful.

I knelt down and brushed my palm over the layer. The surface was soft and flat, except that there was a repetition of a small ridge every centimeter or so. I dug my fingers in and scraped off the moss.

"Here!" I said, looking at Patrick and pointing to the thin lines that now became visible.

Patrick raised his eyebrows. "This? Really? Even if I'd seen it, I wouldn't have recognized it. It just looks like a roof design." He bent down as well to clear other surfaces.

"Anything?" we heard Peter shout from below.

"Yup," Patrick called back. "We have it."

Then he looked up at the cloudy sky and said in a low voice, "Though we might need to wait a bit to get any electricity with this kind of weather."

I automatically looked up as well, but then I shook my head. "No."

He looked at me. "No, what?"

"The cloud cover does not influence cell's ability to absorb radiation."

"Really? Don't we need sun for *sun cells* to charge?"

"As long as it's not night, they will get charged."

He nodded. "Okay. How long, do you reckon?"

"I don't understand."

"How long do you think it will take?"

"The types we use on Senthia get charged within a few passes."

"Is our sun stronger than what you guys have?" Patrick asked.

"Yes, much stronger," I said. "In fact, it got so strong that people ran away."

"Ha…" he said, looking uncertain whether I'd actually attempted a joke. "That's funny."

"All right, let's assume these cells are a lot weaker and probably partially worn-out," I said as I wiped the last bits of soil and moss from the solar cell lines. "I would… reckon… sixty passes."

Patrick nodded and then said louder to the group below, "We'll probably need to wait an hour or so."

Then he turned to me. "Shall I help you get down? Here, take my hands and I'll lower you." I came close to the edge and held his hands. "Turn the other way, so you can hold onto the edge with your feet." Then he shouted, "J? Ready to hold her?"

"Ready as I'll ever be," said J.

"Finally," said Peter and everyone but me laughed.

I did not know what that meant, but it seemed to me it was said in good spirit.

Patrick lowered me down and J grabbed my waist, holding it tightly as he brought me down.

He smiled at me and said, "Do you want me to show you around?"

CHAPTER 26

J and I walked farther up the hill until we reached the end of the once-inhabited area, the edge where the forest started again. He turned around and sat down. I sat next to him.

"The whole city is too big to walk through now, but I thought I'd pick a spot where I could show you a few places."

"Okay," I said and looked around. He was right. From this spot, we could see a large part of the deserted city.

"Here," he said, pointing to a place halfway down to the rugby stadium. "That was the place where I worked."

I looked, then frowned. There was virtually nothing left on that spot. "I don't see anything."

"I know," he said. "There wouldn't be any. The building was made out of wood. It was all very natural."

"What was it?"

"A recuperation center."

I looked at him. "And what was your role in society?"

Something about my question made him smile. "Well, I don't know what my *role* in society was, but I was a trained physiotherapist. First, I worked with stroke and paraplegic patients."

I paused. "What are those?"

"Well, a brain stroke typically happens when a blood clot

blocks the blood supply to a certain part of the brain by clogging the artery."

"There is no such thing in Uni."

"Really? How can that be? Strokes are the third leading cause of mortality in the first world."

"Were."

"Okay, yes, were. But how can you guys control that?"

"I do not know the details. All the information about bio-medical enhancements is proprietary to the Anas and Booleans."

"And they are?"

"They are a species of Descendants. Anas are focused on medical science, and Booleans perform molecular and genetic experiments."

"Do you guys have any diseases at all?"

"No," I said, and then I lowered my gaze. "Not unless we come to Earth." My thoughts went to Stevanion. J didn't say anything, but he must have been thinking the same thing and we shared a few moments of silence.

"What was the other one?" I asked.

He raised his head. "The other what?"

"You said you worked with stroke patients and paraplegic patients. What are paraplegic patients?"

"Paraplegic patients had a trauma—ah, injury—to their spinal cord that blocked the use of their legs, and sometimes, depending where the injury was, also the arms. But I mainly worked with those where the injury wasn't as serious, and there was still some use of the lower extremities, as well as the arms. In both cases, the goal was to train the body to recover movement and coordination."

"But you said you worked with those patients in the beginning. What happened afterward?"

"Right. So the building was originally built for stroke patients, but it was repurposed as a facility for… hmm, *Scrambles*. It's… not a nice word, but that's what everyone called them."

"Who were Scrambles?"

"Well… the people with scrambled brains."

I shook my head slowly. "I do not understand."

"No, I know. So here is the story. At some point—it must have been about five years after I finished my studies—a new drug appeared. It turned the world around. It activated all the brain centers. It hyped up the brain bigtime."

"Hyped up the brain?"

"A normal person—in my time, at least—used ten, maybe fifteen percent of their brain at any given moment, okay?"

"Okay."

"This drug made it possible to use several times that capacity. You would not believe what people were able to do! Luckily, for some reason it remained extremely rare and not many could get hold of it."

"Why do you say luckily? Isn't it a good thing to use the brain to such a capacity?"

He shook his head hard. "No. In the very beginning, people thought there were no drawbacks, but after one or two months of use, they—broke. They could not talk anymore, they had no coordination of their body movements, even their vision centers failed, so they could not see. They were… scrambled. Half of the patients died in the days after the scramble started, but some didn't. And as you can imagine, they had all the symptoms of the people I'd worked with before, so I was transferred to work with them."

He looked to the front, his gaze far beyond the stadium. "I can't escape the feeling that the thing had been manufactured."

"What had been manufactured?"

"The drug." He turned to me. "This wasn't some natural plant that got dried, chopped, mixed with cement, or dipped into gasoline. This drug came out of nowhere, all of a sudden, and it was available on different continents at different locations at the same time. As if someone was trying it out on the people."

"Trying it out? You mean like an experiment?"

"Yeah, exactly like that: finding out how it works on Humans."

I searched my nanoprobes, trying to gather more information on pre-Ev history.

"I don't understand." I looked at him and said, "This historical fact is significant enough to be saved on the nanoprobes. I should have some information saved on this topic. But I don't have anything."

I looked at him again.

"Is that surprising? It might not be so important for the Descendants."

"Unless it was."

In that moment, the gray ruined city disappeared in front of my eyes to give way to a Vision.

> The brightly lit lab is crammed with people in white coats, bent over their lab benches, observing robotic manipulators, talking in groups of three or four. I know where this is: University of Neurotechnology and Innovation. UNI.
>
> The next moment, a group of people enters the laboratory. The first person, holding a secured suitcase, places it on the lab bench. One of the scientists takes several small sealed tubes from the large refrigerator next to the robotic system, opens the suitcase with his

fingerprint and places it in tube-formed soft pouches. Without saying a word, the man closes the suitcase and leaves.

"Dora?" J was holding me, both of his hands on my shoulders. "Dora, are you all right?"

I looked at him.

"You were… you were zoned out. Did you hear me at all?"

"No. I didn't."

"Are you—"

"I had a Vision. It's somewhat similar to the deep sleep stage, so it is very difficult to wake me up."

"Ah," J said in relief. "I was starting to get wor—"

"If my interpretation of what I saw is right," I interrupted, "then what you said before is true."

J shook his head, confused. "I don't understand. What are you talking about?"

"The Scramble drug. It was made. It was made at the University of Neurotechnology and Innovation. And the field trial was planned. They wanted to test it."

J looked at the ground. "At the University of Neurotechnology and Innovation? Didn't you say that was the place where the first prototype of the Mind was made?"

"Yes. And Tania's husband—"

"Deceased husband."

"Yes—deceased husband— he worked there."

J looked at me.

"It's all connected, I am sure of it," I said, looking at J's eyes and hoping, somehow, it would suddenly become obvious to me.

It didn't.

I exhaled and lowered my gaze.

Two beeps sounded on my E-band.

I looked at my forearm and nodded. "The solar cells are sufficiently charged. It will just take a moment for my E-band to siphon the energy. It won't be fully charged yet, but it should be enough to open the door."

CHAPTER 27

The heavy-looking doors moved sideways, peeling away the moss where they slid into the wall, as a gust of air escaped from the building.

"Hermetically sealed," said Patrick. "That's a good sign."

J entered first, I walked behind him, and the rest followed. We climbed down three metal stairs and found ourselves in a dark hallway, the only light coming from the entrance as well as from weak purple auxiliary lights on the ceiling. The hallway was shaped like a tube, and the floor was a metal grid running along the base. Our leathery shoes made no sound.

"It's a new building," said Patrick in a quiet voice. "I don't really know where to look first."

"You think you're gonna wake up the ghosts?" said Frank loudly.

His voice echoed in the hallways and came back to us metallic and distorted. No one said anything for a few moments.

"Let's not worry about ghosts," said Peter. "Let's find a computer that works." His last words were so quiet it was as if he'd said them only to himself.

"Ghosts?" I asked J quietly.

"Some people believe that after the death, the spirit lives on and becomes a ghost."

"Why would the ghosts be here and not outside of these premises?"

"Good point, because officially, ghosts can cross through walls. But much of this is linked to stories of haunted dungeons and castles."

"Haunted dungeons and castles?"

"Old stuff, wouldn't even be in your memory data. It's an—"

"Stop that." Peter turned to us. "Bust the ghosts stories and follow me. We need to get this working."

When we came to the first door on our left, Peter and Rick walked in first and the rest of us followed. As the last person entered the room, the entry gate behind us slid closed, leaving us in the dim light of the purple light tubes on the ceiling.

"Does anybody see a control for the main light?" I asked and looked at the others.

"You mean like a light swi—who-*hoa*!" Peter jumped back.

The others looked at me as well and stepped backward too.

"Freaking hell! What *is* that?" Frank shouted out.

The only person who actually took a step toward me was J.

"Now, that is something else!" he said.

"*What* is something?" I was getting annoyed.

J raised his head to look at the purple-colored tubes. "UV," he said, pointing with a finger to the ceiling.

"Oh." I looked up and understood: the auxiliary lights were in fact the UV lights and they made my eyes fluorescent green.

J came to me, his face a few inches away from mine. He bent down and kissed me, his eyes open to look at mine.

"Very cool," he whispered and smiled.

"All right, the show is over! Let's find the light switch, shall we?" said Peter and went to the right edge of the wall, placing his hands on the surface and feeling around for the way to activate the lights.

The next moment, bright lights flickered on, and we all shielded our eyes.

"Anything else I can do here?" Rick said proudly, dusting off his hands as if they were sandy.

"Well done, boy!" Peter clapped Rick on the shoulder, causing him to almost fall forward.

With all the room lit, I could now take in my surroundings.

Three gray concrete walls. Covering all three were large transparent screens—OLEDs—dimly reflecting our silhouettes. In the middle of the room there was a desk made out of a smooth material. I stepped closer.

A Proto system?

"Wow," I whispered as the realization hit me.

"Wow, what?"

"That's... that's ancient."

"Ah, thanks!" said Peter, rolling his eyes. "I almost feel for the dinosaurs."

I turned to them, realizing how it must have sounded.

"No, no, I'm sorry. It's not that *you* are ancient," I said and turned back to point to the console. "It's just that we do not use anything like this at Uni anymore—but this here is the same kind of computer system that was used during the voyage." I turned again to face them. "This is the mainframe used on the early Seedships."

"Do you know how to start it?" asked Patrick.

"No, I don't," I said and heard an intake of breath in the room. "But I have a manual," I said, smiling, and lifted up my E-band.

I checked my E-band to see if by now it had connected to

the local computer system and I quickly zapped through several information displays until I found what I was looking for. I tilted my head to the side.

Interesting.

I looked up from the small screen, lowered both of my hands, and then quickly raised my arms upward, palms up.

"SYSTEM START. INITIALIZATION," a metallic female voice announced.

"What was that?" Rick asked.

"Gesture commands." I turned to him. "It's unusual that they used it for the start of the system, though. I would assume the start would use touch controls—or voice."

I was almost talking to myself when I realized I had the attention of everybody.

"Do you use voice control at Uni?" asked Rick.

"Yes, in a majority of the cases. In private quarters, AI systems are voice-printed; they only respond to the voice of the owner. But there are many public places where the computer reacts to anybody's voice."

"SYSTEM READY."

My E-band sounded a signal. I lifted my arm to check. The surge of power to the mainframe computer had accelerated the wireless charging of my E-band. At this rate my E-band would be full already within a few passes.

That was my original plan: to fully charge my E-band so that it had enough power to generate a hyperspace resonance field and potentially tap into the porting channel. However, now that Stevanion was gone, and I was where I wanted to be, I didn't need it anymore. I didn't want it anymore.

"Whoa, look at that," I heard Patrick saying.

I looked up.

The three transparent screens dissolved into large images. Everyone turned to stare at them, their faces showing awe at the sight. The screens were so large that we were surrounded by them.

"This is so cool," said Rick.

Each screen showed a beautiful image of Old Earth: large mountains with white on their peaks and blue lakes at the bottom mirroring the rocks. A forest of tall pine trees, thick with layers of fresh snow. The blue depths of the ocean, with sun rays fanning through and a humpback whale emerging in the distance.

I gazed at all of them, more amazed than any of my companions, because I was seeing these kinds of images for the very first time.

No one talked for a long while.

On the bottom and the sides of each screens were little cover-flow icons, each showing a different program, file, or folder.

I checked my E-band to confirm and said, "These are touchscreens."

I walked forward to the middle screen and touched one of the icons to move it to the center.

Nothing happened. I looked back at my E-band to check. It was definitely touch-sensitive.

Why isn't it working?

"J, can you try? Perhaps I have the wrong temperature."

J came close and mimicked the movement.

Still nothing.

"Perhaps it would react to gesture commands?" asked Rick.

"If this were the case, it would still have reacted to the movement I did. It has to be something else."

I scrolled through more information and halted on an image.

I moved my hand to J so he could have a look at my E-band screen and asked, "J, what does this look like to you?"

J looked at it and pressed his lips together. "It looks like… like some kind of a… a glove."

"Ah, of course! It makes sense!"

"I don't understand," said Simon.

"The signal for the computer—it cannot come from just anyone in the room who touches the screens. It has to be from one particular person who is currently in control of the system. And that person needs to wear a tracking glove."

I lifted up my wrist to show them the image on my E-band. "We need to find that glove."

The group spread around, searching. Most of the room was empty except the back wall, which had several metal cupboards. All of them were locked.

"Keys, anyone?" asked Rick.

"No, but let's try brute strength," said Frank, and he kicked the first cupboard with his foot. The door shook and there was a cracking sound, but it stayed closed.

"It's not going to work."

"I can tell you've never tried breaking through a door, Rick." Frank grinned and kicked the door again.

Another breaking sound, and the door swung open.

"Wow!" Rick jumped backward as Frank kicked the other two cupboards open.

We all gathered around the first cupboard. On the top shelf there was a single plastic box. Neatly arranged chip-disk racks lined the rest of the cupboard.

The second cupboard held ten large metal boxes, one on each shelf, each with a series of blinking green and red lights.

"These must be the servers," said Patrick.

The third cupboard contained one metal box, cube-shaped, one quarter IP in length. It was fastened to the back wall.

"What is that?" asked Simon.

I crouched down. I was fairly certain what it was, but I checked my E-band nevertheless.

Of course! The extra power surge for the computer, which also accelerated the charging of my E-band, had to be generated by something other than just solar cells. The power source had to be something stronger. "I know what this is."

They gathered around me. "Yes?"

"It's what you're looking for." I smiled at them.

"What are we looking for?" asked Peter.

"Power. This is a fission battery. A nuclear microgenerator."

"Holy shit!" shouted Simon.

"Oh, no!" several others said and moved backward.

"Dora, is it radioactive? Can you tell?" asked J.

I turned away from the container and looked at them, seeing alarm on their faces. "You do not need to worry. These types of batteries are completely safe. They were safe even in the pre-Ev time."

"But what about the uranium?"

"There is radioactive material there, yes, but first of all, there is only a minimal amount: this battery was not made to power a whole city, only one building, perhaps. And also, the casing is radiation-proof," I said, turned back to the container and put my hand on the top surface.

"No, Dora," J said and pulled me back.

"J, there is no danger. Look!" I said, showing him my E-band.

J looked at the band and then at me. "This doesn't tell me anything. Why don't you move away from that thing?"

I had to laugh at that.

"Is it working?" asked Rick pointing to the generator.

"Yes." I nodded. "I think it activated when we first opened up the door. These types of batteries shut down when they are not used. Once the power is needed again, they turn on automatically. And because they contain uranium, they last for a very long time.

"Now, what we need is a specific interactive system which works with these screens." I walked back to the cupboard and pulled out the plastic box. Inside was a glove made out of rubber finger cups connected to a textile wristband.

I pulled it over my right hand and turned around to face the computer walls. With my gloved hand, I tapped on the folder. The folder then rolled out from a thumbnail to the size of the whole screen.

It was a map. *Of course. The map I saw in my Vision in Mike's cottage.*

Everyone came close to the screen walls, forgetting their fears of the microgenerator behind them.

"Okay, what are we seeing here?" Peter crossed his arms over his chest.

"This looks like a map of some sort. Do you recognize it?" I asked.

"Isn't this… this is *here*! Look!" Frank touched a spot on the map where the green and blue areas met. Everybody leaned forward, but for a few moments no one said anything.

"You're right, Frank. This is a map of this area, and we must be right… here." J touched the screen lightly, pointing to a small red square with a white dot in the middle.

"What is that there?" asked Frank, pointing to a section of the map north of our position.

Everyone looked at the little white square, which was blinking from white to a shade of gray.

"It looks like… it's the location of our village, isn't it?" said Simon, tipping his head to one side.

"Yes, you're right."

"This map was created before the Evacuation. It cannot possibly show our tree village—it wouldn't know where it is, right?" Frank said, still looking at the screen. "Right?"

"Aye. But what is it, then?" asked Peter standing to my left.

"Perhaps it's your underground installation," I said and looked at them.

They all looked at me, obvious surprise on their faces, and then back to the screen.

"Hmm, I think you're right. This must be it," Peter said.

"And what is that?" asked Patrick, pointing to a small yellow icon between the underground installation and the ruined city.

They all shook their heads. I came closer. "This looks like a classic symbol for energy or power."

"Really?" said Simon. "It's different from any of our symbols."

"We label power plants like this," I said, pointing with my finger to the yellow icon.

"Well, if that's the case, this is getting really interesting. Dora, can you tell what kind of power plant it is, by any chance?" asked Peter.

"I can't." I shook my head slightly and looked back at the screen. "And I'm not familiar enough with the system to find out. You will probably need to go there and check."

Everybody was quiet again.

Patrick, looking at the map, leaned his head first one way and then the other.

"You know, J, I can't seem to escape the feeling that the path we took two days ago is the path to this place." Patrick looked at J and arched his eyebrow.

"You actually might be right," said J.

"That means we need to go back there again. And this time, with some tools," said Simon.

"This is good," said Peter. "At least we know where to look now. The problem is that we'll need to wait a few months."

"Why?" asked Rick.

"It's too late to make another expedition, my boy. By the time we're back to the tree village and get ready again, the river will be overflowing. We wouldn't manage to cross it. We'll need to wait."

"I have an idea," I said as I checked the power level of my E-band.

"What is it?" asked J.

"I'm not sure if it will work."

"If *what* will work?"

"Let me try something. I'm not completely sure yet if it is possible," I said, paging through the information on my E-Band, "but my E-band should be able to project the power of the microgenerator to other computer systems within a certain distance."

"I don't understand. What does that mean?" asked Peter.

Before answering, I confirmed with a few more swipes of my E-band that rerouting power was indeed possible. I set the radius to the maximum: all computer-linked electronic equipment within this range would be charged.

I turned to Peter. "It means that my E-band can initiate a power surge to your underground installation and its computers."

"Really? You can do that?" asked Rick.

I looked at Rick. "It's not me doing it. It's just standard Descendant technology."

Then I looked back at my E-band and tapped for execution.

Within moments, we heard a low beeping sound coming from the computer wall screen. We looked to the map again. The underground installation icon now shone a brighter white, and very close to it another white blinking square had appeared.

Momentarily, the sides of my vision blurred, the sounds dimmed, and I could tell another Vision was coming.

Cheering. Loud voices. Happiness.

But also - sadness. Deep, deep sadness.

I closed my eyes tight and pushed it away.

I am not a Senthien.

I am not.

I am not a Senthien anymore.

I shouted it in my head and kept pressing my eyelids shut till it hurt.

Not anymore.

I am—Human.

I am Human now.

"Dora, are you okay?" I heard J right next to me.

I opened my eyes slowly. I saw clearly again.

I exhaled. "Yes, yes, I'm fine. Thank you."

He kissed my forehead and whispered, "Let me know if you need anything, okay?"

"What do you think, Dora? It looks like it worked, aye?" said Peter.

"Yes, Peter. I do think so," I said.

"Good work!" He patted me on the shoulder, but then pulled his hand back. "Oh, sorry, Dora, I wasn't thinking!"

"It is all right, Peter." I turned to J and smiled. "I am getting used to it."

"Uh, guys?" said Rick. "Why is there another blinking square next to our village?"

"Perhaps it's just a different part of our underground installation? Who knows…" Peter shrugged his shoulders.

I felt a Vision building again, gradually, to the edges of my field of view. I closed my eyes and pushed it away.

I am Human now.

Human.

Human.

Let me be. Human.

My heartbeat increased for a moment, but the Vision subsided and disappeared. I opened my eyes again.

"Damn, I'm so curious if it worked!" said Frank.

"Why do you have doubts?" I asked.

"If you lived in our time, Dora, you'd learn never to trust a computer system. It always turns its back on you when you least expect it."

"You make it sound as if it were alive," said Patrick, half laughing.

"Well, you know, sometimes I had a feeling it was and it did stuff just to piss me off."

They all laughed.

"I'm not joking, you guys. I swear, one of my computer's most important tasks was to quit a program unexpectedly right when I was in the middle of it. And, of course, before I thought to save my work."

Patrick smiled and said, "Well, that's because you were using the wrong system."

"No, it's because computers don't like me." Frank crossed his arms over his chest.

Peter shook his head and then turned to me. "Dora, do you want to look through the other folders in the system? See what else can we find out before we leave?"

"Of course, Peter, the Senthien in me is always eager to browse through new data," I said and turned back to the screen.

CHAPTER 28

We were making good time going back to the village, though our backpacks were now a lot heavier from many items we scavenged in the ruins. Most of the first day, J and I walked behind everyone. He kept holding my hand, and I kept smiling for no particular reason.

On the afternoon of the second day, J suggested to camp after lunch and continue forward on the third day. Some of the group went hunting, but J declined and said he had something else in mind.

"Come, Dora. There is something I want to show you," he said, hiding his excitement by suppressing a smile.

"Okay. Should I take anything with me?"

"No, no, I've got everything."

He called out to Peter and Frank, who were sitting in front of the place prepared for the fire. "We're off for the falls, guys!"

Frank, cleaning and preparing some fish, answered without looking at us, "Don't do anything I wouldn't do."

"I guess anything goes then," J said with a grin as he slung a small backpack over his shoulder. "C'mon!"

We made our path through a dense part of the forest, watching our steps. Birds singing high up in the trees accompanied our hike. J didn't talk. He was walking in front, bending hard branches and holding them for me to pass.

Despite his silence, I felt a strange excitement that I could not explain. My heart was pounding, and it wasn't due to our strenuous walk. There was something else.

Is this only about the surprise he had prepared?

"Where are we going?"

"You'll see!" He didn't turn, but I could tell he was smiling.

We pressed on.

As the path turned uphill and some of the vegetation changed, I heard a rumble, first quiet and then louder and louder, though I couldn't identify the sound.

"Do you know what that is?" he said, turning to face me.

"No."

"Good! Now, close your eyes."

"Again?"

"Yes, again. Come!"

"Okay," I said and closed my eyes, holding J's hand a bit tighter.

We continued walking, my steps careful. The rumbling sound was getting so loud I could hardly hear anything else.

"Okay, slowly…" he shouted above the noise. "Step up. Now straight a bit more. Okay, now wait here."

He let go of my hand. I had to use all my willpower not to open my eyes at that moment.

"Don't peek!" he called from somewhere in front of me.

"I'm not!" I shouted back.

It was several passes before he returned. He took my hand and led me a few more steps forward.

"You can open your eyes now!"

And I did.

In front of me was the most amazing sight of a river falling down a several IPs high smooth black rock into a small circular lake. The sunshine found its way between the trees and refracted off the cloud of water drops from the falling river into an arch of six brightly colored stripes.

This was – magnificent!

I turned to him and smiled, because I could not voice my feelings. This was more than beautiful.

"You like it?" His smile was plastered from one cheek to the other. "There's more. Follow me."

We circled around the lake, my hand in J's, until we came to the right side of the waterfall.

He turned to me and mouthed the words without a sound, as it was obvious I couldn't have heard him even if he was shouting. *We'll walk behind the falls* is what I thought he said, but this was so unbelievable, I grimaced a question with my eyes. He smiled and tugged my hand to follow him.

Behind the curtain of free-falling water, there was a small ledge wide enough for only one person to use at a time, so I walked behind him, holding his hand tightly, mindful of the slippery floor as water splashed our clothes with fine drops.

Ten IPs in, he stepped through a narrow opening in the rock wall and pulled me in behind him. We entered a small tunnel and I had to rely on him leading me because it was pitch-dark. The deafening sound of the waterfall got quieter, and I could hear our steps again. The passage gently curved to the right, and my impression was that we were walking slightly uphill.

The next moment, we stepped out of the tunnel and into a large cave. The roof of the cave was open to the sky and the orange light from the setting sun streamed in, transforming the rough walls of the cave into a mosaic of different hues. A soft mat was laid out on the flat sandy floor.

All of a sudden, I realized—this was my dream, my Vision of him in the cave. My adrenaline spiked, and my heart started racing.

I tried to steady my breathing but my heart pounded madly against my rib cage. I was afraid I would faint again.

"I found this place," he said, "a few years back, just by accident. And I remember thinking… that it would be a nice place to bring someone special. Although at the time, I never thought I'd do that." He looked at me. "But, then you came. And changed everything." He stepped closer and took my hands in his. "Changed me."

"Changed you?" I asked, somewhat breathlessly. "How?"

"When the crèches revived us, we all woke up, we started living again, but somehow, I was missing…" he pressed his lips together in a thought. "…life."

"I do not understand you, J. You were alive."

"No," he said, shaking his head. He raised one of my hands and pressed my open palm to the middle of his chest. "You see, I was living, but I wasn't alive. I was missing—fire, here, within me."

His eyes smiled as he looked at me, such a clear nonverbal communication I could not misunderstand it.

"Now, everything is different. The flowers smell better; the air is fresher; the days are brighter; people are nicer; food tastes finer; everything—everything!—is so much better with you here." He released my hands and gently placed his palms on my cheeks, his fingers warm on my skin. "De-freezing made me start breathing, but only when you came into my life did my heart start beating."

I was speechless, overwhelmed by his words, and—without any doubt—completely in love with him.

He bent down and kissed me, the touch soft and gentle. We stayed like this for a long time. It was perfect.

He was perfect.

He drew back and gazed down at my body. He inhaled, keeping the breath locked in for a few moments, but then said, "I know… I know about the interpersonal space and all those things you have in your Uni world, but…" He looked up into my eyes. "I so want to be near you." He touched the back of neck and pulled me closer, whispering, "I want to hold you really, really close. I *need* you, Dora." His body was now completely touching mine, his lips next to my ear.

My heart was drumming and I could hardly catch my breath. The need, the wish, the desire boiled deep inside me. I knew what he felt because—I felt it too.

"This," I whispered, "this was the place I saw in my Visions. Before I came here."

"You did?"

"Yes."

"Is… this when we kissed?" he asked in a low voice.

I nodded, not trusting my voice anymore, then looked up into his dark eyes, his irises indistinguishable from his pupils in the dim light. I could feel the warmth of his body; I could smell the scent of his skin.

His lips parted as he touched my face, gently stroking my lips with his thumb. All of his movements were slow, every motion a question.

But my desire was impatient. It burned fast, scorching and desperate. And it wanted him *now*.

I rose onto my toes and kissed him.

For a moment he was still. Startled. But the next second, he took me in his arms, opening his lips, his tongue finding mine. I wrapped my arms around his neck, the depth of his kiss electrifying the core of my being, pooling all my senses in an exquisite aching need.

The stillness of the moment before was replaced by frantic and wild movements of passion. I slid my hands over his neck, shoulders and arms, feeling his tight muscles through the wet shirt. I could not get enough of him.

But then he stopped and moved away, his lips only an inch from mine. "I want to make love to you," he whispered softly. "But I need to be sure that you want that too."

Oh, J, my body is on fire. You have to feel it. But my voice was gone, so I lifted on my toes again, accidentally sliding my breasts against his skin, and kissed him. He closed his eyes for an instant, looking unbalanced before he took another heavy breath.

"I want you too," I managed to whisper.

There was a moment's pause, and then he leaned in for a kiss, a passionate response to my words. His lips left mine and traced down my neck, a tickling sensation mingled with a very deep, very primal anticipation.

As he slid his hand underneath my shirt, I stopped breathing all together, waiting.

His lips next to my ear, he whispered, "Breathe, love…"

The moment his warm palms started sliding upward, I took a breath. His fingertips left trails on my skin wherever he touched it, and my whole body tensed when they slid across the soft crevice under my breasts.

I stopped breathing again.

He nipped my earlobe, his palm sliding upward, softly

pressing the tight pebble between his fingers, the touch sending jolts through my body, pooling at my base, rousing it awake.

I lost tension in my knees, and I would have fallen if he hadn't been holding me. The craving I felt for him, no, the craving my body felt for his, was nothing I had ever experienced before. I had IC sessions in my life, but how my body reacted to J now, caused my mind to spin, caused my body to shift out of control.

A random thought intruded: *Why couldn't Descendants experience these extreme, exquisite feelings? Why were these bodily responses suppressed?*

But the thought was gone as fast as it came, as J lifted my shirt, the wet fabric sticking to my skin as he slid it up, my hair still wrapped in its folds. He gently pulled it over my head and dropped it on the ground, my damp hair falling on my back again, cooling my skin. Then he loosened the waist string of my dress and it sank to the ground too.

J took a step backward and holding the tips of my fingers he raised my arms slightly and gazed down the length of my body.

"Wow," he whispered, his breaths heavy. "You look... *beautiful.*"

The hunger in his eyes was unmistakable, and for a fraction of a moment, his stare looked almost predatory. Then he took a step forward, cupped my face and kissed me so deeply, I felt its rousing power rippling in every part of my body.

Feeling his hot breaths on my skin and the cool touch of his tongue, I felt him biting my ear lobe, licking my neck and collarbone, then gently sliding down my body. I closed my eyes, anticipating, trembling from within.

His kisses became more urgent, more desperate, as his lips explored my body. I moaned involuntarily, an invigorating anticipation gathering somewhere deep inside me, tightening my inner muscles.

The moment his lips touched the tip of my breast, the soft pressure between his tongue and teeth sent an intense sensation through my body that made me lose all control.

Engrossed in my own fireworks of sensations, I was barely aware that he'd slid off his clothes too, until he lifted my knee, wrapping my leg around his waist—and I felt it, his heated body next to mine, his arousal touching the slippery entrance.

My eyes locked onto his, arms and legs embraced, in the warm orange light of the setting sun, our heavy breaths echoed in the cave. Then J lifted me up and knelt on a mat. As my knees touched the floor, I lifted up slightly, adjusting the position, and then without a second thought, I finally indulged my inner craving: I slid onto him. The motion induced the sweetest agony of desire deep inside my belly.

J moaned as I pressed myself on him completely, arching backward, purposefully bringing my breasts close to his mouth. And then everything became a haze. The exquisite fullness I felt inside me, the burning feeling his kisses left on my skin, the thrusting movements he now began... It drove me *insane*.

I was unaware, crazy, breathless, as he moved my body in a rhythm that matched his breathing, lost in this new sensation that peaked a little bit every time our bodies connected.

My mind was spinning and I was barely aware of my surroundings, of the sounds, of anything else that wasn't the increasing need I felt inside me.

Suddenly, he lifted me up and then pushed me back down, lifting his hips up at the same time. And in that moment, the pressure building up inside me exploded into a thousand pieces, my inner muscles contracting instinctively, releasing me to the most exhilarating and overpowering sensation of my life.

For the next few moments, everything was a blur. I thought I heard him calling my name, but I wasn't certain. I was lost in this unique moment in my life, shivering from my head to my toes.

Tears rolled down my face as I looked up at the open sky. I couldn't stop them. I was so immensely happy, my body ecstatic.

All of a sudden, J took my face in his hands. "Dora! Oh, my God, I'm sorry. Did I hurt you?"

He wiped away my tears, but new ones came tumbling down. I looked at him, his face blurry through tears collected on the rims of my eyes.

"No, no, no... no," I said, shaking my head.

"Dora, why are you crying?" His voice was urgent.

I looked up again and then started laughing out loud. "What—was—that?" More tears spilled as I continued laughing.

"Oh, you mean the orgasm?" His voice relaxed.

"Ah, the orgasm! That's what Tania was talking about! I understand. Finally."

I laughed again.

The strongest driver of evolution. She is so right.

I looked at him and then hugged him tightly. "That was out of this world."

He squeezed me back and rested his cheek on my chest. "Maybe out of your *old* world, but it's definitely part of this one."

CHAPTER 29

I opened my eyes to the fresh morning air and the golden rays of sunlight streaming though the small holes in J's tent. I rolled over on the mat. J was still sleeping. His face was relaxed and beautiful.

I smiled.

I was so happy that I'd found him, that my recurring dream had actually been a Vision, and that he was now here, with me.

I gently placed my palm on his face and left it there.

It feels so wonderful to touch him.

J yawned, stretched his arms, touching the sides of his tent, and then relaxed them again.

He opened his eyes. "Hello, beautiful." His lips curled into a half smile.

"Hello, yourself." I smiled back.

"Are you okay?"

I nodded and smiled again, unable to express just how perfect everything was. I moved closer to him and leaned my head down on his chest, hearing him breathe, my head gently moving up and down in the same rhythm.

"Tell me about your home, Dora," J said.

"My home… is rich with different scents, full of the most diverse plants and old trees; it smells of fine salty droplets of the sea, feels like fine sand grains underneath the feet. My home is mixed with different emotions, sad and happy, strong and weak, but all so essential—for life."

"That's a very poetic way to describe Earth. But what I meant was: what is *your* home like?"

"J, this is my home," I said, lifting my head up to look at his face.

"Yes, Earth is your home." He smiled and kissed my forehead.

I placed my head back on his chest.

"I'd like to hear about the place you spent more than three hundred years of your life."

"What would you like to know?"

"What's that world like?"

"I guess it would seem very complex to you."

"Okay, now I feel like a three-year-old," he said, grinning.

Realizing how it sounded, I shook my head and said, "No, what I meant is, most of the people living in Uni are used to the different species and worlds and porting, and the politics connected to all of it. We all grew up with it."

"I think I know what you mean. It's like a mother tongue; no matter how complicated it is, you can still speak it fluently, because you grew up with it."

"Tongue… of a mother?"

He laughed out loud. "You know, I do love these little lessons I have to give you sometimes. It makes me feel like I'm not so far behind you."

"Why would you feel behind me at all?" I leaned on my elbow, looking at him with surprise.

He looked at me silently for a moment, his face serious now. "Because you are three hundred and fifty-six years older than me. Because the world you lived in is five thousand years ahead of where I left off. Because you have the knowledge of all the things people discovered during those five thousand years. Because you are a Senthien, and you see the future."

I paused for a moment, before I quietly said, "I might be three hundred and fifty-six years older, and my world might have five thousand years of technological advancement more than yours, but I have never lit a candle, I have never sung a song, I have never come so physically near to people surrounding me, and I have never—ever—felt sensations that come even close to those you induce in me when you… when you love me with your body. And neither has anyone else in Uni experienced anything similar… except perhaps the Zema4 Humans."

He smiled gently, listening to my explanation.

"Why are the Humans in your world so oppressed?" he asked.

"I don't know for sure. I have some theories, but that's all they are."

"Okay, let me hear them." He folded his arms behind his head as a pillow and looked at me.

"Remember when you asked me about Zlathars?"

"Yeah. Those are the guys who hold the strings."

"And you also asked me why the Zlathars didn't tell me what to think, as I had a different opinion."

He nodded. "Yeah, I remember."

"Well, you were very precise in describing their special ability."

J raised his eyebrows, a clear question on his face. He pressed his lips together and said, "I don't follow you. At all."

I let out a long deep breath. "Zlathars can… hear thoughts, somehow."

"You're kidding me! I thought that was just sci-fi stuff! Mind you, that's what I thought about seeing the future… so, is that how they rule the Uni, by making sure no one organizes a mutiny on the *Bounty*?"

Mutiny on the Bounty? *Really?* I looked at him with my own eyebrows raised.

"Sorry—it means that someone is trying to take command. The mutiny on the Bounty was a famous rebellion that happened a long… actually, a *really* long time ago, on a ship called the Bounty. So, is this the way they keep the power, by knowing people's thoughts and preventing potential uprisings?"

"That's definitely one aspect of it, but…"

"But what?"

"This is the part I'm not sure of. I think that besides reading thoughts, they can influence others' thoughts and actions as well."

"You mean like, make you think or do something you normally wouldn't?"

I nodded. "I think the Descendants are… *told* what to do and think. And they are not aware of it."

He leaned his head back, staring emptily at the roof of the tent. "That makes them a dangerous opponent." Then he turned back to me. "So, this thought-control power they have—how do you know about it?"

"I don't… know about it for certain. It's just a… hunch. Thoughts that came to me—"

"In a Vision?"

"No, this wasn't a Vision. These were just… thoughts I had, like a memory. Only I never saw or experienced any of it."

"Can you *remember* anything else?"

"No, it's not like memories from my own life, which I can access. These memories appear as single thoughts… and they're very rare. In fact, I think they mostly appear after porting."

"After teleporting? Hmm. Yeah, that is funny… perhaps someone else has had these thoughts or memories, too. Perhaps you're not the only one."

I pressed my lips together. "Well, if they did, they never had a chance to talk about it."

There was a moment of silence as we both contemplated the hard reality of the Uni worlds.

"All right, so they can read thoughts, and maybe they can influence thoughts and actions as well—of the Descendants, right?"

"Yes."

"What about Humans? The Zema4 Humans—can the Zlathars do it to them?"

I shrugged. "I don't know. My guess would be not, because otherwise they wouldn't have to be kept under surveillance all the time. They would do what the Zlathars wanted them to do. But they continue to resist."

J looked at me. "That might be the reason, then."

"Reason for what?"

"The reason they didn't influence your thoughts as well. That you can actually see the situation as it is!"

I nodded. "Possible. Probable, even."

"So, is that the reason the Zlathars pushed Humans to the very bottom of Uni society: that Humans can resist their mind control? Or is there something else?"

I turned my gaze away from him and shook my head slowly. "I… I don't know. I don't think that's the only reason. My feeling is that… Zlathars are afraid of Humans."

"Afraid? But why would such an advanced Descendant species be afraid of low castes like Humans? What can Humans do that is a threat to them?"

"And that is the question, isn't it?" I looked at him and nodded.

I realized I was slipping into my Senthien mode again. I did that whenever I analyzed. I smiled within.

There is something special about Humans that Zlathars fear. What is it?

I closed my eyes and sat very still, barely breathing.

I knew it was there, somewhere, I just needed to reach it.

J was waiting, not making any sound.

Nothing came, however. I exhaled and opened my eyes. "I can't see it."

I looked at J and gave him a weak smile. "I will see it though. I can feel it's really close. Close to my mind."

He smiled a gentle smile and kissed my forehead. "I don't doubt it."

CHAPTER 30

I t was late afternoon when we crossed the rope slide. The river was more turbulent and much higher than it had been on our outward journey, only a few IPs beneath our feet as we slid across. Peter said that a few years ago, the river had overflowed to such an extent that it flooded the village. After that, they raised the village and built it up in the trees.

We had only one day to go before we reached the village, and I realized I was afraid. One part of my anxiety was this little bubble of a small group of people with whom I'd learned to open up, to let go, to become Human completely. I was not sure if I would be able to remain Human in a large group as easily. And second, the Vision that I kept pushing away—and that kept coming back—scared me so much that I was now afraid to see it. Something was obviously there, something that at first I didn't want to know, and now I was too afraid to face.

All of this kept me silent over dinner, and J kept looking at me with worried eyes. After the meal was done, J and I stayed sitting by the fire while everyone else went to set up their tents.

"Hey! You okay?"

"Yes," I said and forced a smile.

"Soon home."

"Yes." But now I couldn't even force a smile.

J hugged me with one arm. "Hey, don't worry about it. One step at a time, all right?"

He understood me a lot more than I thought.

"So, tell me something."

"Yes?"

"How come your dad managed to hide his relationship with your mom?"

"He took a sabbatical."

"Okay?" said J, with a clear question in his voice for me to continue.

"Senthiens, as you know, give predictions of things that might come to be. For that they need access to a vast amount of data. They either collect that via the Uni computer interface or port to different worlds to interact with other Descendant species."

"And this is how your dad met your mom, right, when he went to Zema4?"

"Yes, that's right."

"So, what about the sabbatical he took?"

"Senthiens are constantly gathering and analyzing information, and it's actually hard to stop. Frequently experiencing intense Visions is exhausting, so periodically Senthiens are allowed to take a sabbatical. That was the first sabbatical my father had asked for, and it was approved."

"Why was this sabbatical so important?"

"Because this was the time when my mother and father were together. And a Senthien sabbatical means privacy."

"What does that mean exactly?"

"On a sabbatical, Senthiens have six years with no obligation to gather any information that could induce Visions. And that also means no access to the Uni computer interface or holo communication."

"Hmm—so by taking the sabbatical, he made sure no one knew what was happening to him, and whoever was with him, at the time."

"That's right."

"But weren't there other people on this planet? Someone else who could, I don't know, inform the Zlathars about the two— well, three of you?"

"Sabbaticals are really supposed to be a solitary period with limited interaction with other citizens. All the residences on sabbatical worlds are quite isolated to ensure this privacy. So I didn't meet anyone else during those six years."

"What about food and all the other things your family needed?"

"All of that was automated."

J wrinkled his eyebrows, thinking, the dying fire coloring his face. "But how about transportation?"

"You don't need to go anywhere once you are on the sabbatical world."

"No, I mean, how did your mom and dad get there, to this sabbatical world?"

"Porting, of course."

"Exactly—so how come no one noticed when they ported there?"

"They ported separately. Some Humans were needed on that planet for certain physical work, so a few hundred Zema4 Humans ported there and back every few years. She joined one of those groups."

"How did she manage to do that? Wasn't there proper control of the portation?"

"She swapped places with another woman."

"Oh. Was she already pregnant then?"

"Yes."

"How was that possible?"

"What do you mean? Why wouldn't it be possible?"

"Well, the love-making… what we did," he said, smiling, "is how babies are made, normally. And you said your folks—your parents—did it like that, right? No tubes and stuff."

"Yes." I smiled, remembering the experience we'd shared.

"So, they would have needed space, time, and privacy. How was that possible before they got to the sabbatical world?"

"They had that on Zema4."

"Didn't your father need a reason to teleport there so often?"

"He didn't have to port there. He was stationed on Zema4 for several years to do ongoing surveillance."

"What about the privacy? How could he meet your mom without anyone noticing?"

"By being undercover," I said and smiled, remembering my newly learned word.

"He disguised himself?"

"Yes. And it wasn't so difficult. The clothes that Zema4 Humans wear don't reveal much. It was easy for him to hide who he really was."

"Ha, interesting…. All right, and you were born on this sabbatical world, then?"

"Yes."

"And that was… a real birth?"

"I do not understand."

"Like, a vaginal birth? A normal Human birth?"

I wrinkled my eyebrows. "I cannot tell you. I don't remember."

"No, you wouldn't. No one does. I just thought you might have asked."

I shook my head. "No. It never... really crossed my mind."

"Well, I would assume that was the case. Even if there were automated medical treatments available there, they wouldn't be set up for normal Human birth, would they?"

"I would assume so too."

After a few passes, J asked, "Tell me again, how do Uni babies come into the world? How are Descendants born?"

"I don't know much about the process. The majority of that information is available only to the Anas."

"The medic Descendants?"

"Yes. They control the Office of Progeny. They keep track of how many Descendants stop their rejuvenation processes and how many new individuals are needed."

"So when Descendants decide to stop their rejuvenation processes, they die?"

"They continue aging from that moment on."

"How many years do they still live?"

"I know of some individuals who lived more than two hundred years after their last rejuvenation."

"Two hundred years? People don't normally live that long."

"That is correct, but in Uni, there are no diseases. And all our cells have been reprogrammed during previous rejuvenation treatments to remain at a very young stage."

"So... if you never get another rejuvenation treatment, you would live another two hundred years?"

"Yes, that's what I would expect."

"Huh." He looked sideways, thinking about it. "That's... different. You'd outlive everyone here, even... uh, never mind!"

I tilted my head to one side. "Outlive who?"

"Never mind, I'm just rambling, pay no attention. So, let's go back again. These Uni babies—we don't know how they are born, right?"

"No, this information is not available as public knowledge."

"All right. So, they are born, somehow, and then what?"

I frowned. "Then they continue living." I wasn't sure what was he getting at.

"No, I mean, who takes care of the babies? I certainly hope *that's* not automated!"

"Ah, I see. No, it's not automated. Most new individuals—"

"Babies?"

"—yes, babies, are raised in dedicated centers, called EruLocs, with caretakers until they reach the age of their first rejuvenation. They are raised and educated based on the Descendant species they belong to."

"And they never meet their biological parents?"

"No. Only in rare cases is there a need for a personal meeting between the germ cell donor and the new individual."

"I find that sad, don't you?"

"That's the Descendant way. They don't know anything else."

"But you were not raised like that, right?"

I had to smile at the look on his face when he said that. "No. For the first six years, I was raised by my mother and father."

"And after that?"

"After his sabbatical was finished, my father needed to return to Senthia, and… they both decided that I would go with him."

"What about your mom?"

"My mother joined a group returning to Zema4. I never saw her again."

There was a moment of silence.

"That must have been very difficult for you."

"My recollection is that it was difficult for the next several years after. But that was a long time ago, and I only have a few memories of that family time."

"I am sorry."

"It is all right. I do have many optic nerve cam recordings of her as well."

J nodded and lowered his gaze. "Still, it must be difficult to grow up without a mom. But you had your dad with you. How did he manage to smuggle you back to Senthia?"

"I…"

He frowned. "What?"

"I took the place of an official Office of Progeny individual that originated from my father's germ cell."

"You took her place?"

I looked at the ground. I didn't want to look at him. "Yes."

"And where did that girl end up?" he continued.

"She didn't."

"Oh, I see…"

"I don't want to talk about it anymore." I stood up to leave, but J quickly caught me by my elbow.

"Hey, it's okay. This wasn't your decision. There is nothing you need to feel guilty about."

I looked down.

He put his hands on my shoulders and stroked them as he spoke. "It wasn't your fault. And… I understand your father's decision if that was the only way to protect you. A parent will do anything, and I mean anything, to save his own child."

Which is exactly what my father said when he first told me about it.

I swallowed. "Even preventing another one from being?"

J took a moment before responding. "Yes. Even that."

My father had told me about this after my first rejuvenation. And I turned away from him and left. I ported from one world to another without any contact with him for a very long time. In the end, I realized he was the only person who knew me for who I really was. And I made peace with his mistake.

But right now, looking at J, I wondered if it was a mistake at all. If he even had a choice. *If I had... a child... of my own, in the same situation, would I act differently?*

"Hey!" J snapped me out of my deep thoughts. "Let's change the topic. All of this makes me gloomy."

I smiled. "Yes, you're right. What would you like to talk about?"

"Well, I was wondering: you told me before that when you have your rejuvenation thingy going on—"

"You mean the treatment?"

"No, I mean, you said it was called... uh, Interactive Coupling or something. The eleven-second one."

"Yes. What about it?"

"How come women do not get pregnant, then? Or to rephrase it, how *do* women get pregnant?"

"Descendants don't get pregnant."

"Why? Aren't you—I mean, Descendant women—able to carry a baby?"

"I do not know the details, but from the information I have, I can tell you that the embryos are fully developed extracorporeally."

"But... do you—ah, Descendant woman—have female internal organs, like uterus and ovaries?"

I quickly searched through my nanoprobes. "Yes. The organs are there. But their function has been lost."

"Oh," he said, an indecipherable expression on his face.

"This information is important for you. Why?"

"Ah," he said and waved his hand, "old habits die hard." Then he smiled a crooked smile and looked at me.

"What?" I asked.

"Your tent or mine?"

I blinked. "I do not understand."

He leaned in and kissed me on my nose. "You're so sweet, you know that? Where do you want to sleep tonight? I am ready to set up one tent for us, not two."

I understood and smiled. "All right. My tent, then."

"Rise and shine, everyone!" We heard Peter shouting outside.

"What?" Frank moaned from his tent.

"The sun's not out yet!" Now Rick was complaining.

"It is," said Peter, "a wee bit."

I smiled at that, my eyes still closed.

"If we hit the road now," Peter continued, "we'll be home by late afternoon. I want to see my wife."

I heard J shifting his position next to me, so I turned to look at him. He was already looking at me.

"Good morning, sunshine!"

Sunshine… *Sweet.* "Good morning. How did you sleep?"

"Perfect. I wish we could lie here longer."

"Me too, but I think it's time to go."

I placed my hands on the ground to push myself to the tent door, but J moved his hands to my arms to stop me. He looked at me for a long moment without words, and then he moved his gaze to my lips.

Whenever he did that, it raised my heartbeat in an instant because I knew exactly what he was going to do next. It had nothing to do with my Senthien Visionaire capabilities, but everything to do with that fine and instinctive premonition Humans seem to have.

He propped himself up on his elbow and then bent forward to kiss me. We stayed like that, his lips on mine as if glued together by some invisible microgravitational force. Then we both smiled, our lips still touching, each of us knowing what was on the other one's mind.

I looked at him again and said, "We should go. I wouldn't want them to peek in here because we're delaying the start."

"Yeah, yeah… you're right."

Then he looked at the floor for a moment and then back at me.

"We still have time to try the Uni speed, you know." He smiled a mischievous grin and winked at me.

I bit my lip, glancing at the entrance flap. *We could, couldn't we?*

My heartbeat instantly quickened. Trying to hide my smile, I leaned in and kissed him.

After a midmorning break, we continued our trek. Although we now walked in the shade of a dense forest, it was still extremely warm. J and I walked hand in hand a few IPs behind the rest, hearing a lot of good-spirited talking and laughing ahead.

"What are you thinking about?" J asked, seeing me watching the group ahead.

"I'm still wondering about the cryo-preservation," I said and then looked at him. "How can a person living in a truly life-rich world, with no two trees the same, with no path symmetrical, with magnificent animals all around, believe there is no other choice for them but to stop living for the next hundred years? What could be so bad? Apart from the medical cases…"

What I really wanted to know was: Why had *he* chosen this path?

I wanted to know, but I was scared to find out. J looked at me and smiled, but did not answer.

"J, why did you freeze?" I finally asked.

He looked down and sighed. Then he raised his gaze to look at our path and said, "I was among the people who hoped there would be a medical miracle in a hundred years."

I stopped, a sharp stab in my solar plexus. "Why?" I looked at him.

"It doesn't matter anymore." He smiled sadly, squeezed my hand once, and continued walking.

"I don't understand. Do you need some kind of a cure?"

"No, no!" He shook his head. "I'm fine."

"But?"

He sighed and his face saddened even more.

He took a deep breath, held it in for a few seconds, and then began. "Monica… Monica and I wanted to have children, but we couldn't. Everything we tried had failed, so we decided to jump forward in time. We hoped that in a hundred years there would be some medical miracle that would enable us to have children. So that's what we did."

I remembered our talk the previous evening, and how he wanted to know more about pregnancies in Uni worlds. I now realized he wasn't interested in the pregnancy of Descendant women. He wanted to know about *me*.

I lowered my gaze. "I am sorry," I said, answering his question from yesterday.

"Hey!" He looked at me, then hugged me with one arm

and squeezed me closer to him. "That's past. It's time for a new beginning."

And at that moment, my breath was ripped out of my lungs and my sight blinded, a white veil concealing the real world around me.

A Vision: fast, unanticipated, and so strong that the only thing I could do was watch the scene unfold before me.

> Long red hair. She's hugging J, covering his face with her kisses.
>
> What does his face tell me?
>
> Happiness. Surprise. Shock, maybe? I cannot tell.
>
> Who is she?
>
> I know this.
>
> Monica.
>
> Why is she here?
>
> I know this too.
>
> I brought her here.
>
> "I can't believe all that's happened..." Her red hair bounces as she shakes her head in excitement. "Jonathan, I am so happy that you are here, and I am here, and we are together." She hugs him tight, folding her hands around his neck. He hugs her back, her red curls partially trapped under his arms.
>
> Jonathan.
>
> I frown. I never realized J wasn't his full name.
>
> Jonathan.

I inhale sharply. My lungs, devoid of air for too long, hurt sharply as I push the air inside. My eyes are stinging.

J's hands are on my shoulders, his expression worried as he looks at my face.

"Dora! Dora, what's the matter? Are you okay?" He moves a strand of hair off my face, and folds it behind my ear, keeping his hand on the side of my neck. "You saw something, didn't you?"

"No!" I say, much too fast.

"Hmm… All right, you can tell me later. But tell me in time to change it if it's something bad, okay?"

In time to change it…

How could this be changed?

Pain.

Again.

Deep in my chest, bringing tears to my eyes.

I try to fight it.

What am I going to do?

What am I going to do?

It's late afternoon. The others are talking constantly, excited to be returning home. J and I are silent. He keeps holding my hand, keeps glancing at me every few seconds.

What can I tell him?

I don't have to.

He will see it soon enough.

As we approach the village, the group begins to realize that something is different.

There is a lot of commotion. Many people are on the ground, standing in the open field where the bonfire was. They are clearly expecting our arrival. As we come closer, my nanoprobes notify me that there are many faces I haven't seen before. Human faces. The new arrivals are talking to the villagers.

They all seem – joyous. Carefree.

It looks like a moment of true happiness.

Except for me…

Because I have seen what will happen next.

And there was nothing I could have done to prevent it.

I look down at my hand in J's, as he pushes forward like the rest of the group, eager to find out what has changed.

Then – I release his hand. And he doesn't notice. He walks on ahead, and I fall behind. The villagers walk forward to meet us. Their voices are mixed-up as everybody tries to explain what has happened.

And I look at this firework of joy and feel like an outsider.

An alien.

A Descendant.

I turn my head a bit to look at several more people joining the gathering.

And that's when I see her.

Curly red hair.

She's beautiful.

She keeps turning, stretching her neck, looking through the crowd. She is searching for J.

I move a step backward, trying to distance myself and my feelings from what is about to come.

And then she sees him, her lips spreading into a broad smile, she pushes ahead and starts to run. She's coming from his side, so he doesn't see her, then she hugs him tightly. He turns to look at her, speechless and pale. She's still holding, not letting go. Realization finally sinks in, and he turns to her and embraces her in a strong grasping hug.

And keeps holding on.

Everything is silent for me now. I know there are sounds, laughter, cries, and shouts.

But I can't hear any of it.

I am hollow.

As I retreat back into my safe Senthien, my Human sheds tears to see me go. And cries for a life that could have been.

CHAPTER 31

My feet are bare on the ground. Earth, a patch of grass, some fallen dried leaves under my feat. I walk. I can see green all around me. It calms me.

I just walk, my thoughts drifting aimlessly.

Then I stop.

In front of me is a tree. Thick, with a smooth brown-beige crust reaching up high before the first branches start.

Around the bottom of the trunk there is another plant, growing tightly around it. A bright green plant hugging the large tree with many fingers… trapping it with its grip… closing on it…

I step closer to the tree and touch it, my lightly green nails are the same shade as the bright green of my eyes, the same shade as the bright green plant crawling up the tree, strangling the wooden trunk, not wanting to let go.

I close my eyes.

I need to let him go.

I will let him go.

And the pain deep inside my chest pushes out the tears I was fighting against. They flow like a stream down my cheeks, blurring my sight, soaking the dry earth next to the tree with salty drops.

I'm sobbing.

I cannot stop.

I fold the soft beige dress, and place it on my bed, gently brushing my hand against the fabric. I leave my hand there for a moment, half bent over the bed, clenching my teeth and fighting tears.

I remember my mother telling me something: she said that there is no reason to fear if there is only one choice to be made. And there is no other choice but to leave.

I close my eyes, heavy tears drip onto my folded clothes.

What other choice could there be?

I stand up, swallow, and open my eyes, then let out a deep, long breath with a deliberate attempt to calm myself. I breathe in again and empty my mind.

And it works.

I hear footsteps coming over the bridge and recognize Tania's gait. She knocks quickly and enters without me answering. I turn around. She looks into my eyes, then my skinsuit, and then back into my eyes again. She tilts her head and narrows her eyes.

"Dora… are you going somewhere?" Her voice is higher than usual.

"I need to collect specific information from some locations outside the village. My E-band is fully functional now, and I can collect the data."

"Data? What data? Why do you want to do that now? And why are you wearing your skinsuit?" She shakes her head while piling up her questions.

"My E-band functions optimally when connected to the skinsuit."

Tania looks at me without saying a word. Then she lifts her

head slightly and says, "Should I still call you Dora, or do you prefer Dana now?"

I open my eyes wide. My Senthien is speechless and my Human feels hurt.

For a moment, I fear that all the emotions will pour back, making me soft, powerless, and vulnerable again. I relax my shoulders and breathe out.

"On Earth, as I have learned, the first name is the preferred calling name. I would still like to be addressed as Dora. Thank you for asking."

Tania sighs and comes close to me before I have time to move backward. She holds me by my shoulders and looks into my eyes. Her close proximity is uncomfortable.

"Dora, I know… I can imagine how you feel… I really can. But—" She stops and closes her eyes for a moment. "Please, don't do anything that you might regret afterward."

She looks at me and I can feel the emotions behind her words. For a moment, I am tempted to put my Human in front of my Senthien, but I realize that I can't. Not if I am about to do what I had planned.

I take one step backward. Her arms remain frozen in the same position as if unable to believe my reaction, but then she sighs and drops them again.

"There is no reason for you to worry, Tania. I do appreciate your concern. I just need to collect some information."

Tania's shoulders drop a bit and she whispers, "All right."

She is silent for a moment and then she says, shaking her head, "I never expected … I don't know how this—"

"I do."

She looks up. "You do?"

"Using my E-band, I sent a power surge to your installation. This also initiated the de-freeze of the second batch."

She keeps looking at me, not saying a word.

I take a deep breath and slowly say, "I… brought her here."

We look at each other for a long moment, and then Tania says, "I am sorry, Dora. I really am. Take the time you need, but let's talk once you are back, okay?"

I nod.

She turns away to leave but then swings back quickly. "Don't go too far from the village… please."

I force a smile. "Okay."

She walks to the door but turns to me once again. "And don't go swimming anywhere!"

I almost laugh. "Agreed."

I will miss her.

She smiles back and turns around to walk through the door, but bumps into J. They look at each other, neither of them saying a word. Tania shakes her head slightly and straightens her body.

I have the feeling that she is trying to communicate something to J without saying a word. J turns to me and looks up and down at my skinsuit. Then, opening his mouth slightly, he looks back at Tania.

I leave them to exchange their nonverbal communication and walk to the table. I have four small sticks of bread that I push into the thigh pockets of my skinsuit. I take the flat leather water bottle and hold it in my hand for a second, looking down at my skinsuit. I wish I had a suitable pocket somewhere on me. I bend down and strap the bottle securely to my thigh.

"That will not last you longer than a day, you know."

I turn around. Tania has left and J is standing calmly, blocking the exit of my cottage.

"I am aware of this, Jonathan. I do not need supplies to last me longer than a day."

He swallows, and I can see that his calmness is leaving him.

He steps closer, and I move backward.

His breath catches in his throat as he stares at me.

There is a long moment of silence while I fight the urge to run to him and hold him in a strong embrace and never let go.

But I don't.

Because this needs to be his decision.

"Is there something that you wanted to tell me, Jonathan?" I say, and I can feel that I'm hoping for an answer I want to hear.

"I'm sorry, Dora," J says and deeply bows his head. "I am so sorry."

And the sharp pain pierces straight through my rib cage, bleeding my heart. And for a moment, I cannot take a breath. My throat is shut, and I can't even begin to call out for my Senthien.

I can't see J's face, but his shoulders are shaking.

He is crying.

"Monica," he whispers. "She… she doesn't know… for her it has only been two days since we last saw each other. This is where I was nine years ago. I can't… I can't…" And his voice fails, tears streaming down his face.

I make a deliberate effort and walk over to him. I place my palm on his face, wiping away tears on his cheek.

"That's okay, J. I understand. You need time."

He looks at me intently with a question in his eyes and then nods slightly. "Yes, time. I need time."

Then he suddenly takes me in his arms and hugs me so tightly that my ribs hurt. We stay like this for a very long time, and I am tempted to change my mind.

Then he lets me go, takes a deep breath, and looks at me.

His eyes narrow slightly and he asks in a stronger voice, "Are you… are you all right?"

I am—shattered in pieces, J. "Yes, I am fine. Take all the time you need."

I smile, but he still looks serious. I wonder for a second if my words didn't have the right intonation to sound like a truth.

He nods, lowering his gaze to the floor, and I realize I am getting impatient to leave.

"I want to use the daylight."

"Yes… I see… all right."

He starts turning, but then stops and asks, "Do you want anyone to accompany you? Someone who knows the area, so you don't get lost?"

I lift up my forearm to show him the E-band screen. "My E-band works properly again. I won't get lost."

"Oh, right. Well, don't go too fa—never mind." He looks at me and attempts a smile. "You're self-sufficient. You can take care of yourself."

I clench my teeth. Self-sufficient. And alone.

"Yes. I can take care of myself. Always have." *And always will.*

He looks at me and frowns, sensing a hidden meaning behind my words.

I look down at my skinsuit, checking that I have everything I planned to bring.

"I will see you later," I say with a confident tone, then loop around him and leave.

CHAPTER 32

My skinsuit seems tight and gripping to my body, and I make exaggerated movements when walking to release the pressure, but the pressure stays. I lift my left arm to look at the screen, walking in the direction the E-band is showing me. The scan I did for a natural porting field resonator resulted in specific coordinates on the Earth's surface. Comparing these coordinates to the map my nanoprobes compiled while traveling with Stevanion, I assume this is the place where Stevanion and I ported to, and where all other Jumpers arrived as well.

I continue walking.

Ferns slide and gently touch my legs, but I can't feel them; my skinsuit completely blocks physical contact. I look down at the plants.

It's better this way.

Still, I brush my open palm against the ferns as I walk, the soft leaves tickling and stroking my skin. I keep looking at these green fountains around me, covering the moist brown soil and giving way to the tall, broad, curved trees, their first branches starting high up the air. I look up at the crowns of the trees, but walking in this position gives me a slight neck ache.

I continue to be amazed at this world, this wealth of green and blue that Humans decided to leave.

I bow my head, realizing that I am about to do the same.

I lift my arm again, checking the way, and then change my direction just slightly to follow the map.

What am I going to do?

Where am I going to go?

I don't know, but I can't stay here.

Not here.

J has what he's wanted for a long time. And I'm happy for him.

I think I'm happy.

But I can't stay. I need to go. Anywhere but here.

I wish that my Senthien were strong enough to keep my grief contained so that I could still stay here, in this amazing, natural, rich world.

But it is not, because my Human has become too strong.

Ahead of me I see a tight net of lianas webbed between two large trees, making an obstacle I'd need to walk around. And the next moment, in my mind, I see J's dark eyes, very close to mine. I see his untidy hair, one strand falling over his forehead. And I remember him smiling. And I realize I will never see it again.

And I cry.

Once more.

Tears rolling down, cooling the skin on my cheek as they dry on the light breeze. My throat is tight and burning, and I fight hard not to sob. But I fail, and I'm happy the birds above are the only ones to hear me.

After a few moments, I take a deep breath and wipe my eyes with the backs of my hands. I hold my breath, then exhale shakily and start walking again.

I had no Vision. I have no idea whatsoever if my plan to port will work—and if it does, I don't know where I'm going to go. But I don't really care.

After an hour, I find a short thick tree with large teardrop leaves, making an umbrella cover over its surrounding. I don't think it will rain tonight, but I realize I like this natural green roof on top of me. I peel soft white bark from the neighboring tree to cover myself and lie down.

Sleep doesn't come for a long while, but I keep my eyes closed, listening to the sounds of nature, trying hard to remember and keep every one of them, not on my nanoprobes, but in my memory.

By midmorning the next day, I reach my original porting site. I look around. Nothing here makes me think this place is different from any other place on Earth, but it must be.

I search for information about this place using my E-band and as I scan all the different variables in this spot, suddenly, the E-band gives me an unmistakable answer.

Underneath me, covered by five thousand years of soil and undergrowth, lies a portation chamber. The same type that was built into all the Seedships to enable portation once the Mind was completely functional.

I look down at the dark, moist soil, thinking of the chamber underneath me.

Humans left one porting chamber here before they left. Perhaps they were hoping to come back when the time was right? I checked my nanoprobes' data. The coordinates for this porting chamber were never listed in any of the porting registers. Somebody had made sure to keep it a secret.

I sit down, cross my legs, and wait. Countless thoughts cross my mind, but every second one is of J. *It will pass,* I tell myself, *it has to.* The deep throbbing pain inside my chest starts again and I close my eyes to fight the tears, starting to hate this useless Human part of me.

I open my eyes and exhale, bringing the strong, calm, and unemotional Senthien back. I feel the muscles in my face relaxing and my face unfolds from the painful grip of sorrow.

I lift up my E-band and enter the instruction to generate a hyperspace field.

The icon blinks on my screen.

I look around one more time, then tap for execution.

The bright daylight of the morning shifts into a purple hue as if dusk had swept in. The sounds of the forest change, the songs of the birds fade, the wind in the high branches distorts into a moaning howl, as the portation kicks in.

I can feel it in the whole of my body. It hurts, as if every muscle's coming back to life after being deprived of blood flow. I ignore the pain.

And I leave the most beautiful planet in the universe.

ACKNOWLEDGMENTS

First of all, a big thank you to my family.

To my husband, thank you for your constant support, for being there to bounce off ideas, for being my in-house editor, for encouraging me to finish my book and for being my tireless fan. To my children, for their cheering and support, and for simply being in my life and making me happy. To my parents, for their unconditional love and continuing life-long encouragement.

To my developmental and copy-editor, Sarah Kolb-Williams, thank you so much! Your constructive comments, your attention to detail and your contagious optimism are exactly what I was looking for. It was a real pleasure working with you and I am looking forward to our next project together.

To my final proof-reader, Barbara Tenner, who also read the very first draft of *The Senthien*, thank you so much for your early comments which helped me to bring the book forward and for making sure the final version was ready to face the world.

Huge thanks to my beta-readers: Karin Brown, Vanda Pogacic, Mara Jacob and Tammy Hollister, for your tips, insightful and valuable comments, and your support for me to continue.

For many techy discussions over pizza and wine, my big thanks to Karin Brown, Stephen McEwen and Tom Brown.

KCFC, microgenerators and E-bands are all products of those late night discussions.

Rico Leuthold and Thorsten Kramp, I very much appreciate your IT inputs.

Thank you to an amazing Deranged Doctor Design team who made a stunning book cover. It looks better than I ever imagined!

Streetlight Graphics, thank you so much! You did such a wonderful job formatting my book.

And last, but not least, to my readers: I am immensely grateful that you decided to read *The Senthien*, therefore, bringing Dora and J to life.

ABOUT THE AUTHOR

Tara Jade Brown lives in Switzerland with her husband, two sons, two cats, and a dog. Before becoming a full-time writer, she worked as a neuroscientist, an entrepreneur, and a marketing manager. Her works include her debut novel *The Senthien* (the first book in the *Descendants of Earth* trilogy), *The Mind, Swift Escape*, and a few short stories: *Dante's 9*, *Forbidden*, and *Far Away*. To find out more, please go to www.tarajadebrown.com.